Lake

Lake

The Preacher's Sons 1

Mary E. Hanks

www.maryehanks.com

© 2022 Mary E. Hanks

This book is a work of fiction. Names, characters, dialogues, places, and events are either products of the author's imagination or are used fictitiously. Any resemblance to real situations or actual persons, living or dead, is entirely coincidental.

All Rights Reserved. No part of this book may be stored, reproduced or transmitted in any form or by any means without express written permission of the author.

Scriptures taken from the Holy Bible, New International Version®, NIV®. Copyright © 1973, 1978, 1984, 2011 by Biblica, Inc.™ Used by permission of Zondervan. All rights reserved worldwide. www.zondervan.com The "NIV" and "New International Version" are trademarks registered in the United States Patent and Trademark Office by Biblica, Inc.™

Suzanne D. Williams Cover Design
www.feelgoodromance.com

Cover photos:
Andrii Kobryn @ shutterstock.com
Anastasiia @ depositphotos.com

Visit Mary's website:
www.maryehanks.com

You can write Mary at
maryhanks@maryehanks.com

In memory of

Mountain Man,

a gentle giant who loved to run

And to Chip,

Our empty-nest puppy,

who holds a special place in our hearts

"…redeem us because of your unfailing love."

Psalm 44:26

Chapter One

"Let's go, Pal! Run hard, Ice!" Lake North shouted to his huskies as they exited the snow-covered trees and raced into the half-mile straightaway toward the finish line.

Hoping to have a better two-day combined time than his fiercest skijoring competitor—Irish Markham and her sleek, swift dogs—he skied fervently across the packed snow on his cross-country skis. Pal and Ice were clipped to his hip belt with eight-foot bungee lines, running strongly ahead of him. "Come on, guys! Let's go!"

Lake's legs burned, and his chest heaved with each powerful stroke of his legs and arms moving in unison with his dogs' matching strides. For weeks, he and his team practiced for this two-dog skijoring event. He had the stamina for the three-and-a-half miles of skiing. His dogs were in great shape. He'd already crossed the challenging passage of hilly terrain and forest to reach this clearing, leaving an easy finish if all went well.

He'd never beaten Irish before. To do so, he needed to get farther ahead of her. In yesterday's race, he had a faster run than she did, which gave him hope for a possible win today. But from past experiences, he knew she always finished strong!

"Yip-yip-yip!" Irish called from somewhere behind him. Was she closing in on his team already?

Since they left the starting line in one-minute intervals, her catching up to him meant she was ahead of him in their combined times. He'd advanced yesterday, but she'd made up time today. She must be skiing even faster than usual!

Tension mounting in his shoulders and neck, Lake leaned forward, skiing harder. "Go, Ice! Faster, Pal!" He pushed himself to cut deeper into the snow with his poles and forced his skis to fly across the snowpack.

He barely felt the icy wind brushing against his cheeks. He was hot, his body sweating with the physical effort to beat the regional favorite. If he and his dogs held the lead, this would be their only time coming in first place since he started competing in skijoring races two years ago. But was that even possible now that Irish had narrowed the gap between them?

"Yip-yip-yip!" She shouted again, closer this time. "Passing!"

Fortunately, the trail was wide enough for two teams to pass here without Lake pulling over and stopping his team. "Gee! Gee!" He veered his dogs toward the right. Clenching his jaw, he pushed himself to keep skiing strong, even with his competitor closing in on him.

"On by!" Irish shouted a familiar warning for her dogs to pass and not become distracted by the other team.

Out of the corner of his left eye, he saw her mane of red hair flying out from beneath her knit hat. With her body scrunched low and her ski poles tucked under her armpits, she seemed to ride the wind as she and her dogs—Aurora and North Star—glided past him. "Yip-yip-yip!"

"Pal! Ice! Run hard, boys!" His shouts seemed ineffective as Irish took the lead.

Still, Lake skied with every ounce of strength he possessed. Even as he mentally prepared for a second-place finish, he wouldn't slow down. He wanted to keep the seconds between their racing times as close as possible.

But then, as if Irish passing him in the straightaway wasn't frustrating enough, fifty feet from the finish line, Pal abruptly stopped. Lake nearly toppled over the husky as he tried stopping his skis. Right on the trail, Pal relieved himself and left a steaming pile.

Just great.

Pal glanced back, his eyes sparkling as if to say, "Look what I did, Dad!"

The sounds of another racer approaching sent the crowd into a frenzy of cheering and calling to their favorite dogs to run faster.

Above the din, Lake yelled, "Let's go, Pal! Run, Ice! Let's finish this thing." He forced his legs to move again despite his muscles cooling down while he waited for Pal to do his business. He didn't want the temporary setback to make him lose second place too.

His dogs took off running again, and Lake skied strong as before. He glanced over his shoulder. Morris Collins bore down on him with his Alaskan huskies.

"Sprint, Pal! Bring us home, Ice!"

Amid cheers, Lake, Pal, and Ice crossed the finish line. The third-place competitor followed close behind them.

"Hey, Pal! Nice work. Good job, Ice. I'm proud of you guys." Spur, Lake's brother and his assistant with the dogs, grabbed Pal's and Ice's harnesses and led them back toward their parking area. "You did good, too, Lake!" he tossed over his shoulder like an afterthought.

"Thanks, bro."

"That Pal, huh?" Spur's red cheeks, which nearly matched his hair, widened. "Always wants to take a dump in the worst places."

"Isn't that the truth?" Lake headed for his dirty forest-green pickup.

While he unclamped his skis and retrieved his winter coat, Spur clipped Pal and Ice to their tie-out lines next to the pickup. Then he gave them water and a hydration snack, praising them for today's efforts. Both dogs, brothers from the same litter and nearly identical in off-white coloring and dark markings, panted and grinned wide at Spur like they usually did.

Lake removed his skis and gloves, then pulled his thick coat on. He was searching for his knit hat when Irish strode up to him, right hand extended.

"Good job, North!"

"Thanks. You, too." He shook the redhead's hand good-naturedly. She beat him fair and square. But she must know he wanted to beat her badly. For a few minutes, the taste of near-victory had been sweet. "Aurora and North Star did great pulling."

"Thanks. I skied my share, too." She gave him a flirty grin.

His awareness of her flirting with him made a gulp of emotion catch in his throat. He wouldn't deny an attraction to this female competitor, but he'd left a two-year relationship only two months ago. He and Laurie should have been married by now. Lake and Laurie. With those "L" names, they were destined to be together, or so he thought. In his family, names were a big deal.

Since his internal wounds felt too fresh, he wasn't prepared to flirt with another woman. Still, this redheaded beauty stirred his interest. Maybe just on a competitive level. Ever since they'd begun racing in the same events, he admired her determination and ability to succeed. He respected the way she treated her dogs with care and affection. And he could gaze at her smiling lips all day. Perhaps he did feel something more toward her than only wanting to beat her at racing.

"You skied better than any of us today." He nodded and smiled back at her.

"Not to rub it in, but you're getting harder for my team to pass." Irish walked over to Pal and Ice. She patted each one on the head and rubbed their necks like she knew where to soothe a dog. Both his pets wagged their curled tails and panted up at her with big grins. "Sweet babies, you are delightful! You did well and ran with all your heart just like my girls did."

Lake understood Irish's devotion to her dogs. His love for his three dogs—these two racers and Rambler, a young trainee at home—made him feel connected to anyone who had a bond with their animals. Especially those in the co-racing world of dog-powered sports.

"Thanks for stopping by, Irish." Lake picked up the water dish Pal knocked over in his eagerness to greet their visitor.

"Of course. Uh, Lake?" She stood near the edge of his pickup, nodding for him to come over to her.

"Yeah?" Did she need something? Maybe she required assistance with her dogs. Or help with loading her racing gear. The racers often assisted each other with various tasks.

"I've been meaning to ask you something." Her skin tone was still rosy from racing, but she flushed even rosier. "When we get back to Thunder Ridge, can we meet up?"

His jaw dropped open. Was she asking him out?

"Not for a date," she amended quickly. "Just to talk."

"Okay. Good."

Her eyes widened.

"Oh, uh, not good as in I'm not interested—" Although, he wasn't, right? "It's just—"

Spur snickered from where he picked ice chips from the dogs' fur.

"It's a business discussion. Nothing personal." Irish eyed him with deep green eyes that looked jade beneath the gray skies threatening to drop snow any minute.

"Business?" Surely, she didn't know about him nearly inheriting a bundle of wealth. That wasn't happening, anyway.

"I'd rather not discuss it here." She glanced in the direction of her dogs. "We'll meet up soon?"

"Uh, sure." He felt a need to be honest with her about his previous reaction. No doubt they'd cross paths in their small town of Thunder Ridge. With her working at Nelly's, and their competitor's status, he didn't want any awkwardness between them. "I didn't mean anything disparaging about not being interested in—"

"Don't worry. I'm not interested in you either. What I want to discuss surpasses my feelings. Or yours." She huffed out a breath. "We get along, don't we?"

"As competitors? Dog lovers? Sure." Now, why did he have to say "lovers?"

"Right." She grinned. "Let's chat. If you're not interested in my offer, so be it."

Her offer? So she must have heard about his grandfather's will!

She waved and strolled back to her parking area.

Whatever request she spoke of Lake couldn't help her with it. Since Laurie broke their engagement right alongside his heart, he didn't meet the criteria for receiving his grandfather's money. His thirty-fifth birthday was ten days away, and he was still single.

No marriage? Goodbye, inheritance!

Chapter Two

"How could I be so stupid?" Irish muttered on her way to check on her dogs. A business plan with Lake North? She was as broke as a potato. And they were competitors! Her drive to win superseded any other ambitions when she was racing with her dogs. She was gritty, tough, and determined to stay ahead of every team, including Lake's!

So why did she think he'd be open to helping her?

She squatted down and petted each of her dogs. This was what she loved most about her life and skijoring: spending time with Aurora, North Star, and Pleiades—her babies.

While Pleiades was a brown female Lab that didn't race, Aurora and North Star were a combination of German Shorthaired Pointer and Siberian Husky, whose ancestors were bred for dog-sled pulling. Aurora was russet-colored with russet freckles across her white chest. North Star was black with dark freckles on her lower body and a splotch of white between her ears. They were her teammates, but they were also her family. She dreamed of traveling with them to other races across the country, maybe even competing internationally.

In her lineup of aspirations, she wanted a spread of land for her big dogs to run and practice on, too. But the lease on the quarter-acre where she stayed in a single-wide trailer was up in a week. Since the owner planned to sell, it wasn't renewable. She could barely afford the place on her server's salary, anyway. Time to move again. But where? Finding any rental available to her and her three dogs seemed impossible!

She'd thought her financial troubles were dreadful until she recently heard that the Thunder Ridge Animal Shelter, where she got Aurora, was having severe difficulties. It sounded like they might close! On the same day, someone at Nelly's Diner mentioned Lake North's inheritance. Irish's ears perked up like radar antennas. She knew Lake! He loved dogs. If he were wealthy, maybe he'd help the shelter.

Wasn't he one of the brothers known around town as the preacher's sons? With a nickname like that, they must be compassionate and caring toward all God's creatures.

Irish had heard other gossip about the North brothers from her coworker, Tiffany. "Nine hot single men in one family! And not one of them is married. That should be against the law!"

Chuckling at the memory, Irish petted Aurora, North Star, and Pleiades again. Then she made sure they had enough water and food. Finally, ready to relax, she grabbed her thermos and poured a cup of tepid coffee. She dropped down on a camp chair, heaved a sigh, and let all the race-day stress ooze out of her pores. The air had a chill in it. She shivered, wishing her thermos kept her coffee hotter.

Thick gray clouds overhead looked like a storm was coming. The regular four-and-a-half hour drive from south of Darby, Montana, to Thunder Ridge, Idaho, might be rough. Fortunately, she drove an all-wheel drive vehicle. Although her Subaru was an older model, it would get her home safely. One of these days, with her dreams of having more dogs to form a mushing team, she'd have to obtain a bigger rig. Maybe a pickup like Lake drove.

Yeah, right. Her meager finances didn't allow for new truck payments. She spent all her extra cash on registration fees, gas, and dog supplies to attend these racing events—not to mention vet bills. But she would never skimp on her dogs' care, no matter what.

So, what would she do if she had to pay more for a rental property? Pick up additional shifts at the diner? She groaned. She wanted to spend more time training her dogs. Not less! What if she couldn't find a place that allowed three dogs? She'd sleep in her car before giving up any of her babies. But it was the coldest time of the year.

Her troubled thoughts roamed back to Lake. Why did he act so shocked by her suggestion that they meet up?

She took a couple of drinks of coffee and allowed the fleeting image of her and Lake as something other than competitors to tease her thoughts. She pictured their lips touching, arms wrapped around each other, just testing the idea. A few times, she had imagined he might like her as more than a skijoring contender. But she must have misinterpreted a look or something.

"Hey, Irish." Spur strode over and went straight for her dogs. Aurora and North Star jumped up, barking and panting. "Hey, girls. How are you doing?" Lake's brother petted Irish's dogs, itching their ears and chests. Soon, all three animals were lying down on the snow, stretched out for him to scratch their bellies too. He was good with dogs. Lake was lucky to have a traveling assistant and handler like him.

Nice to have money for such a luxury. A knot of jealousy twisted in Irish's gut. *Stop with the envying.* Wasn't Lake's wealth precisely what might help save the animal shelter?

"They love the attention."

"Don't we all?" Spur grinned.

She chuckled, knowing he liked to tease.

"See you guys next time. Maybe Lake's team will have better luck then."

"Ha!" Not if she could help it.

"Irish, you did good, too." He tucked his hands into his jacket pockets.

"Thanks."

The dogs remained on the snow, completely relaxed. Too bad she couldn't curl up in the back of her car and sleep for a few hours. Instead, as soon as Spur left her area, she'd pull up stakes and hit the road. Do her best to outdistance the storm.

"You guys heading out soon?"

"Any minute." He shuffled back and forth in his snow boots as if his feet were chilled. Or else he wanted to say something.

"Do you have something on your mind?" She'd always been more direct. That's why she asked Lake about meeting up with her.

"What you said back there." He lifted his chin in the direction of his brother's pickup. "I'm glad you're nudging him out of his funk."

"What funk is that?" Did Spur assume she asked Lake on a date, too?

"Women trouble. What else? I say, go for it!"

"You've got it wrong." She didn't want any confusion here. She needed to speak with Lake about his philanthropic possibilities. That's all! Even if she had pictured them kissing, she didn't plan to do anything about it.

"You have dogs in common." A wide smile crossed Spur's face. "You're not bad to look at."

"Thanks a lot." She felt offended and amused by his insincere compliment.

"I just meant you should help him get his feet unstuck from the mud." He shrugged and marched away from her parking area.

Help Lake get unstuck from women problems? No thanks!

Chapter Three

For the last half hour, Lake had been letting his young, blue-eyed husky, Rambler, run on the groomed trails of his property while he skied leisurely behind him. His usual routine involved working with Ice and Pal in a more disciplined manner. Today, Rambler was getting some needed exercise and a lesson in following instructions while attached to Lake's hip belt.

He practiced basic instructions—Gee! Haw! Easy! Then suddenly, the dog lifted his nose, sniffing the air intensely.

"Rambler, stick to the trail! On by!"

The dog must have caught a strong whiff of an animal. He bayed and lunged over the mound of snow to the left of the trail faster than Lake could stop him.

"Whooooaaa!"

Lake flailed his arms in the air, taking an intense off-trail bounce, and tried to rebalance himself. He rammed his ski poles into the snow, attempting to anchor himself and stop Rambler. Instead, he toppled forward, hitting the crusted snow hard with his right cheek, and was dragged, strapped together, human and dog.

"Rambler! Whooooaaa!"

He grabbed a leafless bush and clung to the branches, fighting the husky's pull to get to whatever animal scent he chased. Finally, blessedly, the dog came to a halt.

Groaning, Lake sat up and wiped his sore face with the sleeve of his jacket. His cheek burned like jagged ice particles were embedded in his skin. His chin felt on fire.

"What were you thinking?" He stood and dusted himself free of snow particles. "No off-trail adventures for you, buddy! You've got to stick to the path, no matter the distractions!"

Rambler panted noisily, his turquoise eyes gazing longingly in the direction he'd been running. If Lake had unclipped him, he would have been gone in a flash.

"If a moose or a rabbit crosses in front of us, it's off-limits to you. Got it, bud?" He petted the dog, smoothing his hands over Rambler's legs to clear the fur of small snowballs and making sure he didn't injure himself. "You must focus on the trail in front of you. Not on any other stuff."

That was good advice for him too. He needed to focus on the essential things in his life—trying to follow God's leading, spending time with his dogs, and putting energy into his dreams for the future. Not focusing on what went wrong in his life—Laurie breaking off their engagement, him forfeiting the inheritance, and his current job that he detested. He never wanted to be an accountant. He got a business administration degree with the goal of having his own company, not to balance another company's checkbook. However, the job paid the bills and allowed him to work from home and be closer to his dogs.

Lake did a quick body check of himself. Shoulders ached. Neck, fine. Face? Hurt like crazy.

"Let's head back." Disappointed their training session didn't go better, he aligned his skis, and double-checked that he fastened the clasps correctly. Then he directed them on a course toward his cabin.

At their approach, Pal and Ice bayed and yowled.

As soon as he reached the dogs' play yard, Lake unfastened his ski boots from his skis. Then he unclasped Rambler from the carabiner on his hip belt. After putting him in his large kennel, Lake made sure the youngest of his trio had water and a few healthy treats.

Before he even had time to take care of his facial injuries, an engine turning off in the driveway alerted him that he had company. On his twenty acres, sounds echoed off the nearby snow-covered mountains, creating a sense of his being the only human within a hundred-mile radius. It also made unusual sounds seem exaggerated in the stillness. He didn't recognize the vehicle engine like he did some of the noisy rigs his father and brothers drove.

"We have a visitor, guys."

By the dogs' furious barking, they already knew a stranger had arrived.

Lake rubbed a handful of clean snow over his stinging face. His cheeks must be red and scratched looking—nothing to be done about that now.

Chapter Four

Irish exited her car at Lake's address, and the brisk air hit her, momentarily taking her breath away. Another cold front was moving in already. Only two days had passed since their race and the treacherous journey home from Montana. She nearly slid off the road several times. At least another dumping of snow meant the trails would be good until enough dogs' feet and skis traversed them.

She peered at Lake's cabin and the clearing with the woods and mountains creating a gorgeous backdrop. Even from here, she noticed a couple of trails leading off in different directions. Lake was fortunate to have such a spread for his dogs. She envied him that. But the tiny cabin didn't look like much to brag about. Certainly, nothing a rich person would live in.

"Irish?"

"Hey, Lake."

"What brings you out this way?" He sauntered across the frozen path toward her.

"Sorry to intrude. I should have called first." As usual, she had impulsively followed her instincts.

"No problem." He wore a full-body winter garment like he'd been skiing. A thick fur hat covered his hair. And his face—

"Oh, my goodness! What happened to you? You look like you shaved with a cheese grater!"

"Something like that." His gloved hand moved to his red cheek. He winced. "Rambler thought he'd have some fun at my expense."

"Oh, no. Is there anything I can do? Do you need to go to the doctor? I'll drive you."

"Does it look that bad?"

Up close, she recognized the ice burns. She could almost feel them, since she'd also taken her share of face plants in the snow.

"Those trainees, huh?" She grinned, hoping to keep things light between them. "We all start somewhere."

"Yeah." Grimacing, he nodded toward the cabin that looked even tinier than she first thought.

The rumors about him being rich must be false. Maybe she drove out here for nothing. When would she learn not to be so impulsive? After thirty-four years, she hadn't learned yet.

"Want some coffee?"

"Uh, sure. That would be great." She'd drink coffee, make her apologies, and leave.

He stared at her quizzically before leading her toward the cabin.

Inside the cramped yet tidy cabin, Irish clutched the large mug of coffee Lake set on the table in front of her. She caught him staring at her a few times as he set his coffee down and took a seat. He must be curious about her unexpected visit. Or downright confused like she was.

Tomorrow she'd give Tiffany a piece of her mind! She was foolish for being naïve and falling for the server's gossip.

An awkward silence simmered between her and Lake. Wishing she hadn't driven the twenty miles to his property and that she'd never heard about his supposed wealth, she rotated the warm cup in her hands. "You're probably wondering why I'm here."

"I am. Excuse me. I'll be right back." He jumped up and dashed into a room at the back of the house. The water ran for a few minutes.

This was her chance to bolt! Why not leave before he returned and she humiliated herself even more? But she wasn't the running type. She'd cope with what needed to be faced. Then go, head held high.

"Sorry about that." Lake dropped into the chair again, his face all red now. He must have put a hot cloth on his cheeks.

"Did that help?"

"Not much." He grimaced and grabbed his mug. "I thought a good washing might make my face less wretched to look at."

"Don't worry. I've fallen plenty of times."

"A casualty of the sport." He sipped his drink. "About why you drove out here?" He gazed at her with dark brown eyes that appeared almost black in the natural light coming through the windows.

"I came here with a question." She pressed her lips together for a moment. "A proposition."

"A proposition?" Coughing, he set his cup down with a loud thud.

"Not in the romantic sense. Heavens, no!" She brushed the back of her hand over her chin where she felt a coffee drip. An image played through her mind of what she'd thought kissing Lake might be like, of them involved in something more than skijoring events.

Get a grip! She came here to beg him for money. Not to stir up any emotional connection between them. Especially not after what Spur mentioned about his older brother having women problems.

"Okay. Then, what is it about?"

"It's a business proposal."

His eyes glinted at her like she had suggested they run their skis over rocks instead of snow.

"This is embarrassing for me to admit." She gulped. If she could walk out the door without explaining and not look like a fool, she would. "I overheard someone at work talking about you being wealthy. By the looks of where you live, I heard wrong."

"I'll say." Lake barked out a harsh-sounding laugh, which made her feel worse. "What's this about? Please, explain."

"The Thunder Ridge Animal Shelter is closing its doors unless a benefactor helps it get back on its feet."

"I'm sorry to hear that."

"Me too. At Nelly's, two board members yakked about the problem rather loudly, and I am concerned." Glancing around the cabin, she fought an eye roll. "Before I came out here, I thought you might be able to help."

"How's that?"

"If you were wealthy, which you obviously aren't, and if you love your dogs as I love mine, I thought you might have a heart about the animals at the shelter too." Even admitting she was wrong about assuming he was rich dug at her pride. If she had the funds, she'd donate the money. She would never have approached Lake like this.

Groaning, he pressed his fingers to his temples like he had a throbbing headache. No wonder, after his fall and being dragged by Rambler. "This is legit? I mean, the animal shelter will go down if someone doesn't provide funding?"

"Yes. That's what I said. Wait. You think I made this up?" She bristled. "Like I'm after your money, if you had any? I'm no gold digger!"

"I didn't say that. I just—" He groaned again. "Those board members may have been airing complaints. Businessmen talking over breakfast is hardly actionable."

"No kidding." She crossed her arms and peered at the man she beat on the racecourse many times. She had never thought of him as being rude until now. "I've made a profound mistake in coming here.

For that, I apologize. But I called an acquaintance at the shelter. She assured me they were in dire financial difficulties. Have been for over a year."

"I am sorry they are struggling. I picked Rambler up there."

"And my Aurora."

Lake stared into his coffee cup. "What were you hoping I'd do?"

"That you'd have enough compassion for the animals to donate whatever they need at the shelter." She tossed her hands up. "I thought you might take pity on the animals waiting for good homes. The ones that might be on some kill list!"

His Adam's apple bobbed up and down. "Of course, I feel compassion for them. As I said, I got Rambler at the shelter. And a few others over the years." He drew in a slow breath like he was controlling his emotions. "I wouldn't mind picking up a couple more racers there."

"Same here. But you live in this—" Irish waved her hand toward one of the smallest living room and kitchen combos she'd ever seen. "You must be as dirt poor as me. How did you ever afford this land?" It wasn't her business, but she asked anyway.

"My parents loaned me the down payment."

"You're blessed to have such generous folks."

"I am. As far as money goes—" Lake thrummed his fingers against the table. "It's hard to talk about."

"I should leave." She stood quickly. "I'm sorry for bothering you. My coming here was a mistake." She took two steps toward the door. When would she learn to think things through before jumping headlong into a situation?

"Wait." He stood also. "I don't have the money *yet*."

"What?" She twirled around and met his troubled-looking gaze.

"Whoever you heard talking about me falling into money didn't know the truth. You've heard the saying, 'Don't count your chickens before they hatch?'"

"Yeah?" She shuffled her boots, hoping her soles didn't leave a puddle beneath her. She should have taken off her footwear at the door.

"That's what I did. I had big plans. Marriage. The good life planned out." He smiled, but his smile didn't reach his dark eyes. "With my engagement off, I was denied access to the family fortune." He peered at her as if trying to decide her worthiness with the information. "A domineering grandfather had the last word even in death."

"I'm sorry for putting you in this predicament of having to tell me your private business." A humility she rarely felt came over her. "I'm embarrassed to admit I listened to someone at the diner who mentioned your enviable affluent status."

A provocative grin crossed his soft-looking lips that she found quite attractive. She'd better not stare at his mouth too long, or she'd again be imagining what kissing him might be like. In her past, she had a string of bad dates, lousy kissers, and generally oafish male companionship lacking any chemistry. Now, being in the same room as Lake North, gazing into his eyes, and temporarily thunderstruck by staring at his mouth, a strong feeling stirred within her.

"So, some of your coworkers, or clientele, were talking about me?"

"I can't divulge any secrets." She made a zipping motion across her lips.

His gaze followed the movement of her fingers as they brushed against her lips. Thinking of him watching her and possibly imagining a kiss between them, her mouth went dry. She coughed. Either because of her nerves or the dryness in the cabin, she needed some liquid. She returned to the table, sat down, and took a long drink of the lukewarm coffee.

Lake returned to his chair, staring at her like he needed to say something but couldn't find the words to express himself. What did he want to tell her? And why was he taking so long to say it?

Chapter Five

A daring idea scrambled through Lake's mind, creating turbulence in his thoughts. With his thirty-fifth birthday only eight days away, what if he and Irish got married? That would fulfill the prerequisite of him having to be wed before he received the inheritance. She'd get to help the animal shelter the way she wanted. He'd have the funding to get his kennels up and running come spring and pay Mom and Dad back for helping him with the down payment for the land.

A marriage of convenience was a ridiculous idea, right?

He couldn't propose to Irish Markham. He barely knew her outside of the skijoring circuit. Sure, she was gorgeous. Just sitting across from her, his heart pounded out a wild cadence. His brain whirred with thoughts of pursuing her as more than a competitive racer.

But marrying her? Was marriage to a woman he didn't love, a woman like Irish, even plausible? Hadn't he already determined he wasn't ready to date anyone yet?

He gulped.

What if they circumvented the whole dating part of a relationship and jumped right into marriage? Surely, he was foolish for thinking of it. Daft. Idiotic! He couldn't suggest that kind of marriage to Irish!

Plus, he felt strongly against such arrangements. He and all his brothers did! When they were kids, Lake and Hud overheard some older women in the church gossiping about how "those North boys would amount to nothing and wind up in awful marriages of convenience like their parents did!" He and Hud had vowed that even if it meant their deaths, they would never do such a thing! How could he go against their brothers' pact?

Yet the woman sitting in front of him was stunning in loveliness. Athletic. Spoke her mind. And she cared deeply about dogs. All good traits!

She came out here hoping for financial assistance. What if they helped each other and both got what they wanted? What if he asked, and she said yes?

God, this isn't Your idea, right? If I am ruining Your plan for my life, stop me cold! Open my eyes. Because right now, what I see is a gorgeous woman who could help my dreams come true. And I can help her with the animal shelter she's passionate about protecting.

No stop signs flashed red in his brain. No neon warning signs, either.

Could he and Irish have a relationship built on shared goals? On doing good for the animals they both loved?

"Lake?" Irish waved her hand in front of his face, drawing him from his introspection.

This was a now-or-never situation. Once he asked Irish what he imagined asking her, there was no going back. If she laughed riotously at his proposal or stomped out of the cabin hurling insults at him, he might never be able to show his face on the racecourse again.

"Uh, Irish?" He stood slowly and stuffed his hands into the back pockets of his jeans.

"Yes?" She stood also.

"What would you think about marrying me?" Heat flamed up his injured face, but he forced himself to meet her gaze.

"What?" she yelped, reminding him of her "Yip-yip-yip" during their races. Her eyes bugged like jade stones set in snowballs.

"This is sudden, I realize."

"It sure is."

He took a breath and rushed on before he lost his nerve. "You want a financial endowment from me, correct?"

"A philanthropic thing. Not marriage! That's crazy!"

Her blushing cheeks were cute.

"Maybe. However, if you took a chance on me, and I took a chance on you, something good might come of us being together. Of us joining forces." For the oddest split-second, he wanted to take her in his arms and find out what kissing her soft-looking shiny lips would be like. *Steady, North.* "Here's the thing. I must marry within the next week—"

"A week? That's insane!"

"I must stay married for at least five years to receive my full inheritance."

"Wait. You're not kidding?"

"I'm not." He took several deep breaths. Leaping into marriage was absolutely unlike him. What would his brothers say? What would Hud, the brother who would be the most affected by Lake's decision, say? "To get the finances left to me by my biological grandfather, I must be married by my thirty-fifth birthday. I was engaged and thought it might work out. Then we broke up. The clock is ticking."

Even suggesting a less-than-real marriage to access the money was distasteful to him. He and Hud became blood brothers over the pact they took. Hud would be so angry if Lake went against that and married Irish.

"What do you think?"

Irish removed her knit cap, showing off her long wavy red hair to its fullest potential. He had always been drawn to her red locks flying in the wind behind her during a race.

A mischievous grin crossed her mouth. "If you sent out invitations to all the eligible women in Thunder Ridge, asking them to try out for marriage like one of those Bachelor shows, you'd have a lineup of girls in your driveway."

"I doubt that. Why would I want to do that, anyway?"

"So you and some babe could grab the money and live happily ever after." She gnawed on her lower lip, drawing his attention to her mouth again. "Some lucky woman would jump at the chance to be your wife."

Some lucky woman?

"What about you?" His tone came out sounding huskier than he intended.

"Me? I care nothing for money." She backhanded the air and shook her head. "Other than what it takes to feed and shelter my dogs. Maybe to get some property of my own one day."

"And provide for the dogs at the animal shelter, right?"

"Sure. I care about them too." She tugged her hat back on her head. "When I heard about their possible demise, I had to do something. I won't sit idly by while they are denied basic rights! But to change my whole future?" She glanced around the cabin. "Based on how miserly you live—no offense—and since I've heard your sorry tale about having to marry some hapless female, I've wasted my time. And yours."

First, she called the woman who might marry him lucky. Now, she contradicted herself and referred to such a woman as hapless. Which was it?

"Not necessarily. As I said, you could marry me." What Irish wanted to do for the animal shelter sounded like a worthy cause. If any woman within a hundred miles of Thunder Ridge would marry him on the fly, he guessed a free-spirited woman like her might do so.

"You mean a marriage of convenience?"

"I guess." His brothers would disapprove, but Lake had to act quickly.

"I've never heard of such a thing happening in modern times."

"It's rare. However, my parents had such a marriage."

"No way! Mr. and Mrs. North act totally in love, even at their age."

He laughed. "One, they are in love. They still go out on dates to celebrate their monthly anniversaries. Two, they'd find it humorous that you commented on their age like a love thermometer."

"I wasn't trying to be offensive." She frowned.

"Talk to my mom. She'll tell you her marriage to my dad wasn't a love match." Lake touched a tender place on his cheek and squelched a groan. "She agreed to marry my dad so he could become a pastor here."

"Like she was forced?" Irish's brows rose.

"Not that. Mom was pregnant with me. She agreed to the arrangement for personal reasons."

"Oh."

"I'm saying sometimes people choose to get married other than for love. There are even some stories in the Bible about those kinds of marriages. It can still be genuine."

"That's hard to imagine."

Lake clasped Irish's hand briefly and felt a zing of attraction for her. Marriage might be challenging, and sometimes a daily choice to stick together, but having observed his parents' commitment to each other, he believed it was possible for him and Irish to find love ... someday.

Chapter Six

Marry him? Seriously? Could Irish consider such a disingenuous offer, even if doing so saved the animals at the shelter? She thought of her own three dogs and how much she loved them. If any of them were in harm's way, she'd do anything to save them. She couldn't stand by and knowingly let any animal suffer.

But marrying a mere acquaintance? That was stupid!

Was this just about Lake gaining access to his inheritance? His one final, desperate opportunity?

Still, she asked, "So, if I consented to this plan—which I'm not saying I will—you'd invest in the shelter? Save the dogs?"

"Yes. It's a worthwhile cause." He touched a sore-looking place on his cheek and winced. "I'd use the money for some other things too. But rescuing the animals would be at the top of my list."

"Where would I live?" She glanced around the tiny living room and kitchen combo.

"Here." He swallowed hard.

While she preferred a minimalistic lifestyle, how could the two of them and six dogs share this shoebox? Even though she'd have land to run her dogs, this would be close quarters. "Would this be a ... a real marriage?"

A soft smile spread across his mouth.

Her gaze lingered too long on those masculine lips. Her heart pounded a chaotic beat. Her fingers tingled with the desire to reach out, grab Lake's shirt, and plant a romantic kiss on his mouth. There was her impetuous nature trying to get her into trouble! She controlled herself and waited for his answer. Still, everything within her wanted to try kissing Lake North before she even considered marrying him.

"It would be a real marriage in the future, if you're referring to love and intimacy."

Intimacy? He must be delirious to bring up that subject! They barely knew each other. But she was attracted to him. No denying the thundering way her heart pounded ever since he asked her to marry him. Yet how could she consider his proposal? How could she not?

"I'm sorry to put pressure on you." He clenched his hands together in what appeared to be a nervous gesture. "The week deadline makes this urgent."

"If we discover we don't get along or if our marriage doesn't become genuine in two or three months, can we opt out?" She wanted a guaranteed bad-kisser escape clause.

"No."

"I'm not pledging my life to a man who might—" She clamped her teeth shut and finished in her thoughts—*"kiss like a frog!"* She wasn't desperate enough to jump into marriage with him, even with her lease expiring and nowhere else for her to live with her dogs, without knowing they had some chemistry.

If they didn't have that, the shelter would have to find another benefactor. Could they find someone before it was too late? Shelley, the receptionist at the animal shelter, said they discussed getting rid of some of the animals as if they were already in danger! Irish would do anything to protect them.

But marriage was such a colossal thing. Nothing to be taken lightly. Nothing to jump into like she leaped into so many other things in her life. "I need to think this over."

"Sure. Me too." Lake tipped his chin down, eyeing her. "What is your biggest concern about marrying me? Do you find me repulsive?"

"Not repulsive. Although, your face is a mess today."

"I'll say." He ran his hand over his dark hair. "So, what is it? Do you prefer blonds?"

His grin brought her attention to his lips again. Something unexplainable—a passionate curiosity, perhaps—compelled her to investigate his kissing skills. To not leave this cabin until she decided if he was husband material or not. He'd been bold with her. Why couldn't she be bold, also?

"You asked me to marry you in a shocking proposal! There's a detail I need to know about you."

"Okay. What's that?" His dark gaze met hers.

"This may seem forward of me, but one daring thing deserves another. I need to find out if you—" She crossed the few steps between them, grabbed his suspenders, and pulled him toward her. His eyes widened. So did his mouth. Perfect!

His cool lips met hers with surprising accuracy and heat. The kiss was soft initially, a tender exploration of each other's lips. He didn't resist when she went for a deeper, hungrier kiss, tugging him closer to her. His mouth met hers, kiss for kiss. Heatwave with heatwave.

Stunned, exhilarated, and out of breath, she backed up. "Okay."

"Okay? I'd say that was—"

"Too much?"

"Not nearly enough." He grinned.

"Good answer." Reining in her thoughts and her desire to jump back into his arms, she strode toward the door. After opening it, she glanced over her shoulder. "I accept your proposal, Lake North. I will marry you." She stepped onto the porch, closed the door, and released the longest sigh humanly possible.

Kissing Lake would be just fine!

Chapter Seven

Lake rushed to the window and watched Irish confidently stride from his front porch to her mud-splattered car. She agreed to marry him!

"Whooooeee!" What a kiss!

Wait until he told Mom about him and Irish getting married! She wouldn't believe it. Gran either. No doubt, his brothers would razz him mercilessly. He was going to marry a woman he barely knew to get his inheritance, and he was ecstatic about it!

Lord, I hope You are guiding me in this. I'm taking a giant leap of faith. Irish and I both are! Please catch us if we fall.

This morning he prayed that God would help him find a wife. One just landed in his lap. Not literally. But their kiss? Man, oh, man. Talk about sizzling hot! If marriage to Irish would be full of kissing like that, he'd say, "I do," today!

One week. Lake had one week to prepare the cabin, his family, and his heart for Irish to be his bride!

Later that day, he dropped by his parents' house and found Mom baking in the kitchen. "I have news! I asked Irish Markham to marry me!"

"What? The skijoring racer?" She dropped a bag of chocolate chips on the counter and frowned at him. "Lake Daniel North! You didn't!"

That wasn't the happy reaction he imagined.

"Yes, I did! I can accept the inheritance now since I found someone willing to marry me. I'll be able to pay you and Dad back."

"Found someone? Pay us back?" She thrust out her arms. "Who cares about any of that?"

"I do."

Mom was usually level-headed and didn't yell or act emotionally when dealing with Lake or his brothers. Typically, she took chaos in stride. Not today.

"Do you realize what you've done?" she nearly shouted.

"Yes! I'm going to marry a woman I don't love. But one day, I will, just like you and Dad fell for each other after you married. I already like her a lot!"

"Like her?" Mom gawked at him.

"You and Dad have had a long marriage that started with friendship. Irish and I can do the same thing."

"Oh, Lake." Moaning, she covered her face with her hands. "I can't believe you did this."

"Why not? I've heard your love story my whole life."

Mom lowered her hands and glared at him. Without speaking, she measured flour into a large bowl in jerky movements.

Did it bother her that he was going to accept money from the father who disowned her, even though he was already gone? Or did she worry about her oldest son marrying a woman he didn't love?

They'd talked about the inheritance enough times over the years. He was eight years old when he first found out about it. That's when

Hud and Aiden came to live with them after their parents died in a tragic car accident.

Since then, Lake and Hud, the two eldest of Richard Dupont's grandchildren, knew they must marry someone before their thirty-fifth birthday or forego their grandfather's bequest. They agreed to the latter, although Lake had wavered on that decision.

"Are you going to tell me about this woman you asked to marry you?" Mom asked in a more resigned tone.

"You've probably seen her at Nelly's. She's a server there. Long red hair. Deep green eyes."

"Hmm. Does she attend church here?"

"Not at Dad's church. A lot of our races are on the weekends."

"What about Laurie?"

"What about her?" His shoulders stiffened. He didn't want to talk about his ex-fiancée to Mom or anyone else.

"You loved her. You would have married her. How does asking another woman to marry you so soon after the breakup make you feel?"

"Let's not discuss Laurie, okay?"

"Lake, honey, I know what it's like to be married to someone who hasn't gotten over someone else." She clasped her hands around his wrists. "Don't do that to this woman, okay?"

"I wouldn't intentionally hurt Irish."

"Of course, you wouldn't." She let go of his arms. "You're a nice man. Your dad didn't mean to hurt me either." She dumped some salt onto the flour and ran her fingers through it. "We had some tough times. But things worked out. I love your dad. Always will."

"So you approve?"

"Of a marriage of convenience to get your grandad's money? No!" She tossed up her hands, sprinkling flour dust like rain. "Honestly, when you and Hud agreed not to take the money, I was thrilled. And thankful. What will your brother think of your decision?"

"He'll be madder than a bear whose honey has been stolen. But saving the animals at the shelter is a worthy cause."

"What's with the animals?"

He explained about the shelter possibly closing and Irish's desire to protect the dogs and cats there.

"I'd say you're too blinded by love to see the cost of entering a marriage this way, but that doesn't appear to be the case." Mom rested her hands on the countertop. "Am I missing something? Do you care for this woman?"

His and Irish's kisses flitted through his thoughts. "Just support me in this, will you?"

Mom gazed at him for several seconds. "Invite her to dinner tonight and let Granny Trish meet her." She flicked some flour in his direction. "She has the best intuition about a person's character."

"Mom—"

"You want my blessing?"

"Yeah. I do." He sighed.

"Dinner is at six."

"Will you ask Gran to go easy on Irish?"

Mom chuckled. "Afraid of her digging into the real reason behind this proposal?"

"You might say that."

"I'll tell her. But Gran is eighty-eight. Don't blame me if she doesn't listen!"

Chapter Eight

Irish agreed to marry a man she didn't love, and, on the same evening, she was expected to sit with her fiancé's family for a spaghetti dinner? She needed more time to sort out her thoughts.

No doubt the other seven Norths seated at the table—his parents, grandmother, and four of his brothers that she could barely keep straight in her mind—were questioning Lake's sanity in asking a woman he knew only as a racing competitor to marry him. She intercepted some grumpy expressions sent her way by Spur. After what he said about her helping Lake get out of his funk, he should be on her side. Apparently not.

Lake's grandmother, Trish, wore the most welcoming smile, her pale, seafoam eyes shining. But their depths held questions Irish imagined and squirmed over. *Why are you cavorting with my grandson? Are you a gold digger?*

What a laugh! She cared nothing for money other than how it provided for her and her dogs. And for the animals in the Thunder Ridge Animal Shelter. She'd do anything to save them, even if it meant marrying Lake. Although she cringed at the way she had agreed to his proposal so quickly. All because of one unforgettable kiss? Was she that desperate?

A spaghetti noodle stuck in her throat. She coughed and guzzled some water.

"Are you okay, my dear?" Trish asked.

"Yes. Sorry. I didn't mean to splatter tomato sauce everywhere."

"Don't worry. This table has seen far worse." Liv chuckled.

"Mom was a horrible cook when Dad met her!" The youngest brother, who had light blond hair, blue eyes, and appeared to be in his early twenties, grinned.

"Thanks for mentioning it, Finn." Liv smiled good-naturedly. "I made this meal alone, without your father's or grandmother's assistance. Thank you very much."

"It's about time after thirty-five years of marriage, huh, Mom?" Spur guffawed.

The younger guys chuckled too.

Pastor North, seated at the head of the table to Liv's left, kissed her cheek. "You're a marvelous cook, Livvy. The best inventor of new recipes!"

"Here. Here." Trish lifted her water glass like a salute. "Anyone who keeps nine sons fed and alive has learned the art of cooking. Olivia, you have my admiration." Compassion and appreciation oozed from her kind expression.

"I couldn't have raised a big family without you." Liv lifted her glass in the older woman's direction.

Observing a wife and a mother-in-law acting so kind-hearted and loving to each other, especially after thirty-five years, was a novel idea to Irish.

Beside her, Lake twirled the noodles around his fork, staring at the food as if in deep thought. Any chance he was having second thoughts about his proposal already?

"So, Irish." Trish smiled at her. "That's a lovely name, by the way."

"Thanks. With my red hair and green eyes, my dad couldn't resist calling me that."

"Where is your family?"

"Dad moved as far across the country as he could from my mom." She cleared her throat. "He lives in Florida. Mom and hubby number three live in Portland, Oregon."

"Any siblings?" Trish asked softly.

"One younger sister."

"How did you meet my grandson?" The older woman tilted her head, gazing at Irish.

"Oh, um." Now, why did she flounder over the simple inquiry? "He and I were in a race together. Our dogs got their lines tangled."

Beside her, Lake chuckled.

"So, you're a ski racer like our Lake?" Trish smiled proudly.

"I am."

"It's called skijoring, Gran. And Irish is a lot better at the sport than I am. She's won first-place awards." Lake nudged Irish's arm. "She's the one I'm always chasing."

Spur belted out a loud laugh.

"I meant in the races, bro."

"Sure you did."

Irish focused on eating her pasta without choking on it. She'd let Lake field his family's questions from here on out.

"So, how long have you two been dating?"

"Gran—" Lake shook his head.

"Is that too personal of a question?"

"More spaghetti, anyone?" Liv asked, probably attempting a diversion.

"Yeah. How long have you been dating?" Spur asked. "Last I knew, you were barely speaking to each other. Lake just stared gaga at Irish every chance he got."

"Spur," Lake said gruffly. "That's enough!"

"I didn't think you'd be so touchy about taking a wife."

Irish coughed again. How would she get through even one meal with this boisterous, inquisitive family of Norths?

Chapter Nine

"Tone down the juvenile questions, will you?" Lake appreciated Spur's work with his dogs, but that didn't give his brother the right to pester him and Irish. Or to pry into their private lives.

"You asked a woman you hardly know to marry you, and I'm the one who's juvenile?" Spur stuffed noodles and sauce into his mouth like he hadn't eaten in a week.

"Hey, guys. There's still no troublesome talk allowed at the table!" Mom tapped her knuckles on the table.

It took every ounce of restraint for Lake to remain quiet and not say something rude to his brother.

Silence prevailed for about two minutes.

How was Irish handling all of this? They'd barely had time to figure out how to be engaged, let alone act like an average couple around his family. Even with their passionate kissing earlier, what was he thinking asking her to marry him before they had a real relationship? They shared a common interest involving their dogs. What about faith? Or having kids? Good night. What about everyday stuff, like who would wash the dishes or pick up groceries?

When he and Irish discussed getting married quickly, it seemed like a good solution for keeping the local animal shelter from closing and solving his financial woes. Her heated kiss seconded the motion! He had never kissed anyone like that in his whole life. Not even Laurie.

Just then, he made the mistake of glancing at Irish. Her eyes twinkled back at him. Was she imagining the same thing he was? She winked at him. She *was* thinking of their kisses!

A wide grin crossed his mouth. One fantastic thing about their impromptu marriage would be his marrying a woman who liked to flirt. Her smile alone took his breath away.

"Irish, tell us about yourself," Granny Trish said. "I don't mean to put you on the spot, dear. I just want to get to know you better."

"I don't have much to tell. Three years ago, I moved north from Portland to enjoy snowy winters and do more skijoring." She shrugged. "It's just me and my three sweet pups."

Lake enjoyed listening to Irish speak and watching her interact with his grandmother. It was as if he'd never witnessed a woman's mouth moving. He noticed every lifting of her upper lip. The way her tongue slid slightly across her mouth. She didn't wear lipstick. But he recognized the clear glossy sheen that drew his attention to her mouth earlier.

"Sounds like you love your dogs as much as Lake loves his. I hear it in your voice." Mom smiled toward Irish.

"I do. They are my babies. My three girls. I hope to build my team so I can participate in four-dog and maybe even six-dog mushing events, but that takes—" She shrugged again.

Cash—Lake filled in the unspoken word. Despite their romantic interlude today, they were marrying each other so they'd both get what they wanted. He needed a wife to help him fulfill the demands of a grandfather he had never met. In doing so, he could pay off his parents, his college loans, and the mortgage on his twenty acres. Irish would get to rescue the animals in the shelter. Then build her team with more dogs.

While he would have preferred that they fell in love first, he hoped love would follow.

"It's wonderful that you and Lake have a bond with your dogs and racing." Mom glanced back and forth between them. "Lake received his first dog as a Christmas present when he was eight. He's owned a dog or two ever since."

"Brownie." Lake ran his thumb over the condensation on his water glass. "He was my first rescue pup from the shelter."

"Aww." Irish set her hand on his arm like she'd been doing so for months. "You have a gentle way with your dogs. I love that about you."

Did she purposefully say "love?"

Spur snickered. "You should have seen him with his poodle, Molly, in high school. She chased off every girl he dated. Molly wanted to be the only woman in his life. Was for a long time."

"I can understand why." Irish winked at Lake again.

His cheeks felt hot. He took in a dry breath, his pulse racing a mile a minute.

His brothers chortled.

By the end of dessert, almost everyone at the table had regaled Irish with some childhood or teenage incident between him and one of his dogs. Throughout the storytelling, she acted interested in their tales, laughing and saying "Aww" or "How cute!"

He was intrigued by his fiancée. When they said good night, would they kiss like an engaged couple might do? After her kisses earlier, he didn't know what to expect.

"Thanks for coming over," Mom said as they were getting ready to leave.

"Thanks for inviting me." Irish shook Mom's hand, then turned to Granny Trish. "It was nice meeting you."

Lake almost put his arm around her and led her out the door before his meddling grandmother, whom he dearly loved, pulled an embarrassing question from her proverbial hat.

"You as well, dear. Can we expect to see you in church on Sunday?"

"Oh, maybe." Irish smiled at Gran, and Lake appreciated her kindness toward his grandmother, even if the older woman was a little pushy. "I often work the Sunday morning shift at Nelly's. Or else I'm attending skijoring races."

"There's always Sunday evening." Gran smiled back at her.

"Uh, right. Thank you for mentioning it."

Dad reached out and shook Irish's hand. "You are welcome here anytime. Call on us if you need anything. I mean that."

"Thank you, Pastor North."

"Since we're going to be family, call me Smith."

"Thank you. Good night."

Lake and Irish walked along the snow-packed path toward her car in the single-digit temperature. The crisp air made puffs of steam out of their breathing. Neither spoke. What did his racing-competitor-turned-fiancée think of his family? She had handled herself well under their questions and scrutiny.

At the car, she leaned against the front door and gazed at the dark night sky lit up with a bazillion stars. "I never tire of the view."

"Nor do I." He glanced up at the Big Dipper, letting his eyes train on the North Star, just like he had done ever since he was a kid and thought of becoming an astronomer.

Irish's mittened hands clutched his arms. "You have a lovely family, Lake. I mean that."

"Thanks." He liked hearing his name on her lips. "I'm glad they didn't overwhelm you. Our dinner times were lively with a family of nine boys."

"I can imagine. With four of your brothers present tonight, it was—"

"Energetic?"

"Inquisitive."

"Sorry about that."

"Even so, they made me feel welcome." She dropped her hands from touching his arms. "About what happened earlier between us?" The hesitancy in her tone sounded like a warning. "I may have made a mistake."

He stepped back to gaze into her deep green eyes. "After one meal with my family, you want out of our engagement?"

"Nothing so drastic." She pressed her lower lip between her teeth as if fighting a grin. "I'm determined to rescue the dogs at the shelter. Your offer is still a good one."

"Then, what?"

"The kissing."

"You didn't like our kisses?" That was hard to believe!

She chuckled lightly, and the sweet sound sent shivers racing through him. He could stand in sub-zero weather and still be warm listening to her laugh all night.

"The kisses were remarkable and passed my test."

"Your test? What were you testing?"

"Compatibility. Chemistry. Future potential?"

"We certainly have that!"

"I believe we do." She lifted her chin like she wasn't backing down from whatever she still had to say. "Your proposal took me by surprise."

"It took me by surprise too. So did your kiss."

The porch lights gave off enough brilliance that Lake saw her features perfectly. Her mouth tipped up, her tongue moistening her glossy lips, and the sparkle of her eyes gazing toward him made him yearn to kiss her passionately again. Test, or no test.

"I've experienced some lousy kissers in my dating lineup." She glanced up at the sky again.

"But I passed your test?"

"With flying colors."

"Good. Shall we give it another try just to make sure?"

Leaning toward him, she seemed caught in the same romantic trance he felt. Any second their lips would meet and—

She pushed against the chest of his parka, then opened her car door. The creak of the old relic broke the stillness of the night and the mood.

"So, no kiss?"

"That was the possible mistake I won't make again."

"You want to marry me but don't want to kiss me?"

"Something like that." She winked and slid into the driver's seat. The engine started up with a loud rumble and rattle. "We'll get together and make wedding plans soon, huh?"

Lake squatted down and stroked the back of his fingers down her warm cheek. Her mouth dropped open as if he surprised her with the gesture. It wasn't the same as kissing her. Yet his fingers caressing her cheek made him picture their kiss. And long for it.

"Sweetheart, you can count on that."

Chapter Ten

"When did you get into town?" Lake sat across from Hud in Nelly's Diner two days after the dinner he and Irish attended with his family. He'd received a text to meet him here.

"I flew into Spokane from Ketchikan this morning. Drove straight here." Hud's dark hair, which was rarely out of place, appeared messy, like he'd been strumming his fingers through it. "Yesterday, Mom told me about your plans to marry some woman so you can get the inheritance by your birthday. I had to see you in person. What about our pact? Our brothers' promise? Are you throwing it in the toilet?"

"I'm sorry you came all this way because of that." Lake wished Mom hadn't called Hud. He would have gotten around to talking with his brother eventually. Preferably, after the wedding. "I should have called you, but I decided to marry Irish quickly."

"Not cool, Lake. We promised never to take money from the old man who kicked Mom out. And that we'd never let those old women's predictions about us come true." Hud's brownish-black eyes shuttered nearly closed. "What happened to our agreement?"

"I know. I'm sorry. I didn't mean to—"

"Lie to me?"

"I wasn't lying." Lake clenched his jaw.

"You've changed. I thought we made the same decision when we were kids. That we'd work hard and honestly for every cent we made."

"I want to help the local animal shelter."

"And make your own life easier!"

"That too. Is it such a bad thing?"

He and Hud had been like twins ever since their first Christmas together when they were eight. Lake hardly remembered a time when Hud wasn't his buddy, brother, and cousin all rolled into one.

"Listen. You want to ruin your life by taking the money and offending your brothers, it's your decision." Hud's dark eyes glinted in Lake's direction. "But I couldn't let you do so without trying to stop you."

"Coffee?" A young server buzzed up to their table.

Both men flipped their upside-down mugs over.

"Thanks," Lake said as the woman filled his cup.

"Anytime, Lake." She winked and moved to the next table.

"Still flirting with every passing woman?" Hud asked gruffly.

"No, I wasn't. That's more your style."

Hud glared at him, and Lake wished he hadn't made the snide comment. Their conversation was already tense enough.

"I recognize this matrimonial malarky for what it is—your chance to grab Grandfather's loot. You need funds to pay off your land, so you let a woman hoodwink you into marrying her?" Hud's speech turned impassioned. "When did you ever care about money enough to marry a stranger for it?"

Heat bled up Lake's neck. Glancing around, a few other gazes met his. Just great. Now the rumor mill would kick into high gear about two of the preacher's sons arguing about money in Nelly's.

Fortunately, Irish wasn't working today. Otherwise, she'd be embarrassed by this discussion.

"I don't expect you to understand." Lake sipped his coffee, trying to keep himself from responding rudely again. "I even considered taking the inheritance back when I was engaged to Laurie."

"You what?" Hud ground out.

"That fell through," Lake said in a quieter tone. "Then, two days ago, Irish talked to me about saving the animal shelter. It made sense for us to get married and do good with the money."

"Does she have the capital to invest, too?"

"No. She's a fellow racer. Not wealthy."

"See there! It's all about the money."

"It's not like that." Lake thudded his finger against the table. "Irish wants to rescue the dogs. Will do anything to save them."

"Even marrying a guy who's on the rebound? A guy who falls for the first woman who smiles at him?"

Lake released a growl of frustration. Did Mom tell Hud he was on the rebound and fell for the first woman who paid attention to him? Or was Spur reporting this stuff to Hud?

"What is she after? Half your money when she divorces you?"

Two plates landed firmly on the table in front of them.

"Will this be all for you North boys?" Irish peered down at Lake, a scowl etched on her face.

"I-Irish." How much did she hear? "You are working today."

"So I am." She dangled her bare left hand beneath Hud's nose. "No ring. I don't even need one. I'm not the money-hungry female you think I am."

"Hud, meet my fiancée, Irish Markham."

Hud cleared his throat. "Hello, Irish."

"I'd like to say it's nice to meet another one of Lake's brothers, but—?" She lifted one shoulder and quirked an eyebrow. "I'll be back to check on you boys shortly."

Lake caught her hand loosely. "I'll talk to you later, okay?"

She nodded without speaking.

"Lover's quarrel?" Hud asked in a mocking tone.

"Thanks to you. And not lovers. Racing competitors."

"Yet you asked her to marry you!"

"Keep your voice down, will you?" Lake sliced his sausage and stuffed a bite in his mouth. "The bottom line is I want to pay Mom and Dad back. Pay off my mortgage. And I'd like to stop doing a job I hate!"

"At what cost? A lifetime of suffering through a marriage you can't tolerate?" Hud separated his food so nothing on his plate touched. He'd always been a picky eater. "Are the folks asking for you to repay them?"

"No. But when I was going to marry Laurie—"

"Laurie. Another mistake."

"What do you have against her now?" Hud was too opinionated. Too prideful. Lake guzzled his lukewarm coffee. Then set his cup down with a thud.

When Irish walked past with plates filling her arms, their gazes met. She glanced away first. He hated the awkwardness between them now. The strain between him and Hud was awful too. He'd probably face a firing squad of accusations with each of his brothers for marrying Irish and accepting the funds they all despised growing up.

"What might I have against Laurie? Let me count the ways." Hud held up his left hand, ticking his fingers with his right index finger. "Tepid. Lackluster. Didn't like your brothers. Didn't like your dogs. You deserved better."

Lake was about to disagree.

"Thus, his reasons for choosing me." Irish shuffled her fingers over his hair. "Isn't that right, sweet lips?" What was with the change in her demeanor and calling him a nickname?

"Too bad he didn't find you first." One of Hud's eyebrows arched on his forehead.

"Amen to that." Irish nodded.

Lake's gut clenched at how Hud disrespected Laurie. She may not have been Hud's ideal of a potential wife, but while they were together, she was faithful and devoted to Lake. Would he be able to say the same about Irish? Now, why did he have to go and compare them like that?

Irish frowned at him. What did he miss? "Uh, what?"

"I said you and I have found something special already." She peered intensely at him as if trying to get him to agree. "If you didn't like my kisses—" She shrugged and walked away.

Heat spread up Lake's face.

"You're kissing her already?" Hud rubbed his hand over his several-day-old whiskers that appeared to be a permanent fixture on his face.

"Like I'd tell you." Lake cut his pancake into fourths and stuffed pieces in his mouth. "Let's skip the talk about Irish and get to the financial side of this interrogation."

"But the other part intrigues me. How did you catch a woman like her, even if it is fake?" Hud lifted his chin toward Irish serving food on the other side of the restaurant. "She's fire. Might be too much for you."

"I doubt that." Lake thought of the way she kissed him two days ago. Of the heated way he kissed her back. "She might be a fiery tempest." He met Irish's gaze and winked at her. "But I like her passion just fine."

Hud gave him a grudging nod. "Okay. So, tell me, how can you reconcile our grandfather's betrayal of Mom by taking the inheritance he denied her?"

Lake groaned. How could he hope to explain without causing an even wider chasm between them?

Chapter Eleven

Irish paced in front of the animal shelter, her irritation level reaching its zenith. How could Lake stand her up like this? She agreed to marry him for the well-being of the animals in this shelter. How dare he snub her about the one thing that would get him what he wanted!

More pacing. More checking her phone to see if Lake had called or sent a text. Nothing! How dare he treat her so disrespectfully!

Ever since overhearing his discussion with Hud yesterday, she had struggled with her agreement to marry him. What did Lake still feel for his ex? When his brother commented about Laurie, Lake responded defensively, like he'd punch Hud if he said another word about her.

Marrying Lake so he could get an inheritance and rescue the animal shelter had seemed noble and compassionate. But doing so with a man who loved someone else, especially if Irish was starting to have feelings for him, would be agony. She would lose too much of herself if she fell for him and then had to live in a loveless marriage for five long years. Even a great cause wasn't worth that pain.

That's why she had called for a meeting with Mac Taylor, the shelter's director. The financial situation might not be as dire as Shelley said it was. Maybe she exaggerated. Surely, none of the dogs were on death row. Perhaps there wasn't any reason for her to marry a man she didn't know that well. Plenty of time to cancel their wedding!

She stomped her feet to warm them and paced some more.

Breaking off their engagement wouldn't help Lake with his predicament of having to be married before receiving his inheritance. Maybe he could find another woman in the local lonely-hearts club willing to marry him on short notice. But in three days? Did she want Lake going after his ex, or a man-crazy woman like Tiffany?

She groaned and jerked her phone out of her pocket. It was fifteen minutes past their meeting time. She'd already sent three texts, but she shot Lake another one.

Where are you?

Shelley, wearing a pink polo shirt with "Thunder Ridge Animal Shelter" embroidered above the pocket, opened the door. "Mac says you'd better come on in now."

"Okay." *Lake North, if you don't show up in ten seconds—*

Taking a deep breath, Irish squared her shoulders and strode into the manager's box-like office. She shook Mac's hand, gazing down at the balding fiftyish man. "Sorry for the delay."

"No problem. I have another meeting in fifteen minutes, so I thought we'd better get started." Mac waved his hand toward one of the two seats opposite his. "Is someone else joining you?"

"I hope so." She sat down on the edge of the chair. "Lake North, my partner, should be here any second." She hesitated to use the term "fiancé." Was a man who kept a woman waiting like this, one without the decency to call or text to explain the hold up, a trustworthy enough person to marry? Especially after the conversation she'd overheard between Lake and Hud? "Let's proceed."

"Of course. What is your concern today?"

"I've heard things aren't going well with the shelter financially." Mac's posture stiffened, but she forged ahead. "I care about this place because I adopted one of my dogs from here. And because I love dogs! I'm worried the financial problems might be serious enough to close the place down. Are things that bad?"

Mac's face turned beet red. So did his scalp. "I didn't know folks in town were already discussing our tenuous situation. I can't deny the severity of our current circumstances."

"I don't mean to embarrass you." Yet Irish needed answers today. "I truly care about the animals. Are the rumors true about closing?"

"I care about them also." Mac stared fixedly at her, his voice deepening. "However, caring isn't enough. Caring doesn't feed or shelter the animals coming through our doors. We need solutions. Our funds have dried up."

Lake burst through the doorway and pulled off his knit hat. "I'm sorry for being late. I had an emergency with one of my dogs. I had to wait for the vet and my assistant to arrive."

Irish lunged to her feet. "Which dog? Is he okay? This meeting can wait." Hearing one of Lake's dogs was sick or injured immediately changed how she felt about him standing her up.

"Rambler tore his paw on some jagged ice, a frozen stick, or something. Poor guy."

"How is he now?"

"He's resting. Spur is with him. Doc Cooper says he'll recover fine." He clenched his hat between his hands. "Sorry for holding up the meeting."

"That's okay. Please—" Mac gestured back toward the two chairs.

Irish set her palm on Lake's coat sleeve as they sat down. "Are you okay?"

"Worried sick. But Rambler's okay. That's what matters."

"I'm so sorry he got hurt." She clasped her hands in her lap.

"Thanks."

She would be worried sick too if one of her babies got injured. She wouldn't care about being on time for a meeting with a wounded pet at home, either. Maybe she wouldn't throw in the towel about marrying Lake. His situation had been a legitimate emergency.

Mac tapped his wristwatch. "I'm sorry, but we only have a few minutes. How can I help you?"

"What have you already covered?" Lake set his hat on the thigh of his jeans.

"Not much." Irish eyed Mac. "Is the shelter going under?"

"We're not trying to pry into your affairs." Lake's soothing tone sounded like Pastor North's. "We have personal reasons for asking."

"Our funding is gone," Mac spoke in a monotone. "There's not enough to pay the receptionist or the vet service."

"And the dogs?" Irish asked.

"We'll do our best to find homes. Or pass them off to other shelters. We should be able to move the desirable breeds."

"And the less desirable ones?" Irish's irritation rose.

"I hate to mention what might happen to them." Mac picked at a hangnail as if it were of more value than the topic.

Irish and Lake exchanged glances. If the shelter closed, the remaining animals would probably be put on a twenty-four-hour notice. What if any of those were her dogs? What if Aurora still lived here? Or Lake's Rambler?

Even the thought of cruelty happening to one of her babies made her feel desperate for a resolution to the problem. She'd marry Lake on the spot if it meant stopping injustices from happening to the dogs and cats in this facility.

"You have a moral obligation to the animals in your care!" A rush of heat rose in her temples. "An obligation to the community to do your best to care for all the creatures entrusted to you!"

"Miss Markham, my hands are tied." Mac lifted his empty hands. "I don't have the money. If I did, I'd make sure every animal had food and provision." Yet his tone lacked conviction. He kept glancing at his watch.

"Let's say someone had the money to contribute, would you keep the shelter open? Continue working here?" Irish asked, although, something about Mac made her wary of him. Maybe his emotionless tone. Or the way he seemed to lack genuine concern for the animals.

"What are you getting at? Are you thinking of donating to the shelter?"

"Yes." Lake smoothed his palm across Irish's shoulder, startling her. He probably meant the gesture to show a unified front, so she didn't back away from his touch. "Irish and I are going to be married. I'm about to receive an inheritance. Since we're both dog lovers, we'd like to donate some money to our hometown shelter as a wedding gift to ourselves."

They hadn't discussed the money being used as a wedding gift, but it sounded all right to her.

"Would this happen to be a large donation?" The director's eyes lit up like dollar signs flashed in them, making Irish even more suspicious of him.

"We still have to speak with my lawyer"—Lake's hand nestled against her shoulder, his cool fingers touching her neck—"but we're convinced we want this shelter to succeed and thrive in Thunder Ridge. If that includes us giving a large sum, we're prepared to do so."

"That's wonderful news!"

Irish sighed, moving away from the warmth of Lake's touch. Acting like a romantic couple when they weren't annoyed her like fingernails against a chalkboard. When the day came that she and Lake cared deeply for each other, she'd snuggle right into his arms. But not until then!

"The day just got better." Mac stood and picked up a stack of papers. He tapped them against the desk. "Thank you for stopping by and chatting with me."

Was he dismissing them?

"We want something in exchange," Irish said without standing. She didn't trust Mac, and she wanted to share her idea quickly before Lake interfered.

"What's that?" Mac's movements stilled.

"We want to save the shelter, but we also want a seat on the board. Two, actually."

"Oh, well, I can't—"

"Irish?" Lake tugged on her arm.

"I mean it. We want to sit on the board, see the books, and know how our money is being used for the animals' benefit."

Lake made a disgruntled moan.

If Mac were involved in any dishonest business practices, she and Lake having a seat at the table would keep things on course from here on out.

Mac's already-red face darkened. "Are you suggesting something underhanded is going on?"

"What I'm saying is if we donate a wad of cash, we want a hands-on approach to distributing funds for the shelter in the future." Irish faced Lake and smiled at him as if he were in total agreement. The glint in his gaze defied that notion. "After we speak to our lawyer, that is."

"You heard my fiancée." Lake finger-tapped the surface of the desk. "We want to bail out the shelter. Can you stop it from being closed? Protect all the animals in your care? I assume you have the authority to do that. Call a meeting of your board, or whatever."

Mac dropped the stack of papers on the desk. "I'll see what I can do. Now, if you'll excuse me, I have another appointment."

Lake and Irish stood.

"I look forward to doing business with you." Lake extended his hand toward Mac.

Mac appeared sickly, but he shook his hand, then nodded briefly toward Irish. "Thank you for stopping by."

"Of course." Irish linked her arm with Lake's and held on all the way outside, just in case anyone looked out the window. Ugh. She was the one who didn't like subterfuge!

Lake's arm stiffened beneath hers, but he didn't pull away. However, when they reached her car, he quickly walked away from her, jumped into his truck, and drove off without saying anything.

Chapter Twelve

Lake drove back out to his property, his brain whirring with thoughts of the wringer he'd been through today. Rambler's accident on the trail. Waiting for the vet. Meeting Mac with Irish. Her announcing they wanted to be proactive on the shelter's board! He didn't have time for that. Yes, he cared about the animals. But wouldn't his generous contribution be enough?

They weren't even married yet, and Irish was already directing their lives! As his wife, she'd occasionally speak up for him. He'd do the same for her. But not yet!

The inheritance money wouldn't be in his bank account until after the wedding ceremony. Here they were saying they'd serve on the board before he saw a dime of the funds? Talk about counting their chickens before they hatched! Doing that had caused him a lot of grief before.

He didn't blame Irish for being zealous, especially with the possible danger to the animals. But Hud's questions about her motives twisted through his thoughts. Was she after anything besides helping the dogs in the shelter?

Lake slowed down as he approached his driveway, then pulled into the small area beside Spur's truck. Not far behind him, Irish followed in her car.

She was passionate about her dogs, he knew that much about her. He'd observed her on the racecourses often enough to know she cared deeply for them. The dogs of fellow racers, too. Even today, when Lake told her about Rambler, he heard her compassion in the way she spoke about the emergency. When she said she wanted to rescue the animals in the shelter, he believed she meant it. But how far was that commitment going to go? How involved did he have to be?

He shut off the engine. Nerves on edge, he hopped out of the pickup and slammed the door. His priority was checking on Rambler. Then he'd see to Irish!

"The cabin door is open," he called to her as soon as her car door creaked open. "Go inside. I'll be in shortly." Without waiting for her to say anything, he strode toward the back of the house to the tune of a couple of baying dogs who obviously recognized the sound of his truck.

Not finding Spur or Rambler at the kennels or in the fenced play yard with the others, Lake strode to the cabin and then entered through the back door. Spur was spread out on the floor in front of the woodstove, snoring, with Rambler beside him.

Rambler's tail thumped a steady beat against the wooden floor. Lake squatted down beside his youngest dog. "How's it going, buddy?" He ruffled his whiteish fur, petting him under his chin and gazing into his turquoise eyes. "You doing okay? How's your paw?" He checked the bandage that was wrapped lightly around Rambler's foot.

"You're back." Spur stirred.

"I see you're sleeping on your watch."

"Why not?" Yawning, Spur pushed himself into a sitting position. "If Rambler whined or was in pain, I'd know. He's happy as a pig in a mud puddle. Glad to be inside."

"Good boy, Rambler." Lake stroked the dog's neck and chest. "Everything's okay, then?"

"Yep. He's enjoying the attention while the other two are yapping outdoors."

A sound like boots crossing the porch perked up Rambler's ears. He made a soft woof. Irish must have walked up on the back porch.

"Someone else here?" Spur asked.

"Irish."

"You left her outdoors?"

"Sort of." Petting the dog calmed his irritation a little. "She and I have things to discuss privately."

"Lover's tiff?" Spur thrust his hand through his scraggly red hair. "Remind me never to fall for anyone."

"Why's that?"

"The way you and Hud go through women? Count me out!" Spur's scowling expression spread out his freckles. "Makes me want to swear off marriage for good."

"Sorry we've been such bad examples to you and the others." He and Hud had experienced some bad relationships, no denying that.

"Are you going to leave her out there?" Spur nodded toward the door.

"I told her to come in." Lake set both his palms at Rambler's ears and kissed him on the top of the head. "Feel better soon, bud."

He strode to the door. Time to face the music with his future wife—and whatever it would take to make their marriage work.

Chapter Thirteen

Because she was still annoyed with Lake, Irish remained on the porch, perusing his huskies in the backyard. Pal and Ice barked and howled. They knew her, so it wasn't the frantic yapping as if she were a stranger. Still, they made plenty of noise. "Hey, puppies. How are you doing?"

Normally, she would have tromped over and petted them, but she was too keyed up about Lake's behavior and comments at the shelter to act all loving to his dogs. The whole drive out here, she'd been stewing over their conversation with Mac. By the time she pulled into Lake's driveway, her frustration simmered with a desperate need to tell him just what she thought of him!

The door creaked open.

"Irish." Lake stepped onto the porch.

"How is Rambler?" She'd cut him some slack for having an injured animal.

"He's better. Spur is with him. If we want to talk, we should stay out here."

"Fine. I'm glad to hear your dog is okay." She gnawed on her lower lip, and a few choice words pounded through her brain. *Hey, jerk, the wedding's off! Find another sucker to marry you! No wonder Laurie bailed.* But even with her livid temper, the last one was off-limits. No reason to be cruel. She'd state her facts and be done.

Done with him. Finished with the engagement and trying to save the shelter. But could she take it that far?

"I'm sorry for driving off. It was rude of me."

His humble-sounding words stole some of her thunder, but not all.

"Sure was."

"I didn't like you making assumptions for both of us."

"What assumptions? That we're engaged without being in love? That you asked me to be your wife so you could claim your inheritance?" She glared burning fireballs at him. "What? It's okay for you to have rules and stipulations—marry me by such and such date or the deal's off—but not me?"

Lake shuffled on the porch in agitated movements. "I agreed to donate the money to the shelter. I didn't consider it might require a time-consuming commitment."

"Did you assume marriage wouldn't take a time commitment either?"

"I didn't say that."

"You didn't have to! You want it quick and easy—a done deal. Marry the first female who crosses your tracks with an urgent enough need to accept a fake marriage." She took three steps and thumped her index finger against his thick coat. "I agreed to marry you to save the dogs in the shelter. If you don't want to spend time there, fine. But whether we're married or not, I'll do what I want when it comes to how I spend my time. If I choose to devote my free time to the animals who don't have forever homes yet, I will!"

"You're serious?"

"Don't I sound serious?"

"You still want to go through with the marriage?"

Oh. He was talking about that? Not her involvement in the shelter?

"One disagreement, and you're ready to bail?" Wasn't she ready to bail moments ago, too?

"No. That's not what I said."

"Look. I'd rather not have to marry you to save the shelter. Do you know any other billionaire willing to fork up the money to save the dogs?" Irish tossed her hands in the air. "If so, speak now or forever hold your peace!"

"Did you just quote a line from a marriage ceremony?" He gave her a slight grin. Not a good enough one to make her smile back at him.

"Did you hear the part about me not wanting to marry you?"

"I heard!" Spur yelled from inside the cabin.

"Quiet in there!" Lake called.

"Perfect. Now your whole family knows our business."

Their breaths steamed between them, and they stared at each other for a few seconds. Irish glanced at his mouth, which brought back the memory of the kiss. Still perturbed with him and questioning her sanity in agreeing to marry her racing competitor, she kicked the romantic thought right out of her mind.

"Do you still want to go through with it?" she asked quietly so Spur wouldn't hear.

"Yes. I still want us to get married. Just don't go making decisions for me."

"Likewise!"

"Deal."

His gaze flicked between her eyes and lips. He'd better not be thinking about kissing her. That wasn't happening today! Maybe not for months!

"When do you want to get married?" Lake asked her in an equally quiet tone. "My birthday is in four days. To get the money, I must be married by then."

"In three days, then. No reason to rush anything." She grimaced. The nature of this arrangement made everything rushed.

"Okay. Three days." He exhaled a long sigh. "We'll have to pick up the license together. No waiting time in Idaho."

"Fine."

"Sorry about the accommodations." He rocked his thumb toward the cabin. "It's not much to offer you, but it's all I have for now."

"There are two bedrooms, right?"

His mouth fell open.

"You aren't expecting anything else from this arrangement, are you?"

"After our kisses, I don't know what to think." He scuffed his boot against the porch.

"I told you I had my reasons for that."

"I liked kissing you, Irish." A soft-looking smile crossed his lips. "I'll participate in more of your chemistry testing anytime."

Spur whistled like he heard that too.

Irish rolled her eyes. "Today's episode cooled my embers right down."

"That's a shame. We should get to know each other better since we will be sharing the rest of our lives together."

His sincere-sounding words unnerved her. Did he really think they'd stay married? Even love each other someday?

Chapter Fourteen

Lake left Michael Peyton's office with Dad, who had offered to tag along to the lawyer's office for moral support. Without commenting, his father observed him filling out the paperwork to accept his half of the inheritance left to him and Hud by their maternal grandfather.

Even though his and Irish's marriage wouldn't happen under the best circumstances, Dad hadn't lectured him about waiting for the right person. Nor did he caution him to wait for a spiritual sign from heaven before moving forward with a marriage of convenience. Hopefully, he realized Lake had made his decision and respected that.

Before Laurie split up with him and broke his heart in pieces, Lake usually prayed about situations in his life like his parents had taught him to do. He trusted God to guide him. He believed in the best for his future. Since the fateful day when Laurie told him she didn't love him enough to marry him, had he prayed as sincerely or as faithfully? Outside of his desperate plea for the Lord to stop him if he was making a foolish mistake about marrying Irish, had he taken the time to really pray about him and her?

A glug settled in his middle. Thanks to his fast-approaching birthday, he had been rushing things.

"Are you sure about this marriage?" Dad clapped his hand on Lake's shoulder.

"As sure as I can be." He cringed, anticipating the dreaded lecture.

"Have you prayed about you and Irish?"

"Yes." Lake swallowed hard. "Maybe not enough. But I have asked God to guide me. Us, I mean."

"Why not give yourself more time to pray and seek the Lord about it?"

"My birthday is in three days. It's now or never."

"Right." Dad sighed.

For as long as he remembered, Lake knew Dad wasn't his biological father. But he never doubted he was the eldest son in his dad's heart. They had discussed his biological father and prayed for him through the years. But in every way other than in blood, Smith North was his true father. Even now, with him questioning Lake about praying, he loved Dad and appreciated his wisdom and guidance.

"I can't say I'll have a happy marriage like you and Mom. But marrying Irish feels like the right thing for me to do so we can save the shelter and pay you guys back." Lake shrugged. "I'm going to use the money for good to the best of my ability."

"I'm sure you will, but at whose expense?" Dad looked him in the eye. "Mom and I aren't worried about the money. We trust you to pay us back when you can." He tucked his hands in his coat pockets. "Please. Don't marry Irish unless you're certain she is the right person for you."

"I asked her to marry me, and she said yes. I am going to marry her in two days." Lake blew out a steamy breath in the chilly air and walked toward his pickup. At the door, he turned back. "Were you certain Mom was right for you when you married her?"

Dad's chuckle sounded forced. "You know I love your mom like crazy."

"What about back then?"

"I was engaged before I met her. I had trouble letting the other woman go from my heart." Dad kicked at a snow mound beside the cleared sidewalk. "It was a difficult time for your mom and me."

"Did anything help?"

"Mom. I fell for her. Not immediately. But after a while."

"Then everything worked out for good like you often say it will."

"You're right." Dad stared intently down the street. "But it came at a cost. Be sure of your own heart before you marry Irish. And be willing to do anything to win her love."

"I will." Lake felt the weight of his promise.

"Let God guide you. We can trust Him in everything." Dad wrapped his strong arms around Lake's shoulders. "I love you."

"Love you too. Your being here with me today means a lot."

As Lake drove home, he thought about how pleased he'd be to pay back his parents, donate to the shelter, pay off his student loans, and build the new house and kennels he'd dreamed about for so long. Maybe he'd help some of his brothers in the future too. All he had to do was marry Irish, sign the final e-signature, and the first installment of his inheritance would land in his bank account. It almost seemed too easy.

Dad's comments about caring for another woman when he married Mom and that it came at a cost churned in his thoughts also. Was he implying Lake's feelings for Laurie might come at a cost to him and Irish having a normal marital relationship?

He spent the rest of the drive asking God for grace and wisdom. And to overcome whatever emotional baggage he might still be carrying about Laurie.

Chapter Fifteen

After turning off her car engine at Lake's cabin, Irish smoothed her hands down the ivory-hued sweater and flannel-lined black slacks she wore for warmth. The outside temperature was too cold for a dress. She didn't usually wear dresses, anyway. And with it being five degrees out? No thanks!

She zipped up her coat, exited her car, and walked up the well-groomed trail toward the porch. This tiny structure twenty miles north of Thunder Ridge would be her home in two days. What would it be like to share a small house with a stranger? Since they were racing competitors, and she had kissed him, Lake wasn't exactly a stranger. But close.

Earlier, he called and invited her to dinner, saying he wanted them to talk. That they should find out more about each other before getting married. Irish agreed, but if he attempted to kiss her, she'd put on the brakes as firmly as a dog musher stopping a team. Lip-locking was on hold until further notice!

"Irish, welcome." Lake opened the door and waved his hand toward the inside of the cabin. He was dressed in a navy pullover sweater and crisp black jeans. He looked good. Smelled good too. A spicy, musky aura emanated from the warmth of his body. It made her want to lean in and sniff.

She gulped. "You, uh, look nice."

"You look beautiful."

"Thank you." She liked a man who could express himself. "A girl can't get enough male appreciation these days."

Chuckling, he helped her remove her coat. "You are daringly honest. I like that about you."

"You might not appreciate my forthrightness once we're living together." She coughed. "I mean, once we're married."

Chivalrously, he didn't comment. He placed her coat on a hook behind the door. She slipped out of her boots, leaving only a tiny puddle of water on the doormat. Something in the kitchen smelled amazing. Drawn to the inviting heat from the woodstove, she walked right over to it in her stocking feet. "I'll love this part of your cabin."

"Not looking forward to sharing the coziness otherwise?" Lake grinned, joining her at the woodstove and holding his hands to the warmth.

After their previous kisses, did he assume she wanted more out of this arrangement than she agreed to? Inwardly, she questioned her decision not to let any kissing happen tonight. What was the harm in a little smooching?

"Smells great in here." She avoided his question and her thoughts. The scent of spiced meat made her stomach growl.

"It's venison. I used one of my grandmother's recipes."

"You cook? I mean, really cook?" Her jaw dropped an inch. Completely un-ladylike of her. Of course, men cooked! But she'd never known one personally who did.

"In a household of nine boys, we all took turns helping in the kitchen. As the eldest, I had my share of kitchen duty and chopping wood."

Irish glanced at the neatly stacked pile of wood chunks and kindling next to the small-sized woodstove. "A man who cooks and chops wood might come in handy."

"See. There are benefits to marrying me." He winked.

"Maybe." She liked him flirting with her.

"Do you cook?"

"I do all right. Nothing fancy. Don't love chopping wood."

"Maybe you'll need someone strong like me around then."

Oh, he was pushing it tonight.

"'Need' might be a stretch."

"Not one of those needy females, huh?"

Her hackles ignited faster than she inhaled a breath. "No! I am not! I take care of myself. Do what needs doing to survive. I have worked my tail off to provide for myself and my dogs. So you can douse any idea of me expecting you to be my hero. Because I don't!"

His eyebrows shot up on his forehead. He cleared his throat. "Thanks for the warning."

"Let's get this dinner over with." She stomped over to the small table with a candle shining from the center. Any romantic efforts were wasted on her now. She plopped down in one of the seats, not caring if Lake usually sat there. Picking up her napkin, she glared at him. He hadn't followed her to the table. He hadn't moved at all.

Her words rushed to her mind. *"You can douse any idea of me expecting you to be my hero."* She dropped her gaze to her lap. Why did she take offense so quickly? He probably didn't mean anything personal by the needy-female comment. Her mother had always depended on a man to take care of her. But not Irish. She hated it when men assumed women must be frail and worthless in strength and accomplishments. She hated being put down, but disrespected because she was a woman? That made her fighting mad!

"Irish?"

She didn't lift her gaze, fearing her face must be ten shades of red. But it was rude of her to stomp over and sit down. No reason to make it worse by not speaking to him. "Yeah?"

"Can you come back over here?"

She glanced up then. Lake stood by the woodstove, his hands tucked into his jeans pockets.

"Why?"

He'd better not be thinking of kissing and making up!

"My mom doesn't allow anger at the table."

Irish remembered Liv mentioning that at dinner the other night. "Is she here?" She double-checked the room.

"No. I don't like bringing anger to the table, either. My parents always made us work out our differences before we sat down. Or else leave it until afterward." He stepped toward her, hands outstretched. "Please? It's a tradition I'd like to keep in our relationship."

"Are you kidding me?" He was concerned about his mother's rules here?

"It's about keeping the peace. Good digestion, if nothing else."

Grumbling, she stood and let him clasp her hands. The heat of his palms touching her skin sent warmth through her, melting her annoyance like ice off her boots. She allowed him to lead her back to the woodstove. She didn't need this man, but she liked the gentleness of his fingers surrounding hers and his tender tone when he spoke to her.

"I'm sorry. I meant the needy-female line in humor. Not offensively."

"Let's forget about it." No reason to hold a grudge. She didn't want to explain her strong reaction to his comment, either.

"Not just so you can eat my good cooking, right?"

"Never that." Although, she couldn't wait to taste the delicious food on the table. "How's Rambler doing?"

"Much better."

"I'm glad to hear it."

"May I?" He clasped her hand and settled it around the crook of his elbow.

"Of course."

As if escorting her into a posh restaurant, he walked beside her from the woodstove to the table, then pulled back her chair.

Moments later, she savored the best venison and meat sauce she'd ever put in her mouth. "Oh, my goodness. You weren't wrong about your ability to cook. This is fantastic!"

"Thanks. I'm glad you like it."

"I might have seconds of this."

"You're welcome to have as much as you want." He gave her a warm look. Did he mean the food? Or was he flirting with her? "I've been told I'm the best cook of the North men."

"The best, huh?"

"At a lot of things." He was flirting with her!

A blush ran down her face to her neck and upper torso. If she let him, Lake's flirting might keep her warm for a lifetime. But if she allowed emotional closeness too soon, her heart might become too vulnerable. She couldn't let that happen.

Chapter Sixteen

Lake's gaze snagged with Irish's over the candlelight, and his pulse raced. She drew him to her like a moth to a flame. Ever since he first saw her racing her dogs, he had felt intrigued by her charisma and determination to succeed. He related to how much she loved and valued her pets and racing companions. And she was so beautiful.

Now that she sat across from him, and with them already having kissed, his romantic engines rumbled with the slightest glance from her. It was too soon to know how they'd coexist in this cabin. Or if they'd ever fall in love. Her temper alone might cause a dynamite-like disaster to implode in his calm life.

Wasn't having plenty of space to himself one of the reasons why he bought a rural property? He'd wanted to get away from the chaos of the North household. He craved peace and quiet. Both were rare commodities in a home with nine boys and three adults.

Now he was marrying Irish in two days? A woman who pelted him with eye daggers one second, then sat here gazing at him with wonder or flirtation in her eyes the next. As if she might leap over the table, sit on his lap, and plant another doozy of a kiss on his mouth.

Whew. If she did—

He shook himself. He had asked Irish here to talk—not to indulge in romantic fantasies or whatever. He took a deep breath and tried to ignore the emotional tightrope between them. "What do you see happening here?"

"Happening?"

"With us living together as husband and wife." They would be sharing this modest house. The close quarters wouldn't be easy on either of them.

She glanced over her shoulder toward the three doors at the back of the cabin. A twin bed barely fit in the bedroom on the left. A double bed fit wall to wall in the other room.

"I'll stay in your guest room. You don't expect anything else, do you?" Her eyes glimmered toward him as if she assumed he'd be the one pushing for intimacies. Good night! She was the one who kissed him!

"No expectations." He coughed and took a sip of his water. He was already entertaining thoughts he shouldn't be thinking, but not expectations. Besides, he wanted more than physical closeness with her. He was hoping for a real marriage and a lasting relationship. That meant they had to build a foundation of trust between them.

"Good. I wondered there for a second."

He had too. "Are you okay with my dad marrying us?"

"I assumed it would just be us at the courthouse."

"My parents would like our wedding to be at the church. You remember my dad's a preacher, right?"

"Yes." She gnawed on her lower lip.

His gaze locked onto the movement of her teeth pressing against her soft lip.

"Lake?"

"Mmm? What?" He forced his gaze to lift and meet her beautiful jade eyes. A man could lose himself in those green hues forever.

"I'm okay with it. No fanfare, though. It will be a"—Irish glanced around the cabin—"a formality. Nothing more."

"Even with the kisses we shared?"

She might not want much ado about a wedding—he didn't either, so he wouldn't invite his brothers or his good friend, Jazzy—but he couldn't deny how their passionate kissing affected him. For four days, he couldn't forget how warm and sweet Irish felt in his arms, how he longed to kiss her again.

Her cheeks darkened. "A girl ought to find out what she's getting into before she leaps into marriage. Someday, one thing might lead to another."

"I'm counting on that." He reached across the table and clasped her hand lightly. "This 'formality' is for keeps. I plan to pursue you as my wife. I want to be a loving husband to you and for us to have a real partnership."

Her gulp was audible.

"You kissed me like you meant it. The next time we're close enough to kiss, I'll show you I mean it too."

Their gazes held for about a minute. If heated glances were combustible, the air between them would burst into flames.

They finished their meals without any more discussion about romance or kissing. They talked about faith, music and food preferences, and where her dogs would shelter once she moved here. Despite their platonic discussion, a palpable tension hummed in the air.

In two days, they'd be sharing this little home. Not quite man and wife. Not quite strangers. But married, nonetheless.

Chapter Seventeen

Irish tugged one dress after another across the rack in the dress shop in Sandpoint. Since Liv had insisted on some girls' time for the two of them, Irish agreed to go wedding dress shopping with her. Now, she wished she'd dug in her heels and said it didn't matter what she wore. She hated all these dresses!

"What about this one?" Liv held up a puffy pinkish-white wedding dress and tipped her head slightly. "This soft color would look lovely with your adorable red hair."

Irish smiled at the compliment. But pink? She gnawed on her lower lip, stopping herself from saying what was on her mind. She had rejected five of the elegant dresses Liv held up. How could she politely tell her future mother-in-law she loathed this dress even more than the others?

"You don't like it, do you?"

"No. Sorry. I don't want to disappoint you, but simple is more my style."

"No worries." Liv chuckled. "I've raised nine boys. I'm clueless about picking out fancy dresses and pretty things."

"I rarely wear dresses. Training my dogs fills most of my free time."

"I understand." Liv returned the dress to the rack.

"What did you wear when you married Pastor North?"

"A baggy dress. I was very pregnant with Lake."

"Ah. I see."

"Do you miss your mom being with you for this occasion?" Liv gave her an understanding smile.

"Not really. Mostly, I'm disappointed not to have my dad here to walk me down the aisle."

"Ah, sweetie. I'm so sorry."

"It's okay."

Liv touched a couple of lacy dresses. "What would you like to wear for your wedding? I'd love to buy one of these for you as a gift."

"You don't have to do that! It's barely a wedding, anyway. Lake and I are just—" Irish's face heated up. "I mean, we'll be legally married. But it's not what I imagined. No frills required." She was chattering and probably offending Lake's mother, who'd kindly offered to buy her a dress and take her to lunch. "I'm sorry to sound rude. The circumstances of our marriage make everything about it weird. Not the dreamy stuff, you know?"

"I understand." Liv squeezed her hand. "You're marrying Lake for a good cause. I admire you for being honest about it. That takes courage."

"Thank you for understanding."

"Anyone willing to marry a good man for a worthy cause has my admiration. Especially when they're vowing to stick to the marriage and plan to fall deeply in love with each other." Liv gazed at her as if silently asking her if that was what she was planning to do with Lake.

Irish swallowed what felt like a tablespoon of peanut butter. Would she and Lake fall deeply in love someday? Would their marriage last?

"You look surprised. I don't blame you." Liv let go of her hand.

Since Liv was being honest, Irish felt encouraged to express herself too. "Lake and I barely know each other."

"But that will change. You like each other, don't you?"

"Sure. We have dogs in common. And racing." She wouldn't mention their kissing.

"He isn't hard on the eyes either," Liv said in a playful tone.

Irish felt the roots of her hair burning. "No, he isn't."

"You're beautiful. I'm sure Lake has noticed that, too."

He had mentioned something along those lines last night. But he was just being polite, right?

"I don't know how he truly feels, so I couldn't say." Randomly, Irish picked up a blue dress. She liked blue. This one ought to do. Then her outing with Liv could be over.

Liv set her palm over Irish's hand on the hanger. "You should ask him."

"Ask him what?"

"How he feels or what he thinks. You don't have to marry him just to save the shelter."

Why else would she marry him?

Liv peered at her with the same intensity she felt in Lake's eyes. Like she, or he, gazed into the windows of her soul and knew her deeply already.

"I'm sure he still cares for his ex." Irish clutched the plain blue dress to herself.

Liv cringed slightly. She probably hoped for a love match for her son. She must be so disappointed in the woman he chose.

"May I tell you something?" Liv asked softly.

"Sure."

"I've prayed for the person Lake will marry for twenty years." Liv smiled tenderly, and Irish noticed the resemblance between her and Lake. "I've prayed for you."

"Me?" Irish swallowed hard. Then it hit her. "Oh. So, you assumed Laurie was the answer to your prayers?" And Irish was a poor second-best?

"For a time, I did. When she broke up with Lake and broke his heart, I knew she wasn't the person I hoped my son would marry. I want him to be happy and live a fulfilled life." Liv smoothed her hand over Irish's shoulder. "God has a different plan for him. And you, too."

"You mean like I'm a part of God's plan for Lake's life?"

"Is that too difficult to imagine?"

"Frankly, yes. I can't imagine being an answer to anyone's prayers."

"You, my dear, are becoming that answer right now." Liv gently took the blue dress from her hands and returned it to the rack.

"What are you doing?"

"You'll see." Liv led her toward the exit. "I have a different kind of outfit for you in mind."

Irish followed her future mother-in-law out the door. After Liv saying she prayed for her for twenty years, she'd follow her just about anywhere.

Chapter Eighteen

Lake and four of his younger brothers stood around a campfire in his backyard, cooking hotdogs and marshmallows despite the ten-degree nighttime temperature. Like a hundred other times, the guys laughed boisterously, bragging about accomplishments, razzing each other, telling jokes, and exaggerating stories from their childhood. All of them seemed compelled to one-up each other's tale.

"That's not the way it happened!" Wilks argued.

"I'll tell you how that went down," Spur said.

"You're both wrong. It went like this—" Finn dramatically told his rendition of the tale.

"No way! You're telling it backward!" Sunday laughed.

Some of Lake's closest friends sat around this campfire for his bachelor's party. But a few were missing. Hud had returned to Ketchikan. Coe was on a humanitarian aid trip to India. Stone was off finding himself, or losing himself, somewhere. Aiden, whom Dad nicknamed A.W. when he joined their family, lived in an art community in Denver.

The two brothers Lake missed most were Coe and Hud. Without those two attending this shindig, something felt odd. Growing up, the three of them were inseparable. They used to talk about everything. They were explorers who united for great causes, the three who faced bullies as if they were one, and the trio who stood up for the younger brothers when necessary. They were the eldest of the preacher's sons. The ones with the weight of being the big brothers to their tribe of nine.

Hud and Coe should be here. But Lake couldn't expect them to attend due to the hasty wedding plans.

It seemed impossible that he would be kissing Irish as his wife in less than twenty-four hours. His wife! Fire shot through his veins whenever he thought about his promise to take the lead on their next kiss. Should he pull her into his arms and kiss her passionately when Dad pronounced them husband and wife? Or should he wait until they were alone?

"I looked up to Lake my whole life," Sunday, the second to youngest and the best baseball player of the brothers, said somberly, snagging Lake's attention. "I admired him as the eldest. So why is our big brother casting away our trust? Why is he breaking the pact we all vowed to uphold?"

Uh-oh. The good-natured storytelling just took a sharp detour.

"That's right!" Finn punched the air with his fist. "Why is this honored brother shoving our faces in the mud?"

"Tell us, Lake," Spur said in a snarly tone. "Why are you ruining the brotherhood?"

How did their fun time of laughing and goading each other morph into such serious, ominous expressions on his brothers' faces?

"Come on, guys. This is a celebration." Lake lifted his soda. "Someone should give a toast."

"A toast isn't what we had in mind." Spur's eyes gleamed in the firelight's glow.

Lake gulped and set down his can without drinking it.

"Pain and agony should come to any brother who breaks our pact." Wilks gazed around the group as if garnering support. "Let's do what's fitting and throw him in the lake!"

"Yeah!" Finn let out a yowl.

"Now, hold on!" Lake said.

"I'll do the honors myself." Wilks pumped his fist in the air.

"It's payback time!" Spur shouted.

Chills raced up Lake's back as if he already felt the icy waters of Lake Pend Oreille circling his neck.

Hoots and wolf-like howls followed from the younger brothers. Now, he really wished Coe and Hud stood beside him. But what if they were here and came against him too? What if they were all angry enough at him for marrying Irish and accepting the inheritance to take matters into their own hands?

"Grab his legs, Spur!" Wilks turned toward Lake with wide eyes. "I'll grab his arms."

"You guys are crazy!" Lake backed up, holding out his hands. He should have known this bunch would come up with some idiotic retribution toward him for his bachelor party.

"You figured you'd go through with a marriage charade without your brothers getting upset? Without us doing something to stop you? Think again!" Spur picked up a wooden stick and thudded it against a large rock outlining the fire ring. "I call this court into session."

"Court? Guys, lighten up. Eat more marshmallows."

"Lake is guilty of treason to the brotherhood by engaging in a fake marriage! His guilt demands punishment!" Spur pounded the stick against the rock again.

"Let's leave him in the woods ten miles north and find out if he makes it back for his wedding!" Finn acted out grabbing someone, hurling him over his shoulder, then tossing him into a heap.

Lake clenched his jaw and took a few more steps away.

"How about driving him to Montana and dropping him off?" Sunday, usually the more tender-hearted of the bunch, sounded as miffed as the others. "Then he'll miss the wedding altogether!"

More chortles followed. This uprising was getting out of hand.

"Guys, stop already." Lake shuffled his thick knit hat over his head. "Sure, my marriage is unexpected, even for me. And, yes, I broke the pact that I should never have made. Sorry to disappoint. What you're talking about doing is childish. We're grown men here. Can we let the past go? Just get over it!"

Four intense gazes met his.

"Hud isn't letting it go or getting over it." Spur clenched his teeth in a grimace.

"Stone, either." Sunday shook his head.

"You've talked to Stone?" Lake wasn't aware of anyone being in contact with him in the last year.

Sunday pressed his lips together.

"If you know anything about him, you should tell Mom. She's—"

"Yeah, yeah," Spur cut in. "About the verdict? Will we let Big Bro escape his crime without us taking appropriate measures?"

"Noooooo!" Wilks yowled.

Finn and Sunday made wolf howls.

Lake wanted to run inside the cabin, slam the door, and lock it. But this gathering, and even his brothers' stupid comments, were all harmless fun, right? He could handle a bit of teasing. Even some pranks. He dished them out often enough to his younger brothers over the years.

However, when Spur nodded impishly in his direction, he wished he would have run for it. He could take on any of these brothers one on one. But wrestling four of them?

Like football players rushing a quarterback, they charged at him, knocking him to the ground. Before he could stand, each grabbed one of his limbs and hauled him toward the cabin. He fought their holds. "Let me go, you idiots! You can't do this!"

He squirmed, kicked, and called out warnings all the way inside, but none of his brothers let go. They dumped him unceremoniously in the center of the empty guest room in the pitch dark. Why was the room empty? Spur dug into Lake's coat pocket and removed his cell phone. Lake grabbed for it, but Spur rushed from the room and slammed the door.

His brothers went too far this time!

Groaning, Lake leaped to his feet. Where were the bed and other furnishings? The window must be boarded up from the outside since he couldn't see the moon on this clear night.

Hands outstretched, he crossed the space to the door. He flailed until he found the light switch. It didn't work. He yanked on the doorknob. Nothing gave. Someone had replaced the old doorknob with a keyed one.

Just great.

He'd take the hinge apart, even in the dark, if he had the right tools. Unfortunately, he didn't have anything like that in this room. He felt around the perimeter of the tiny space. Whichever brother did this dirty trick made sure any sharp objects he might employ had vanished.

"You guys! This isn't funny."

"Wanna bet?" Spur chortled from somewhere in the cabin.

The other brothers laughed like this gag was the funniest prank they had ever pulled.

Would they make him stay here all night? They went to a lot of trouble to get rid of the bed and dresser. Maybe they didn't empty the closet. Lake shuffled to the small door and felt around. Empty! However, farther back on the top shelf, he felt a quilt. They must have overlooked this. Or perhaps, one brother had mercy on him. Sunday, no doubt.

Grabbing the only warmth he'd have tonight, other than the parka he wore, he wrapped it around his shoulders and lay down in the middle of the room. It wouldn't be the best sleep. Not his worst one either since he'd slept on the trail with the dogs in bitter winter weather before.

"Comfy, brother?" Sunday asked from outside the door.

"How about letting me go? I'd like to sleep in my room the night before my wedding."

"No can do. Sorry."

"Sunday—"

His footsteps shuffled away from the guest room door.

More laughter and chatter ensued. Now that they'd moved the party inside the cabin, the guys told even more exaggerated tales. Lake chuckled over a few of the stories. Hud and Stone wouldn't appreciate the outlandish things they said about them. Too bad they weren't here to defend themselves.

If Hud were present, would he have joined in on this prank? He would be the type to throw Lake into Lake Pend Oreille in winter!

Groaning, he turned to his other side, trying to get comfortable on the hard wooden floor. This was going to be a long night.

Chapter Nineteen

Even with today being her wedding day, by ten a.m., Irish had already fed her dogs, taken Aurora and North Star for a skijoring run, deiced their paws, given them and Pleiades lots of petting, and worked on training her youngest dog with a leash walk.

"We're moving today."

Three trusting dog gazes peered up at her.

"You have no idea what that means. But it's all going to be fine. Mom is taking care of you." She patted their heads and gazed back at them like a mother with her children. "You and Lake's dogs are going to be best buddies someday. For now, you must tolerate each other. We'll work on being buddies later, okay?"

What about her and Lake? Would they have a companionship that lasted beyond the five-year contract?

How was the cabin going to accommodate them? Lake had tried to convince her all the dogs should stay outside. That wasn't happening! At least one dog would sleep at the foot of her bed at night.

"You three are the best pups in the world. Us living with Lake and his huskies doesn't mean anything has changed. It's a small space, but we don't mind sleeping in close quarters, do we?" The dogs grinned and wagged their tails like they knew what she was saying.

She made certain their tie-out lines were secure so they could be outdoors safely, then headed toward the house to make final packing arrangements. She'd meet Lake and his parents at the church at one o'clock after she and Lake picked up their marriage license, which meant their wedding was really happening. She let out a long, deep sigh.

Inside the trailer, she glanced at the black pants and the sky-blue top with navy piping Liv bought for her. Dressy but simple. She appreciated Liv's thoughtfulness in helping her find an outfit that she could wear for going out to dinner or a party. Not some elaborate dress that would hang in the back of her closet for five years.

Irish stood in front of the bedroom mirror, perusing her appearance. Besides her deep green eyes, she'd always thought her hair was one of her best features. Maybe she'd leave her long, slightly-wavy hair freefalling today. Lake might like that. Even if their wedding wasn't the dreamy here-comes-the-bride event she once wished for, she wanted to look her best.

She picked up her small makeup kit. A little charcoal eye shadow, black mascara, and rosy gloss should do the trick to help her look dressier.

How did Lake feel about their wedding day, especially considering he was engaged to Laurie a few months ago? Was he having second thoughts? She had a few of those this morning. She wouldn't blame him if he did too. However, she hated the idea of him pining over his ex.

She stuck her tongue out at her reflection. Enough thoughts about him and Laurie! Lake was marrying her today. Not the other woman.

Putting on a tiny amount of blush—her cheeks reddened enough without it—she let her thoughts drift over their kissing a week ago. In Lake's arms, she was confident of their chemistry. But would they fall in love? What if she fell for him, and he didn't reciprocate? What then? An annulment. Too many hurts to count. More emotional baggage. She wouldn't stay in a loveless marriage forever.

She groaned at the negative thoughts. *Lighten up! It's your wedding day!*

As far as she could tell, Lake was an honorable man. He loved his family and his dogs. He treated her nicely. He could articulate his thoughts about her and his hope for a good life between them. These were all admirable qualities.

The memory of him saying he'd pursue her danced through her, removing doubt like a feather duster removing dust. What would his pursuing her look like? And when it happened, what would she do?

Chapter Twenty

Lake woke up with sore shoulders and an aching back. The guest room door stood ajar, letting in a stream of morning light. One of his brothers must have pitied him and allowed some heat from the woodstove to reach him before they left after partying last night.

He sat up and groaned. Every muscle in his body hurt. Today was his wedding day, and he felt this lousy?

He pulled off his knit hat and ran his hand through his messy hair and over his scruffy face. He hadn't gotten the haircut he thought he would. But after he fed the dogs, he'd shower and shave. Try to look more human. Then he'd put this room back together for Irish.

He was frustrated with his brothers for pulling that stunt the night before his wedding. They were just blowing off steam. Getting back at him for the tricks he pulled on them with Coe and Hud over the years. Nothing personal. Still, he was annoyed.

A few shenanigans he'd participated in came to mind as he got around. On the day before Stone's high school graduation, they threw him into Lake Pend Oreille at midnight. After an opening night theatrical success, they put whipped cream all over Finn's VW Bug.

And on Spur's first date, they smeared chocolate pudding on the front seat of Dad's car. After sitting down, the backside of Spur's pants looked like he had an accident. And he had to clean out Dad's car, which made him late picking up his date.

Yeah. Maybe Lake deserved a prank or two pulled on him.

Since feeding the dogs was the first task of every day, he donned his outerwear and then strode outside to the yaps and howls of his trio. He petted each dog, fed them, and ensured their water bowls were full. He checked Rambler's paw as he'd been doing each day since his injury three days ago. It was healing fine, which was a relief.

Even after he showered and shaved, he still felt stiff and achy from sleeping on the floor. Fortunately, the facial scrapes from his skijoring accident with Rambler a week ago were mostly healed, too.

His cell phone buzzed.

Was Irish calling to tell him the wedding was off? Hopefully, his brothers didn't pull any stunts on her.

He glanced at the screen. Hud.

Just great.

Lake took a breath. "Hey."

"So you're still going through with it?"

"Sure am." He swallowed hard.

"Is there anything I can say to talk you out of it?"

"Not that I can think of."

"We don't need the old man's money!" Hud's tone got louder. "We're doing fine on our own, aren't we?"

"Are you upset about my marriage or the money?"

"Both." Hud said sharply. "We promised we wouldn't get the money if it meant marrying someone we didn't love. And we vowed never to take money from the man who kicked Mom out of his life!"

"I know. Okay?" Lake hadn't forgotten Hud's question at the diner regarding that very thing.

"Yet you are going through with doing both?"

The day they cut their palms in a half-inch slice and pressed their hands together, they vowed never to take their cold-hearted grandfather's money. Then, when they overheard those cranky women gossiping about the pastor, his wife, and their rebellious sons, they pledged never to have a marriage of convenience, either.

But they were kids back then! Now, they were adults who could make their own decisions. However, Lake was breaking a lot of promises today.

"I'm sorry, man."

"What of our pledge?"

"I promised Irish too. Should I go back on my word to her?"

"Her or me? Her or all your brothers?" Hud's volume escalated with each question. "Is she that important to you?"

"Not yet," Lake said truthfully.

"Then stop this sham of a wedding! Tell Dad and Mom the truth."

"They know I'm not marrying her for love."

"They do?" Hud smacked a desk or something with his hand. "I can't believe it."

"I'm not in love with her like I was with Laurie. I admit that! But I'm hoping we'll fall in love. It happened for Dad and Mom, didn't it?"

"So you're staking a marriage on a slim chance the two of you might make it work? This is a horrible decision!"

"Maybe. But it's my choice to make. You'll support me either way, right?" Lake asked. "If you accepted the legacy and married someone you weren't in love with yet, I'd be there for you."

Hud didn't respond.

"You won't hate me forever because of this, will you? I mean, you'll still come back to Thunder Ridge. Back to the family." After fifteen seconds of silence, Lake spoke quietly, "I'm sorry, Hud. I hate for anything to drive a wedge between us. You should have been the first one I called when I decided to accept the money." He took a breath. "I, uh, feared your reaction."

"With good cause!" Hud muttered a harsh word under his breath. "You going through with a fake marriage without me or Coe present is even more devious. The two of us might have done something to make you reconsider."

"Spur and the others tried."

"I know all about that."

Spur had probably called him.

"I'm sorry you can't be here."

"Would my being there have made any difference?"

"I doubt it. Time is running out. For you too." Lake was being bold, but he forged ahead. "Maybe you should consider doing the same thing—get married and draw from the inheritance. Use it for good like I plan to do."

"Are you nuts?"

"You could give the money away to one of your causes."

"I'm calling to stop you from making the worst mistake of your life. Now you're saying I should marry some poor woman I don't love?" Hud groaned loudly. "Listen to yourself. You've changed, man."

Maybe he had. After Laurie, his heart had hardened. He gave up on any hope of having an ideal marriage. Then Irish came along, making him wish for a relationship again, even if it wasn't perfect. They'd have companionship, if nothing else. And there was always their heated kissing.

Two months wasn't enough time for him to be free of the pain of his broken engagement. But asking Irish to marry him brought life and hope back into his heart. It made him open to taking a risk with her. More open to talking things out with God, too.

"If things go bust, don't hesitate to get an annulment," Hud said like a final parting shot.

"Are you going to wish me well?"

Another pause.

"Are you?" Lake pushed.

"Fine. I wish you a happy marriage. But not for one second do I believe it'll happen. Check your email."

"Why?" Lake pulled his phone back and opened another screen. He saw a notification of a new email. It was from Coe. More brotherly advice?

"I appealed to someone you might listen to more than me."

"Come on, Hud."

"I'm calling Dad next. He has no business performing your ceremony!" Hud mumbled something derogatory and ended the call.

Sighing, Lake poured some coffee before facing his brother's message from the other side of the world. He dropped into a chair at the table and gulped down a few swigs of black coffee. *Stop stalling.* He tapped the screen and opened the email from Coe.

"I love you, Lake. You are a great brother!" Those first words erased Lake's fears about Coe writing him a negative message. He exhaled a ragged breath.

Instead of this brother telling him to back out of marrying Irish, the letter was filled with words of admiration and caring for their sibling relationship. He defended Mom and Dad's marriage as one that had been a long-lasting, loving relationship. Coe didn't mention one hint of condemnation about Lake's unplanned marriage or his accepting the inheritance.

He was taken aback by Coe's kindness and support. His brother, who was one year younger than him, obviously didn't possess the same rage about him getting married as Hud did.

"Do what's right for you and Irish. Let God lead you. Be sensitive to His voice in your heart. Jesus is that close to you. All you have to do is listen to Him."

Listen to Him.

Oh, Lord. Have I been listening to You? Have I been sensitive to Your voice like I was before?

With tears in his eyes, Lake finished Coe's letter. His brother had given him exactly what he needed to hear—encouragement and brotherly love. Good words of advice too.

Let God lead you.

That's what Lake wanted to do. However, he may have muffed it with this rushed wedding and not praying about it as much as he should have. Right then, he asked God to bless his marriage with Irish. And for him to listen to the Lord's voice in his heart more often in the future.

Then he prayed for Hud, his brother who still didn't understand the choices he'd made.

Chapter Twenty-one

Irish stood in the foyer of Pastor North's church, clutching a small bouquet of daisies and yellow roses. Liv insisted she walk down the aisle carrying a bouquet. She even asked if Irish wanted Trish to walk beside her. An escort wasn't necessary, she assured Liv. Besides, she didn't know Trish well. And this wasn't that kind of wedding.

Why did she have to wait in the foyer, anyway? Who cared whether the groom saw her before the ceremony? They'd already seen each other when they signed the marriage license at the County Recorder's office. And she wasn't wearing a lacy gown she didn't want the groom to see. She didn't care about any of those wedding traditions.

Today she and Lake were going to make promises they planned to keep. But if they discovered they didn't get along and wound up hating each other, they'd separate amicably after five years, per the inheritance agreement. The prenup she signed included a fair settlement in case the worst happened. Her parents divorced when she was young. Both remarried other people. Mom, twice. Yet they seemed content with their lives.

Not that she wanted a divorce! Even with the way she and Lake were starting out on shaky footing, Irish hoped for more, expected more, from their marriage. Still, she had to accept that even if Lake's kisses made her feel emotionally connected to him on some fundamental level, she didn't have any guarantees of a happily ever after with him. But what spouse had such assurances besides the vows they promised and the love they shared? Which she and Lake didn't have!

She groaned. Wasn't she the glum bride?

Too bad Dad didn't want to travel across the country to walk her down the aisle. What did he say? The Florida sunshine was too much of an enticement to face a frigid winter in the northern United States? Apparently, more alluring than watching his eldest daughter get married.

Slow music began on a sound system in the sanctuary. That was her cue.

Ready or not, here I come.

She smoothed her hands down her soft blue blouse and black slacks. She would have felt naked in a flimsy fancy dress. Thank God for Liv, who encouraged her to choose clothes she liked and would be comfortable in today. Not ones she thought others expected her to wear.

Taking a deep breath, Irish stepped into the church. She stumbled the second she spotted Lake at the front of the room, decked out in a dove-gray tux with tails. Why did he dress up so stylishly for their simple ceremony? For their kind of marriage?

But goodness! What a handsome groom he was! How sweet of him to go to all this trouble for her. For their wedding. Was this part of his pursuing her?

Their gazes locked. Warmth flooded through her. His steady, confident gaze drew her to him like North Star racing for a salmon treat. In the seconds it took for her to traverse the room from the back pew to the altar, she forgot her doubts about them being together and focused on the man she was pledging her life to. Her bridegroom, Lake North.

A couple of feet away from him, she paused. How close was she supposed to stand? Beyond walking up the aisle, she didn't remember any other instructions Pastor North gave them.

The pastor stood near the center of the altar area. Liv and Trish linked their arms and stood off to the left side, smiling. No one looked suspicious of Irish being here under pretense. Did they approve of their son's rash decision to marry her? Maybe they simply understood that life didn't always turn out as planned. And they loved Lake and wanted the best for him, no matter what.

She could appreciate that, especially since her family hadn't sent her any well-wishes today.

Lake held his hand toward her invitingly, and she clutched it like a lifeline. He drew her forward until she stood right beside him. Even though he smiled tenderly at her, a twitch beneath his eye revealed he wasn't as calm as he appeared in the model-perfect tux.

"You look beautiful," he whispered.

"Thanks. You, too."

"Are you ready?" Pastor North glanced back and forth between them.

Ready as she'd ever be marrying a man she barely knew. And in front of his parents and grandmother, no less. Fortunately, they were having a private ceremony—without his brothers or her work acquaintances present.

"We're ready." Lake squeezed her hand slightly.

"Let's pray first," Pastor North said.

Taking a breath and letting it out slowly, Irish appreciated the pastor's quiet voice beseeching God for grace, wisdom, and love. It gave her a minute to calm her pounding heart. To question whether she could go through with the wedding vows.

" ... and bless Irish."

Hearing her name said in prayer stilled some of her nervousness and doubts.

"We're so thankful You brought her into our lives. Our first daughter-in-law. May her and Lake's lives together be blessed. May they be joined together in beautiful harmony and a special joy that survives and thrives through all the ups and downs of life."

Considering their uncertain beginning, surviving and thriving seemed impossible. But wasn't there a verse about believing in the impossible? Or about God being the God of impossible things? That gave her hope. Pastor North asked God to bless their marriage. Her and Lake's marriage wasn't hopeless. And if it wasn't hopeless, it must be hopeful. Blessed, even?

She sighed.

"Amen," Pastor North finally said.

Followed by "Amens" from the others.

Irish said, "I do," in the proper places during the traditional vows. As did Lake. They remained side by side, hands clasped.

After they exchanged promises and rings, Pastor North grinned widely. "It's my honor to pronounce you as Lake and Irish North."

Liv and Trish cheered and clapped jubilantly.

"You may kiss your bride, son."

The wedding kiss! They hadn't even discussed it.

She met her bridegroom's gaze. What would a wedding kiss with him be like, especially with his parents observing? A slight brushing of their lips?

Lake turned her gently toward him, and it felt like his fingers scorched her skin in every place he touched her. His gaze swept over her as if he admired every part of her face and hair.

He leaned next to her ear. "I'm going to kiss you now."

Why was he warning her? His words about the next time they kissed flashed like a caution light in her thoughts. Surely, he wouldn't give her a passionate kiss in front of Smith, Liv, and Trish!

Slowly, Lake brushed his lips across Irish's cheek. Ticklish sensations. Then his lips met hers with ultimate gentleness. She sighed and relaxed into his embrace. Were her lips trembling? Or his? He took her more fully into his arms and deepened their kissing. Warmth against warmth. Breathing into each other. Taking, giving. Someone in the room let out a soft gasp. Was that her? The kiss ended, and he held her to him for a few more moments, their hearts pounding a drumbeat against each other's chests.

"I promise to pursue you," he whispered. "'Til death do us part."

She was Irish North now. Lake's wife.

The preacher's daughter-in-law.

Chapter Twenty-two

Lake stood on the porch in front of the cabin door, carrying a couple of Irish's bags. They'd haul the rest of her stuff over tomorrow. Her dogs were still in her car. His dogs hadn't stopped barking in the kennels since their arrival. As soon as they changed out of their wedding finery, they'd tend to their animals and settle them for the night.

"Here we are. Home sweet home." His hand on the doorknob, the tradition of the groom lifting his bride over the threshold passed through his thoughts. He and Irish didn't have to do anything just because ritual dictated that they should. But maybe they'd look back on this moment fondly if— "Irish, hold up."

"Why's that?"

He set down his bags, then took her load out of her arms.

"What are you doing?"

"Just this." Enjoying the surprised look on her face, he scooped her up in his arms.

"Lake! Put me down!"

Despite her verbal protests, he carried her into the cabin. "Welcome home, Irish."

"You didn't have to carry me."

"I wanted to." He set her down slowly. She backed up like she didn't want to be too close to him. Did his kiss during their ceremony scare her off? Maybe it made her think he had other things on his mind. If so, she'd be right. But being the gentleman he was, he'd wait for those things to progress naturally between them. "This is weird for both of us. But we had a real wedding. A true beginning for us." Shrugging, he didn't know what else to say.

"So you thought carrying me across the threshold might make me more comfortable with you as my husband?" At least, she smiled now.

"Something like that." He retrieved the bags he'd been carrying and led her to the guest room. He flipped the light switch on, then gaped at the bare room. Someone had replaced the lightbulb and the doorknob but didn't return the furnishings! "Spurgeon North!"

"What's going on?" Irish gazed around at the space, then eyed him suspiciously. "Where's the bed? I'm not sharing your room!"

"I know that." Irritation burned through him. "This is my brother's doing. Or a few of my brothers. They made me sleep in here like this last night."

"What?" She dropped her bags. "Where did you sleep?"

"On the floor, thanks to a bachelor party prank!" He strode out of the room. "I have to change out of my rented tux before I can take care of the dogs. Then we'll sort this out."

"I still don't understand."

"The North brothers are notorious for pulling practical jokes on each other, particularly on special occasions."

"That doesn't sound very nice. I thought you guys were preacher's sons. Honorable, and all that."

"We're not saints."

"No, I don't suppose so." She met his gaze briefly. Then she took her overnight bag into the bathroom and shut the door.

Sighing, Lake went into his room. As he changed into a flannel shirt and jeans, the thought of his brothers not returning the guest room furniture, and wondering where they might have stashed it all, irked him like crazy. He'd like to have a serious discussion with Spur, the ringleader of last night's activities!

Outside, they fed and secured Irish's dogs in a temporary shelter Lake had built. Tomorrow would be soon enough for all the dogs to get better acquainted.

He owned only one other outbuilding, so he'd check there for Irish's bed and dresser.

Irish had a fire in the woodstove when he returned from the shed without finding the missing bed frame and mattress. Pleiades rested at her feet.

"I hope you don't mind." She nodded toward the panting dog. "She's the baby. She usually sleeps with me."

"I suppose one dog inside is all right. The cabin gets smelly with more than one large dog in the small space." He pointed toward his bedroom door. "You can sleep in my room. I'll crash on the couch."

"I don't mind sleeping on the couch. I'm shorter than you."

She nibbled on her lower lip, making him more aware of her mouth. Their wedding kiss pranced temptingly through his thoughts. So did the tender way she gazed at him when he whispered his promise of pursuing her.

He cleared his throat and removed his outerwear. "Are you hungry?"

"After the massive dinner we ate? No. I'm more tired than anything."

"Me too." He crossed the room to the woodstove and held his hands toward the heat. "Thanks for getting this going."

"No problem."

They stood with hands outstretched, not talking, not meeting each other's gaze.

"I'll, uh, change the sheets and get the bedroom ready for you."

"Thanks."

Putting fresh linens on the double-sized bed, he pondered the last twenty-four hours. They hadn't turned out like he had planned or hoped. His bachelor party ended on a sour note. He slept on the cold, hard floor. His and Irish's wedding ceremony was unusual. However, their kiss had been the highlight of the day.

He pictured his parents hugging and congratulating him and Irish at their reception dinner at the restaurant. Even Granny Trish embraced Irish with a long hug before they parted. He was thankful for his family's loving support, especially today.

He appreciated how Mom, Dad, and Gran had always tried to guide him and his eight brothers toward God and living lives of service and love. In many ways, they'd given him and his brothers a legacy of far greater value than the inheritance he'd be accepting tomorrow. Did his siblings even realize what he was feeling now?

He thought of how Mom, Dad, and Gran let each of the North boys go as they matured into adulthood. When some took wrong turns, they allowed them to live their lives without meddling too much. Even today, not one of them said a disparaging word to him about his marriage to Irish.

They could have taken him to task for not waiting for love. Or for not being more sensitive to God's leading. Or not praying enough. But they hadn't. They seemed to believe the best of him and respected his decisions. He thanked God for that!

He smoothed his hands over the comforter on the bed, imagining how differently things might have turned out if he and Irish had married for love today. How long would it be until they cared for each other like that? Tenderly. Sweetly.

Time to get out of this room! Releasing a long sigh that felt dredged from the bottom of his ribs, he left the door open and returned to the woodstove. "It's all set in there. Whenever you want to, uh, go to bed, you can."

"Okay. Thanks." Irish patted her leg, and Pleiades stood and followed her toward the bedroom, panting. At the doorway, she paused. "This is weird. It'll get better, right?"

Hearing the insecurity, or the vulnerability, in her tone, he almost felt sorry for her marrying him in this kind of arrangement. "I'm sure it will. Hey, hold up a sec." He followed her to the door.

"Why?"

"I want to say"—he kissed her cheek quickly—"good night. I hope you have a good sleep." He backed away from her.

"Thanks. Good night." She gave him a sweet smile.

"And thank you."

"For what?" Her hand on the doorknob, she glanced at him over her shoulder.

"For marrying me." Despite being weary of their uneasiness, he let a smile tug across his lips.

"You're welcome." She stepped inside and closed the door.

Standing outside his bedroom door with his wife on the other side, Lake prayed silently for their future. Granted, they had embarked on a peculiar journey. He and Irish didn't love each other. But by her enthusiastic response to his kiss during the wedding ceremony, she was attracted to him. Maybe even secretly wanted more to happen between them.

That gave him hope.

Right then, he made a promise to himself. He would kiss his wife good night every night, even if it was on the cheek. Pursuing her heart had to begin somewhere.

Chapter Twenty-three

Early the following day, the thudding of boots and objects dropped noisily on the porch awoke Lake. Moaning, he sat up on the loveseat where he'd curled up for the night and rubbed his hands over his face and kinked neck. Every muscle in his body cried out for relief from last night's cramped position.

"What's going on?" Irish rushed barefoot into the room and peered out the window.

"My brothers are being a nuisance, no doubt."

"Looks like they brought the bed back."

"It's about time." Realizing how gruff that sounded, he softened his tone. "I mean, they should have brought the stuff back yesterday."

"Are you going to speak with them?"

"I suppose I should." He stood sluggishly. An idea came to mind, and he pondered it for a few seconds before mentioning anything. Would Irish go along with a prank if he asked her to? "Hey, Irish?"

"Yeah?"

He pulled off the sweatshirt he slept in. Bare-chested, he faced her.

Her eyes widened. "What are you doing?"

"Will you go along with a practical joke?"

"Like what?" She crossed her arms over her chest.

More footsteps and stuff dropping on the porch resounded.

"Would you mind if we pretended that my brothers caught us being romantic?"

"Lake!"

"I mean kissing! That's all. They think they won their joke by keeping the bed." He lowered his voice so Spur or Wilks wouldn't hear him. "What if we acted like we didn't mind the missing bed? If it makes you too uncomfortable—"

"I get it. They are your kid brothers. You have your pride. They deserve payback after what they did." She bit her lip for a second. "For the record, I don't like deception. But I'll play along this time."

"Thanks, Irish."

She ruffled her long, gorgeous hair, making it messy and so attractive Lake could barely swallow or breathe.

More thumps came from the porch.

"Ready?" he asked.

"As I'll ever be."

Before he opened the door, Irish slid her arm around his waist. Her palm smoothing across his bare back shot tingles up his nerve endings. He met her gaze and smiled as he opened the door. The way her jade irises sparkled back at him, he didn't know if she was faking flirting with him or had real feelings toward him.

"Are you guys having a pang of conscience out here?" Lake asked in a sleepy tone. "It's too early to be making all this racket."

"Give the newlyweds some privacy, will you?" Irish yawned.

Lake wanted to guffaw at Spur's drop-jaw, stupefied expression.

"Uh, hey, Irish. Lake." He dumped a box of books on the porch floor.

"Good morning." Irish smoothed her hand over Lake's chest until her hands clasped around his waist and her cheek rested against his side.

Heart pounding like a runaway train, he put his arm around her shoulders and tugged her closer. "Some joke you guys pulled. I'm glad you stayed away until after the wedding day."

"You are, huh?"

Lake kissed the side of Irish's hair. "Of course we are. Aren't we, honey pie?"

"You got it, sugar lips."

Wilks and Sunday carried a dresser up the steps and set it down with a resounding *whomp*. Their jaws dropped as their gazes flicked between Lake and Irish.

"Staring isn't polite. Hurry up and leave us alone, will you?" Irish kissed Lake's cheek.

"This is the rest of it." Spur lifted his chin toward various furnishings, books, and boxes. "Do you want us to carry the stuff inside?"

"No! Uh, don't worry about it." Since his blanket rested on the couch along with his sweatshirt, that would be a dead giveaway of Lake's sleeping arrangement in the living room. "We'll take care of all this ourselves later."

"Sure thing. Sorry for any inconvenience," Spur muttered, looking downcast.

"Doesn't appear to be any inconvenience." Wilks snickered. "Congrats on the nuptials."

"Welcome to the family, Irish." Sunday smiled.

"Thank you."

Her hair tickled Lake's chest. His heart pounded out a chaotic beat. What they had meant as a pretend interaction felt genuine, like he could tip her back and kiss her for the next week. That had nothing to do with his brothers still being within eyesight!

"Do you?" Spur asked from the foot of the stairs.

Lake must have missed something. "What was that?" He ran his palm over the back of Irish's hair. Her strands were soft and delicate to the touch.

"I asked," Spur said with an annoyed tone, "if you need help with the dogs this morning."

"Nah. I'll take care of them."

"Happy honeymooning, then." Spur's words sounded anything but congratulatory as he tromped down the trail.

"Happy birthday!" Sunday called.

"Yeah. Thanks."

After the guys hopped into Spur's truck, Irish asked, "Do you think we convinced them?"

"You convinced me." He kissed her cheek.

She smacked his arm lightly but stayed curled against him until Spur pulled the truck out of the yard. "Happy birthday, Lake. Sorry I didn't think about getting a gift."

"No problem. Our wedding was a gift. Thank you for that."

She met his gaze for a long moment. Then she let out a teeth-chattering shiver before running into the house. He heard her bedroom door shut. Was she upset with him for asking her to trick his brothers? Or was she as affected by their tender interactions as he was?

He threw on his outerwear—a sweatshirt, one-piece jumpsuit, hat, boots, and gloves—and prepared to face the winter elements.

While he fed and watered the five dogs outside, the reality of the last twenty-four hours sank in. He was a married man. He was thirty-five. Today he'd e-sign the remaining papers accepting his grandfather's legacy. And he'd be able to resign from his current job.

All because Irish was willing to marry him.

Relief rushed through him, followed by guilt. As a kid, he vowed he'd never marry outside of love and never do so for money. Where were his high ideals of love and marriage now? Hud was right about one thing. He had changed.

Even if some good came of their situation, were the potential troubles worth a lifetime of being stuck in a loveless marriage, if it came to that? He couldn't even contemplate the idea of him and Irish never falling for each other. He told her he would pursue her, and that's what he planned to do. However, he had no idea how to go about it.

"Hey, girls." Irish's soft-sounding voice reached him.

Turning from petting Rambler, he observed Irish interacting with her dogs. The tender way she hugged and petted each one, even kissing them on the top of the head, tugged on his heart. Pleiades was outside now too. Irish cooed words of praise and love to her and the other two.

Lake's mouth went dry. For a few seconds, he felt jealous of the dogs. A ridiculous impulse! Yet, as his wife petted the animals, he wished she stroked his head and ran her hands through his hair. Their playacting from earlier wasn't far from his mind either. "Uh, Irish?"

Her back to him, she continued showing affection to her dogs. "Yeah?"

"Sorry if that thing with my brothers made you uncomfortable."

She stood and faced him, tucking her hands into her jacket pockets. "You mean cuddling in your arms? Why would that make me uncomfortable?" Her face reddened slightly.

"I probably shouldn't have asked you to do that when we haven't—"

"Are you going to tell them the truth about us?" She tilted her head and gave him a perplexed look.

"No. It's none of their business."

"Good. You asked me to go along with a prank on your brothers, and I did. Now, you owe me a mouth-watering post-wedding breakfast."

Her cheeky playfulness dislodged the unrest in Lake's gut.

"Sounds fair. I'll head in and make you a breakfast you won't forget."

"I'd expect nothing less."

Were they talking about breakfast? Or something else?

Forty-five minutes later, they sat across from each other at the small table in the cabin with plates piled with eggs benedict, fried potatoes, and flaky biscuits with homemade jam.

Every so often, she murmured, "Mmm," or "This is so good," or "Where did you learn to cook like this?"

"Dad and Granny Trish taught me."

"Not your mom?" She put a bite of the sauce-covered eggs in her mouth and sighed dreamily.

"When she met Dad, Mom didn't know how to cook." Lake used the side of his fork to cut a chunk of potato in half. "He and Gran taught her. She got the basics down enough to cook for our brood but left elaborate cooking to the other two. Then me, Hud, and Coe were assigned cooking duties, so we learned fast."

"I see." Irish waved a piece of biscuit in the air. "This is flaky and fantastic. I make survival biscuits, but nothing like this. Please make me a batch of these at least once a week!"

"I promise I will."

They gazed at each other for several seconds. Lake felt like he made her a promise of much greater worth than making her biscuits.

I promise to kiss you and fall in love with you ... for the rest of our lives.

Chapter Twenty-four

Even with his and Hud's pledge, as a kid, Lake had secretly dreamed up scenarios about getting the inheritance and how he might spend it. From owning a wild horse ranch in Montana to buying donut shops across the country to dropping one-dollar bills from a hot air balloon, he'd imagined many ways to spend his grandfather's wealth.

An animal shelter in desperate need of funds had never crossed his thoughts. But it was a worthy cause. And the shelter's needs had brought him and Irish together. Writing the large check for the shelter seemed like a perfect thing to do on his birthday. Fortunately, with electronic transfers, the first installment of the inheritance was already sitting in his account. No reason to wait another day.

After dropping off the check at the animal shelter, where Mac thanked them profusely, he and Irish went to the bank and arranged to pay off the mortgage on the land. He'd get a check to Mom and Dad later.

Throughout the morning, he'd received birthday texts from everyone in his family except for Stone and Hud. Some of the brothers commented on his marriage, even offering congratulations. Others were silent about it, and their silence spoke volumes.

En route from the bank to the pickup, Lake was telling Irish how good it felt to be debt-free when Laurie stepped out of the dress shop her sister owned. She paused, staring wide-eyed at him, then at Irish, and then at him again. Lake sucked in a harsh breath. His boots momentarily froze to the pavement beneath him.

"Lake!" Laurie grinned.

"Laurie."

Irish's hand slid into the crook of his elbow and tugged possessively.

This was awkward! Resentment and embarrassment rose in him. He hadn't seen Laurie in over two months. Not since she broke things off between them and left town. Who would have guessed he and his bride of twenty-four hours would bump into his ex-fiancée in Thunder Ridge today?

"I didn't expect to see you so soon." Laurie's face darkened. "I stopped in to talk to my sister."

"I didn't know you were back." He stuffed his hands in his jacket pockets.

Irish squinted at him like she expected him to say something.

"Oh, uh, this is Irish." Both women stared at him. "My wife."

"Oh, right. I heard you—" Suddenly, looking like she was about to cry, Laurie turned back toward the store. "I forgot something. Excuse me." She dodged into the shop.

Lake huffed out a breath.

"So that's Laurie, huh?"

"Yep."

Irish let go of his arm and resumed her stride toward the truck. The physical distance she put between them seemed to mirror their emotional distance.

He sighed and followed her.

"You didn't tell her about us? You didn't reach out to her?"

"Why would I? We were finished before you and me—" He shrugged, not knowing how to express their situation. Married, but not married. Kissed, but not kissing. Sharing a life, but not quite sharing their lives.

Seeing Laurie had unnerved him.

"I should get over to the diner." Irish rocked her thumb in the direction of Nelly's. "My shift is about to start."

"Want a lift?"

"No, thanks. See you later." She strode down the sidewalk without glancing back at him.

Married only one day, the discomfort between them was palpable. Running into Laurie had ensured that!

Chapter Twenty-five

During her afternoon shift, Irish received endless congratulations from her coworkers and customers for her advantageous marriage to Lake. It was as if he was a prince who swept down and saved her from a life of poverty! The idea chafed. She had her pride. Several servers, mainly Tiffany, grumbled about one of the most eligible bachelors in town being snatched away.

"How did you catch Lake North?" she asked woefully. "Was it love at first sight?"

"Not really." Irish wouldn't lie to her. Nor did she feel any obligation to explain. "It's complicated."

"Ohhh! How far along are you?"

Heat flamed up Irish's forehead. "I'm not pregnant!"

"Then why is it complicated? It's Lake North, for goodness' sake! Any single woman within a ten-mile radius would marry him on the spot."

Yeah, yeah. "He's great," Irish said half-heartedly. *Handsome. Wealthy. Good kisser.*

Tiffany huffed. "Don't you love him?"

"I said he's great. The rest is private. Now, we'd better get busy if we want to keep our jobs." She tightened her apron and left Tiffany standing by the silverware trays with her mouth hanging open.

The workday felt endless as customers questioned her about marrying Lake. News sure traveled fast. Apparently, she was the highlight of the local gossip cycle.

Approaching the next table in her section, she groaned. Spur and Wilks sat there grinning up at her. This was all she needed!

"Well, if it isn't our infamous sister-in-law!" Wilks thrust out his hands.

"Hey, fellas." She dropped two menus onto the table, holding a coffee decanter with the other hand. "Coffee?"

"Yes, please." Wilks nodded. "Extra creamer."

Both guys flipped over their mugs. Irish filled each cup without spilling a drop.

"Thought we'd let you serve us a meal today." Spur's mile-wide grin glistened beneath his scruffy face. He was in brighter spirits than earlier.

She grabbed a couple of creamers from an empty table and dropped them into a small basket in front of Wilks. "Do you know what you're going to order? Or do you need a few minutes?"

"I'll take Sam's Sizzling Steak and Eggs." Wilks's smile reminded her of Lake's. Of all the brothers she'd seen, he looked the most like him, only shorter.

"Surprise me." Spur winked. "Like you surprised me by marrying my brother yesterday."

Tired of the North brothers' shenanigans, she scowled at him. "Look. If you want me to choose your food, fine. I'll bring you the best vegan entrée we offer. Tofu egg substitute?"

A sickly look crossed his face. "Never mind."

Wilks guffawed. "I like you, Irish."

"Good. Because Lake and I will be in this relationship for a long time." She eyed Spur sternly. "Now, what'll it be, brother?"

"I'll have the Number Two." He heaved a melancholy sigh.

"Fine choice." She turned on her heel and filled a few cups of coffee for other customers on her way to the kitchen.

She'd barely placed the ordering slip in the queue when Tiffany sidled up beside her.

"Can you put in a good word for me with those adorable North brothers?" She clasped her hands together in a begging pose. "They are so cute!"

"Seriously?"

"A girl needs a little male distraction in this never-ending northern winter."

Would Lake care if she set a hungry female predator loose on his brothers? Maybe they deserved it after the stunts they pulled about the guest room furnishings. "I can put in a good word for you."

"Thank you, Irish. You're a gem!"

"How have you worked here this long without meeting them?"

"I've talked to them as customers. Never as personal acquaintances." Tiffany giggled and rocked her eyebrows. "Could we sit at the table with them for two minutes?" She smoothed her hand over her long blond locks. "Then maybe they'll see me as more than a server in a restaurant."

"How do you want them to see you?"

"As an available woman, of course! You took the North man I wanted. But I'll accept one of his brothers as my consolation prize."

Rolling her eyes, Irish waved Tiffany in their direction. "Come on, then."

"Right now?"

"Yes. Before we get swamped with more customers and don't get a chance." Irish walked back to her brothers-in-law's table. "Got a minute, guys?" She plopped down on the bench beside Spur. By his wide eyes, she had surprised him. "I have someone who wants to meet you."

"Who's that?" Wilks asked.

Tiffany stood at the end of the table, waving demurely.

"This is my coworker, Tiffany Dale." Irish spread her hands toward the grinning duo. "This is Spur and Wilks North, my husband's brothers." She stood up before either of them spoke. "Now you've met. Have a nice chat." She bustled off to gather the plates of food she needed to pass out quickly, or else she'd be reprimanded for dawdling.

A few minutes later, Tiffany returned for more plates too. "Why'd you leave me alone with them?"

"I did my part and introduced you. Now I'm working." She loaded her arms with yummy-looking dishes. "What did you expect? For me to sit there yakking and get fired?"

"No. But give a girl some warning."

"Were they rude to you?"

"Hardly. They asked if I wanted to sit down and have a meal with them." She sighed dreamily. "If only I could have."

"At least they know your name now."

"Yeah. Except Spur called me Terri." She made a pouty face. "But I dig guys with red hair. And his sparkling grayish-green eyes are to die for."

Irish groaned. Wasn't it only a couple of days ago that her coworker had lamented over some guy from Georgia?

She dropped Spur's and Wilk's breakfasts in front of them. "Can I get you anything else?"

"Another server who wants my phone number." Wilks winked. "The last one smiled at Spur the whole time."

"Do you want me to find you a wife, too?" she asked teasingly.

"I'm not marrying anyone the way you and Lake did!" Spur glowered at her.

"I didn't mean—" Irish's face flamed. "Keep your voice down, will you?" All she needed was for folks in the restaurant to catch wind of her and Lake having a marriage of convenience. She'd never hear the end of it!

"Then again, with how they looked this morning, it might not be a bad way to get a wife." Wilks grinned and winked.

Groaning, she marched quickly away.

Chapter Twenty-six

The annoying sound of the phone buzzing awakened Lake from a nap. After sleeping wretchedly for the last two nights, hauling furniture into the guest room, and carrying all his stuff from his bedroom into the smaller room so Irish could use the bigger bedroom, he felt wrung out.

"Hello," he answered groggily.

"This is Irish."

"Hey." He sat up. "What's going on?"

A static noise made her voice unclear for a few moments. Sometimes the rural Wi-Fi was less than ideal.

"—from the shelter. There's a meeting tonight. Some crisis."

"Already? We just gave them a check this morning."

"I know. But we should be there." She made a huffing sound as if warning him he'd better be okay with them going to this unscheduled meeting.

He still didn't like Irish planning things for him. "Are you saying the shelter will still be in a crisis even after the money we donated?"

"I'm saying I don't know what this is about. But we need to—" Her voice disappeared again.

"Yeah, okay." He hoped she heard him.

"We're committed to helping, right? Do you mind if we go?" She spoke in a softer tone. "I know it's your birthday. We could grab a bite to eat afterward."

At least she asked him this time.

"Sure. We can go to the meeting if it's important to you. What time?"

"Six o'clock."

"See you then."

Later, he sat beside Irish and faced the four board members who looked miffed at being summoned to this gathering. What caused Mac to risk rousing anger in this group of volunteer board members by calling an impromptu meeting on a cold winter night?

"I'm sorry to inconvenience you with this gathering." Mac held a stack of papers and tapped them against the table, straightening them. "Shelley? Some assistance, please."

"Sure thing, Mac." The receptionist, apparently also the secretary for this meeting, took the papers and distributed them among the group.

"If you haven't met our new benefactors, this is Lake and Irish North." Mac flicked his hand toward them. "They generously donated a large sum of money to bail out the shelter."

"Hello." Lake nodded.

"Hey." Irish lifted her hand in a wave.

"You mean the whisperings around town aren't true? The place isn't closing, after all?" an older woman asked grumpily. "It would have been nice to hear the truth from you. Then we could have eased the worries of fellow animal lovers in town."

"Thank you for your input, Patricia," Mac said tightly.

"I heard there was a hostile takeover underfoot." Ted Lumberton, a staunch man with a rotund physique, tapped his thick index finger against the table. "What's this about? Why the secrecy and last-minute call for a meeting? These two don't appear hostile." He nodded toward Lake.

"We're not. We want to help." Lake lifted his hands in a peaceful gesture. "Only as silent partners."

Irish jabbed him in the ribs.

He made a soft "oomph" and glared at her.

"I apologize again for the inconvenience of this meeting." Mac's voice sounded anything but apologetic. "I felt it was necessary."

"Cut to the chase." Harley from the gas station shuffled in his seat and seemed agitated. "Whatever this is about, get on with it. Time's money." Turning toward Lake, he said, "Welcome to the club, North."

"Thanks."

What was with the dark glances and irked expressions darting between the board members? Had there been bad blood among the group in the past? Was it aimed at Mac? Or toward each other?

Irish nudged him in the ribs again and nodded at a letter in the stack of papers. He glanced at it. Mac's resignation letter? Did this mean more responsibilities were landing at Lake's feet? Er, his and Irish's feet?

"You're resigning?" Patricia held up a similar copy of the letter, waved it like a flag, and grinned. "Oh, happy day!"

"You've got to be kidding me," Larry muttered.

"Why now?" Harley scooted forward in his chair, assuming a more domineering posture. "We have enough troubles here without people bailing on us."

"I'm hardly bailing. I've kept the ship afloat for years." Mac's face reddened. "If you'll let me explain—"

"I wish you would!" Irish said heatedly. "We're investing our money and time into this program. We didn't know the man in charge was leaving without warning."

Lake grinned at her use of "our money." That their marital status of thirty hours gave her a sense of entitlement was humorous. Kind of cool, also. If only they had married for better reasons. For all the right reasons. He thought of his rough night's sleep on the couch. *Focus, North.*

"The time has come for me to step down." Mac's tone deepened. "With today's debt paid, it's a perfect opportunity for me to go and someone else to step up. Perhaps Lake?"

"Not me." Lake shook his head. "I have enough work to do at my place. I'm building my own kennel business this spring."

"Is that right?" Mac's brows lifted.

"It's my plan."

Irish squinted hard at him. Why was she looking at him like that?

"Why not weather this crisis, Mac?" Harley demanded. "Then weasel your way out the back door." He glared at the director as if they'd previously had words.

"With the Norths sponsoring the shelter, we're out of the woods." Mac ran his hand over his shiny bald head. "I've fulfilled my contract. I'm done here."

"Hardly fulfilled. Your contract ends in two months," Patricia said mockingly.

"Why are you leaving in the middle of winter?" Lake asked.

"For starters, there's going to be a battle with the city council over some outdated ordinances."

"About what?" Irish demanded. "What's the real issue here? I've looked over the papers you gave us. There are complaints about upkeep and repairs. Nothing for the city to be that riled about."

"Welcome to Thunder Ridge Animal Shelter and its current ruling entity." Patricia cast snide glances toward Mac and Shelley.

"Care to enlighten us, Mac?" Ted demanded.

Sighing, Lake settled deeper into his chair. This wasn't turning out to be the quick meeting he had hoped for. He was hungry and eager for the dinner he and Irish planned to get at Nelly's.

Mac loosened his tie. "Financial poverty has made the decision-making process difficult."

"What decision? Giving up? Letting the property get run down?" Irish lifted her chin toward Mac. "Not doing your best for the dogs?"

Lake took note of her agitation. The way her hands clasped and unclasped. Her forceful speaking. She was really worked up about the possible mismanagement of the shelter.

"I must get back to work," Harley said brusquely. "Get to the bottom line, will you?"

"Are you two finally getting married and leaving town together?" Patricia pursed her lips.

"Patricia!" Shelley gaped at the woman.

"I'm a married man!" Mac's face turned beet red.

"So, I thought." Patricia tapped her manicured nails on the table. "Word is spreading—"

"Let's not get sidetracked," Lake interrupted her. "Mac's private life, and Shelley's, are their own business. This meeting is about the shelter and the care of the animals. Let's stick to the topic. And keep our conversation polite. Then we can all get out of here and spend time with our families."

"Good leadership, North." Harley eyed him. "Why don't you take over running the shelter? You care about your dogs. Probably know more about animal upkeep than most of us."

"Not me. While Irish and I are concerned about the shelter, I have my own plans." He felt Irish clasp his hand tightly beneath the table. "We are invested in the well-being of the animals here. That's why we've taken steps to ensure its continuity."

"But you don't want to give your time?" Ted groaned. "Then why are we here?"

"Because Mac called this purposeless meeting!" Patricia glared intensely at the manager.

"I'm more than willing to give my time to protecting the animals." Irish withdrew her hand from Lake's and sat up straighter. "I can fill in as the shelter director. No problem."

No problem? Shouldn't they have discussed this before she advocated for the position? Sure, they were barely married. And they had just heard about Mac resigning. But if Irish became involved in the day-to-day operations at the shelter, they wouldn't have much time to spend together working on their marriage. Not enough time for her to train with her dogs, either.

"I say we find someone with more experience." Patricia twirled a flashy ring on her finger. "Someone who will lead this cause in better ways than the current management has."

"I've done my best, Patricia." Mac rolled his eyes.

"That's hard to imagine."

"Can you stay on for a short time and allow for a gradual change in leadership?" Lake asked.

Irish frowned. "I don't see why—"

"I suppose I could." Mac pinched the bridge of his nose. "A couple of weeks at most."

"Sounds fair." Lake clasped his hands loosely on the table.

"Time enough for someone to look over the books," Patricia said haughtily.

"The books are fine!" Shelley tossed down her pen like she had a personal stake in the matter.

"There are back doors for sticky-fingering funds." Patricia smirked.

"Nothing like that happened!" Mac scowled at her.

"No one is accusing anyone of underhanded dealings." Lake palmed the air, trying to keep the peace. "Let's maintain civility. Mac, you've offered your resignation. We shouldn't try to force you to stay. But if you're willing, an extra two weeks would—"

"Lake—" Irish tugged on the sleeve of his shirt.

"—give us time to get a few things settled."

"If he needs to leave, I'll do it!" Irish said insistently.

Why was she pushing so hard to be more involved here at the shelter? Didn't she want to focus on training her dogs and adding to her team?

"Unless Lake becomes the director," Harley said, seemingly pushing the point. "Why not manage the place the way it should be done?"

"Thanks for honoring me with the suggestion, but my purpose in getting involved here was to provide for the material needs of the animals."

Irish huffed out a noisy breath. What was going on with her? If she wanted the job that badly—

"What better way than sitting in the director's chair making good decisions"—Ted glanced curtly at Mac—"for the animals, instead of for any other reason?"

Heated glances crisscrossed around the table.

"Why don't we postpone this discussion until the next meeting? That will give us all a chance to ponder the situation." Lake shuffled forward in his chair, getting ready to stand up.

"I second that," Larry muttered.

They adjourned amidst some grumbling.

Irish slipped away before Lake had time to ask if they were still meeting at the diner. With her not even saying goodbye and how she'd been sending him glances and jabs throughout the meeting, he was probably in for an unpleasant birthday dinner.

Chapter Twenty-seven

"Coffee?" Talia, an eighteen-year-old server at Nelly's Diner, held up the coffee decanter.

"Definitely." Irish turned over her cup.

As the steaming brew filled the cup, she thought of turning over Lake's and letting Talia fill it too. But she was still irked with him. Besides, she didn't know how long he would take to get over here. Or whether he might head out to the cabin alone.

She had left the shelter quickly. She should have talked to him first. But how dare he override her wishes to be the interim director! What did he have against her doing a job she would love to try? Unless he planned to control everything she did. Oh, if he were that sort of manipulating man, she would let him have it!

She sipped her black coffee, needing the caffeine and intense flavor.

"Am I welcome here?" Lake dropped into the seat opposite her.

"Free country." She gripped her cup tightly.

Talia buzzed back to the table. "Coffee?"

"Yes, please."

Talia filled his cup and then left swiftly. Maybe even she felt Irish's angry vibes filling the air.

"I'm sorry we didn't get to talk about the director's position alone." Lake's tone was quiet but held a slight edge.

Irish stared hard into her steaming cup. "Mac sprang his news on all of us. However, if you think I'm incompetent—"

"I didn't say that."

"But you meant it."

"Not at all." His firmer tone of voice made her glance up. "You and I don't know each other well, Irish. We aren't picking up emotional cues and nuances like a happily married couple. We're second-guessing each other. I have no idea what you want, what you like, or what you wish I would do or say." He took a couple of swallows of coffee, probably burning his throat in the process.

"Here's a fact about me, I don't like anyone telling me what to do!" The fire in her words pulsed adrenaline up her spine and neck. "Or having to report my wishes to anyone."

"Not even your husband?"

"Especially not to him if he ever wants to cross the threshold to my—" Clenching her teeth, she didn't finish the statement. This wasn't a topic for a public place.

"I'll be more careful in the future."

"Good!"

"Do you two know what you'll be ordering?" Talia strode back to their table and winked at Lake. "Or do you need a few minutes to finish your lovers' spat?"

Irish glared at her. The young server was too saucy and mouthy. "I'll have the burger combo."

"Milkshake?"

"Coffee will do."

"And you? What's your heart's desire?" Talia grinned at Lake like she thought he might be the flirting type.

"I'll have the roast dinner. And the milkshake. Chocolate."

"You got it." She pranced away, a cocky grin cast over her shoulder at him.

Irish watched to see if Lake's gaze followed the young woman's swaying hips. It didn't. He stared into his cup, his shoulders curled, his mouth pursed like he was as wound up about what happened back at the shelter as she was.

She let out a long sigh, letting go of a tiny bit of her tension. They were married now. They had to learn how to talk about stuff. Even annoying stuff. He was right about them trying to second-guess each other.

"Why did you shut me down back there?"

Lake met her gaze for several heartbeats without answering.

"I didn't mean to."

"The idea of you thinking it's okay to speak for me makes me so mad!" She jabbed her finger at herself. "I have a mind of my own. A mouth of my own. And I know how to use them!"

A sultry grin settled on his soft lips as if he were thinking of something other than speaking that she could do with her lips. Did he imagine them kissing?

His expression changed. "Do you picture yourself running the shelter?"

"Why not? Someone needs to do it."

"What about all the time it takes to train your dogs? I thought you wanted to prepare for mushing a four-dog team." He circled his hands around his cup.

"I do!"

Wait. Was his concern about her wanting to run a four-dog team and all the time it would take to achieve her goal? Not about trying to control her? She was so quick to leap to conclusions! Had she taken what happened back at the shelter all wrong?

Even if that were true, she couldn't let it go. "I already have a job. So it's not like it would be a huge time difference for me to work at the shelter instead of being a server here."

"I beg to differ. You work thirty-hour weeks at Nelly's." Lake lifted his coffee cup toward his lips. "I saw Mac's time log. He's been working sixty hours a week. No wonder he looks exhausted." He took a long drink.

"Really?" She hadn't noticed his time log or his look of exhaustion. She'd label Mac a weasel or a jerk. Not a weary man. "I wonder why he's there so much."

"Turning the shelter around, getting it out of the red and into the black, and restoring the community's goodwill will take a great deal of time and commitment from whoever fills his shoes." He set the cup down and nudged it forward. "If this is what you want to do, fine. For a time, you'll probably have to give up racing. And no additions to the team." He sat back and sighed like delivering his speech had worn him out.

"I would not give up racing!" How boorish of him to consider her inept at juggling responsibilities. She'd been on her own for a long time. She knew how to work hard and survive. Her marriage to Lake wouldn't change her work ethic or drive to race her dogs. "Believe me. I can juggle workloads. Always have. And for your information, I would make a fine director!"

A couple at the next table turned around and stared at her.

"I never thought otherwise," Lake said softly. "Although, someone with experience running a similar business would get up to speed faster."

Even if he might be right, Irish didn't like conceding to his points, including whether she would race against him and his dogs any time soon.

"Here you go!" Talia set their plates in front of them. "I'll be right back with your shake." She hurried away.

Lake stared at his plate without picking up his fork.

Despite Irish's irritation, the food smelled delicious. She took a big breath and then let it out slowly. "I'm sorry all this happened on your birthday."

"It's fine. In the future, I'll be more careful not to—" Lake opened his hands toward her like he didn't know how to finish the statement.

"Take charge like you're policing our arrangement?"

"Exactly. However, I wasn't trying to take charge. I'm sorry it came across like that."

Dumping a mound of ketchup on her plate, Irish still felt agitated. She stuffed two fries in the condiment before putting them in her mouth.

Talia dropped off Lake's chocolate milkshake, her gaze dancing at him.

"Thanks." He took a sip from the straw, not glancing up. "Do you consider ours a real marriage?" he quietly asked after Talia left their table.

"No. Do you?"

"I want it to be one."

"How you acted back there?" Irish dipped another fry in the sauce, jabbing it against the plate. "Shutting me down when I volunteered to be the temporary director set us back months."

"I'm sorry to hear that. I sincerely apologize. I would never purposefully offend you or harm what we're trying to build here." He sipped his frothy drink. "Married people talk about things. Before we take on responsibilities or financial obligations—"

"Is this about your money?"

Lake glanced around the room. "No, it's not about the money."

"Someone must make the decisions for the shelter." She lowered her voice. "Why not me? I have the animals' best interests at heart. I would make sure your donated inheritance was used for good."

"I'm sure you would do all those things." He picked up his steak knife and operated on his meat in jerky movements.

He probably wished she'd stop talking and let him eat in peace. This was his birthday dinner, after all.

She had one last question. "What about me makes you think I can't do the job?"

"I didn't say anything was stopping you from doing the tasks." He reached across the table and stroked her hand. "We just got married, Irish. I thought we were going to focus on our relationship. And train with our dogs. Owning six animals is a huge commitment."

"I know that. Of course I do."

Yet she couldn't let go of the urge to follow her heart about the shelter.

Chapter Twenty-eight

"Let's go, Aurora! Faster, Star!" Irish shouted to her dogs. The freezing air hitting her face stung her eyes and nose. Despite wearing a ski mask and goggles, she still felt the cold air swirling past her.

She dug in her ski poles, heading up the slight incline around the base of Alder Point. The steady rise of the landscape in this four-mile race was a killer on her calf muscles. But she'd done it a few times before and won each time.

The sound of baying and another driver's voice calling out, "Passing!" warned her of an approaching team from behind. She must have lost considerable time for someone to be close enough to warn her of an impending pass.

Their teams were released in one-minute intervals, so passing was less likely. However, her team had lost some time when Aurora paused to relieve herself. Then North Star's lines got tangled, and Irish stopped and fixed them. Her dogs' safety mattered most to her, even if it meant giving up valuable seconds.

"Passing!" the shout came again. This time she recognized the male voice as Lake's!

Irish moved her team as far right as possible since the trail was wide enough to allow passing. "Gee! Gee!" she called and continued skiing, trying to maintain her lead.

Not glancing over her shoulder at him, she didn't break focus or her body's rhythm as she glided in tandem with her dogs running hard ahead of her. Lake had passed her for sections of the trail during previous races. She'd let him go by her this time, and then she'd pass him when the conditions were safe.

Even though this was only day one of the two-day racing event, she didn't like Lake's team moving ahead of her. This was their first competition since their marriage three days ago. Two days since their heated discussion at Lake's birthday dinner at Nelly's. This was her chance to show him nothing had changed about racing against each other. It was time to kick in some extra effort and spur her dogs to greater speeds. They loved running! She enjoyed skiing competitively.

No way was she letting her husband win today's leg of the race!

"Go, North Star! Run, Aurora!" Her dogs were the fastest dogs on this course, Lake's dogs included. Her team would finish strong and take first place—if she had her way.

"Passing!" The shout came again. "On by!"

Aurora and North Star's ears perked up.

Pal's and Ice's heads came into view on Irish's left. Noses forward, mouths panting, ears back and alert, the huskies raced with determination and obvious joy to run with their pack leader. As they passed her team, their strides were evenly matched. Lake gave her a slight nod.

His team accomplished the passing process more smoothly than many race-day passes on the trails. Even though racers did everything in their power to keep the dogs safe and accident-free, sometimes lines got crossed and tangled. Irish was thankful for Lake's efficacy in managing his dogs and keeping them running straight while he skied. He'd improved a lot since their first haphazard meeting. So had she.

She'd keep a distance between them, and then when it was safe to do so, she'd pass his team and give him a run for his money. Although, with Lake's inheritance, she'd never be able to give him a run for his money entirely!

But in this race? Here? She would fight for the first-place win for her and her team. She wouldn't give up racing like Lake suggested the other night, either. Not a chance!

"Go, Aurora! Fast, Star!"

Putting her all into racing against the clock, the hilly terrain, and her husband's team ahead of hers, she skied forcefully, powering forward. Her legs burned. Her core heated up. She breathed heavily. "You can do it, Star! Go, Aurora!"

She rounded a clump of trees that previously blocked her view and came upon Lake and his dogs not too far in front of her. She scanned the trail farther ahead. It appeared too narrow to pass. But after that section, she should be able to get around his team safely.

"Easy," she said to her girls and backed off skiing. "Steady."

Lake dug in deeper, his muscular legs quickly moving ahead of her. He was taking advantage of reaching the narrow strip before her. Did he think for one second that she'd let him win without a challenge?

She'd show him. She might have to alternate heat and ice packs on her calves later due to sore muscles, but for now, let them burn!

As soon as they reached the broader section of the trail, she shouted, "Go, Star! Run, Aurora! Yip-yip-yip!"

Married or not, following Lake North to the finish line would never do!

Chapter Twenty-nine

"Let's go, Pal! Run, Ice!" Lake fought the urge to glance over his shoulder and check on Irish. He'd been thrilled to pass her. He rarely had the opportunity to get ahead of her and gain some time over her team. Had something happened to slow her down today? There were various reasons a skijoring team might pause, including safety issues.

He wanted to make his best time possible. A faster ski time than Irish's would give him a leg up in tomorrow's race. But he hoped everything was okay with her team.

He heard Irish calling her dogs just a little behind him. She even blasted out her war cry as if challenging anyone in her path, including him, that she was heading for the finish line and competitors better get out of her way!

Not likely!

He skied as fervently as ever, his thighs and calves on fire. He wouldn't back down an inch from racing his best just because he and Irish shared the same last name. This was his chance to beat his most-driven skijoring opponent on the first day of the competition. And he was in the lead! "Go, Ice! You've got this, Pal!"

Irish's wild-woman yowl got louder, signaling she was closing in on him. "Yip-yip-yip!"

Heart pounding, legs burning, ski poles digging into the hard-packed snow, Lake forced his legs to work harder, if possible. "Run, boys! Go! Go!" The dogs must have detected the urgency in his frenzied tone. Even they seemed intent on outrunning Irish's team.

"Passing!" Irish shouted.

How did she catch up so quickly? He veered to the right of the wide path, glad there was enough room for two teams to pass safely here. "Gee! Steady! Good job, Pal. Good work, Ice!"

"On by!"

Irish's pointers came up even with his huskies. Her dogs, one black and one russet, gained a couple of inches, their toned bodies stretching out into the run, outdistancing his dogs with their long noses facing forward.

"Go, Pal!" Lake worked his legs, trying to go faster, still hoping to pull out of this neck-and-neck race with Irish's team, both racing against the clock and each other.

"Yip-yip-yip!"

Her dogs' ears perked up at her command, their strides lengthening even more. They outdistanced Pal's and Ice's noses by two feet now.

"Go, Pal! Come on, Ice. You can do this!" Spur shouted in a feverish tone from near the finish line. "Don't back down because she's your wife, Lake. Don't give up!"

Lake wasn't giving up. He was skiing as strong as he could. His dogs were running powerfully, too. It wouldn't be enough to cross the finish line ahead of Irish, but he'd still have the better race time. Ahead of him, Irish shouted encouragement to her dogs.

So did Lake. "Good job, Pal! Bring us home, Ice! Great job, guys!"

Crossing the finish line to the cheers of the small group of bystanders, Irish had made up some time by finishing a couple of seconds ahead of Lake. In tomorrow's race, he would start with a time advantage. Even so, Irish's team would be tough competition.

Spur ran up and snagged Ice's and Pal's harnesses. "Good job! Your time was better than Irish's!"

"I know. Tomorrow will be another story." Lake chuckled. "But we'll give it all we've got, won't we, fellas?" He petted both dogs.

After the dogs settled down with healthy treats and water, Lake strode over to Irish's parking area. Good sportsmanship, drilled into him since he was a kid on Dad's T-ball team, came easily to him. He walked up to Irish and held out his hand toward her. "Good race, North!"

Grinning, she shook his hand. "Thanks. I had to cross the finish line ahead of you. No hard feelings?"

"No." He gulped down a swallow. "Plan on the competition getting tougher."

"It was pretty tough today."

"Yeah?" It was nice of her to concede to his competitive efforts. His team had worked together more successfully than ever. He saw what he, Pal, and Ice were capable of doing. In the days ahead, he'd work them even more on the trails at his place. His and Irish's place, he mentally corrected.

Irish smoothed her hands over her thighs. "Can't wait to get some heat on my muscles. Either I've been slacking off lately, or you made me work harder today."

"Ah. You're just getting lazy," he teased.

Playfully, she punched his arm. "Better watch out. I know where you live."

"I'm glad you do." He kissed her cheek. Her eyes widened, and she backed up like she felt uncomfortable with him showing affection. "Good job, Irish. I mean it."

As determined as they were to race well, they would have to work at engaging with each other as a couple after their races. He couldn't let their competitive natures hinder their baby steps toward a real relationship.

Chapter Thirty

Irish dropped off two plates at table five, and her cell phone vibrated in her apron pocket. She glanced behind her, hoping her supervisor, Brenda, didn't notice her reaching for it. She wasn't supposed to check her phone while working, but the pad of Aurora's foot had been a little swollen following their races two days ago. Irish was waiting for a text from Lake with an update on how her dog was doing this morning.

She sidetracked to the bathroom entryway and checked the cell screen. The text wasn't from Lake. It was from Shelley at the animal shelter.

Trouble. Get over here as fast as you can.

What kind of trouble? She quickly tapped in.

With Mac!

"What's going on here?" Brenda stepped into the doorway and crossed her arms, squinting at Irish. "Is there an emergency?"

Tempted to answer yes, she shook her head. "Not that I'm aware of."

"You aren't supposed to use your phone during your shift."

"I know. I'm sorry."

"I'll have to write you up for this."

Irish stuffed down her pride and thoughts of resigning. "I'm sorry for checking my phone. My dog's foot has been sore. I looked to see if Lake contacted me about it."

"Did he?" Brenda pursed her lips and tipped her head like she debated whether this situation warranted an employee using a cell phone.

"It wasn't him. I apologize for checking."

"You're worried about your pet, so I'll let the violation go this time." Brenda held up her index finger. "Last warning. This isn't your first phone infraction."

"Thank you for understanding."

"Table number ten is waiting." Chin up, Brenda strode toward the kitchen.

Irish stuffed her phone back into her apron pocket, but she was still worried. Was Aurora okay? What did Shelley mean about Mac?

"You better watch your back." Tiffany scuttled past her, carrying plates.

Irish collected a credit card from a table in her section and walked alongside her coworker. "What's that supposed to mean?"

"Brenda muttered something about finding another server to take your shifts."

Irish groaned. She should quit before she got sacked.

"It's not like you have to work anyway." Tiffany gave her a mocking smile. "Since you married the richest bachelor in Thunder Ridge, you're set for life. Easy Street all the way."

Irish would have argued, but Brenda came into her line of sight, perusing the dining room. She took care of the payment details and returned the card to the customer. But Tiffany's comment hovered in her mind. Did she have to work here?

Whether she continued at this job or took over the animal shelter duties, she would always work somewhere. She was independent and liked working. But three dogs took a lot of time—Lake was right about that. It also meant more work and commitment if they both added to their teams like they hoped to do.

After her shift, she'd stop by the animal shelter and find out why Shelley had texted her. If Irish proved her worth in helping resolve the problem, maybe Lake would see she'd make a good director after all.

Chapter Thirty-one

Lake was on his way to the kennels to check on Aurora again. Thankfully, the swelling in her paw had gone down since Irish left for work this morning. His phone vibrated, then stopped before he got it out of his pocket. He groaned, frustrated with the terrible internet service.

He checked his recent calls. Irish had called twice, so he pushed resend.

"Why did you hang up?" she asked without a greeting.

"I didn't. The service cut out on me."

"What's—" Her voice disappeared. "—animal shelter."

"What did you say?"

"Mac is—" Silence. "He just—"

"We'll talk about it later, okay?"

Nothing.

"Irish?"

The call disconnected. He groaned.

He had to find a better service plan. What if there was an emergency and he couldn't get through? What if one of his family members needed help, and they couldn't reach him? He'd take care of this today and get the best service available. The cost didn't matter!

His footfall came to a stop. Since when didn't the cost matter about something? Oh, right. He'd almost forgotten about the extra funds. Because of the inheritance, things had changed for him financially. With all the extra money in his bank account, he wouldn't have to weigh the price of every item and service he wanted against his limited funds. He'd never take it for granted, but with his new financial stability, a weight lifted from his chest.

"Hey, girl, how are you doing?" He entered Aurora's kennel and petted her. The tall russet-colored dog with lightly freckled splotches on her chest whimpered and wagged her tail. "How's the foot?" He lifted her paw and checked it. Dry and rough, but no more swelling. He took out the tin of paw balm he carried in his pocket and rubbed a little into the bottom of her foot. "Good girl. Rest up. You'll be back on the trail with North Star in a few days."

He spent some time petting each dog and checking their water dishes.

What had Irish called to tell him? Something about Mac. Was there information at the shelter he should be aware of? He'd look into it when he went to town.

Later, Lake stopped in at the internet provider in Sandpoint, talked with a rep, and arranged for an upgrade to his service plan. They assured him a technician would see to the changes promptly. He took care of several other errands before returning to Thunder Ridge. Hoping to talk with Irish, he stopped by the diner.

"She left early," Tiffany said.

"Did she say where she was going?"

"To spend time with her other love." She winked.

"Who's that?"

"You know, the dogs?"

"Oh, right. Thanks for letting me know she went home." He turned toward the door.

"Not home. To the animal shelter."

"Oh." He glanced back. "I see."

"Duty calls." Tiffany nodded toward the kitchen, then grinned. "Congratulations on the marriage."

"Thanks." Lake strode out of the diner, concerned about why Irish went to the shelter instead of finishing her shift. Something serious must be going on.

Minutes later, he pulled into the animal shelter parking lot and swerved around several potholes. The pavement needed resurfacing. The building could use a paint job. Some upkeep around the grounds would be helpful, too. A new manager might value curb appeal more than Mac apparently did. Although the shelter's financial problems may have contributed to the poor maintenance.

Lake parked his pickup next to Irish's car. Her vehicle looked like she'd driven through some deep mud puddles. His rig probably appeared just as bad, thanks to wintry country roads.

"Lake?" Irish met him outside the glass door of the shelter. "How's Aurora?"

"Fine. The swelling is down. I put a few layers of balm on her paw."

"That's a relief. Thank you. When I saw you—"

"Sorry. You called, but the phone kept cutting out."

"I didn't mean you had to drive into town. Sorry to trouble you."

"No problem. What's going on?" He nodded toward the building. "I stopped by the diner. Tiffany said you came here."

"Mac left. Shelley's running the place alone."

"What? He said he'd—"

"I know. But he paid himself a healthy sum and left." She blew out a noisy breath. "He isn't answering his phone. I'd like to drive over to his house and chew him out. But Shelley says he left town already."

"Just great." Lake pulled off his hat and scratched his scalp. "Did he pay the other outstanding debts?"

"We are trying to figure that out. Shelley texted me at the diner."

"Why'd she notify you and not me?"

Irish squinted at him. "We're married. Talking to one is talking to the other, right?"

"I guess." He squelched his irritation.

"I tried calling you."

"I know you did. Thanks for that." He'd deposited a whale of money into the animal shelter, and the director took off with a "healthy sum?" Should they call the police? "I'd like to see the books too. And call the other board members."

"Shelley and I are—" Their gazes clashed. "Fine."

Huffily, Irish marched back inside the animal shelter. Lake followed her, the tension of their interaction tightening his neck and shoulders.

"Lake." Shelley lifted her chin. "I'm surprised to see you here."

"Are you?" They weren't in charge, but he was invested in helping the shelter out of its predicament.

"Irish is doing a fine job of working through the problems here."

"I'm sure she is. What other problems are there besides the missing director?"

"Lake"—Irish shook her head at him—"I'm taking care of it."

Did she think he was overstepping by coming here? She was the one who called him!

"What else happened?" Recalling her accusation about him being controlling at the meeting a few days ago, he kept his tone mellower than he felt.

"Mac fired the other two workers yesterday." Shelley shifted on her chair. "The animals have been on their own today."

"On their own? Didn't you feed them? Take care of them?"

"That isn't my job!" Shelley said emphatically.

"You've got to be kidding me!" He strode toward the kennel area.

"Wait!" Irish rushed after him and grabbed his arm. "I came right over and fed the animals. I already cleaned the stalls too. A mama dog had her litter in the night."

"Irish jumped in and took care of everything." Shelley sounded relieved. "I called the vet this morning. But I'm not cleaning any stalls!"

"No, I don't suppose you would." Why did Shelley even work here when she didn't want to assist with the animals? Sighing, he focused on Irish. "Are you still concerned about the dogs?"

"Yeah. I am." She met his gaze with something other than fury in her eyes. "Investing your money but not your time or your heart is a shame." She stroked her palm against his chest. "We can't just let this place fall prey to charlatans."

"It wasn't my intention to ignore anything. But I thought Mac was honorable enough to keep his word about staying for a while."

"I thought so, too," Shelley muttered.

"We all thought wrong." Irish pulled her hand back, breaking contact between them.

"Where are the books?" Lake sighed. "I'll do what I can to help."

"This way." Irish led him back into the office where they previously talked with Mac. "I'll leave you to it. I'm going to check on the mama dog again."

"Okay." He dropped into the chair behind the desk. Going over the books wasn't his idea of a fun way to spend the afternoon, but it was what he'd been doing for a living over the last two years. He'd do a quick overview and then call in a professional bookkeeper if the task required a longer time investment than he was willing to contribute. "Uh, Irish?" He waited for her to turn around. "It was good of you to care for the dogs and the puppies. Thank you."

Her bunched-up shoulders lowered. She sighed, and her posture sagged. "Sure."

"Was this what you were calling to tell me earlier?"

"Yeah. Dumb connection."

"They should fix that today."

"Good. It's about time some things got fixed." She pegged him with a dark look and then left the room.

What did she think needed fixing? Their marriage of six days? Or him?

Chapter Thirty-two

Irish sat on the porch swing holding Aurora partially in her lap and petting her. She felt guilty about her injured paw and not being nearby to comfort her today. Even though Lake's ministrations helped, she wanted to be the one giving her all the love and extra attention she deserved. Cold puffs of air swirled around her as she breathed the night air, but the blanket tucked cozily around her and Aurora kept them warm.

The front door screeched open.

"Mind if I join you?" Lake held out two cups of steaming coffee.

"Sure. A hot drink sounds good. Thanks."

He handed her the cup and sat on the worn chair across from her. "How's she doing?"

"Fine. Lapping up all the attention."

"I can understand that." He smiled.

Their gazes met, and she pictured herself in his arms. Him showing her affection. Warmth spread through her, alongside a longing to know her husband better. What would it be like if they were already close? Already sharing love, laughter, and intimacies like a married couple on their honeymoon?

"I thought we should talk." While he said the words softly, they threw a cold splash of water over her tender thoughts and romantic desires.

"Are you still upset that I stepped in at the shelter?" She drank a swallow of hot coffee.

"Not upset. But we should discuss it."

"I did what I had to do. And you thanked me for it. All the board members agreed that my being the interim director was a good thing."

"I know." He pressed his lips together as if stopping himself from saying something he'd regret. "Look. This marriage is new to us, but I want it to work. I want us to discuss everything and figure things out as we go. Being on unstable footing from the beginning feels like—"

"It's not working?" She finished his sentence a little breathlessly. "That there isn't hope for us?"

"I wouldn't say we're hopeless. But I don't know how to do this." He stretched his hand wide, palm up, then relaxed it. "I don't know how to be a good husband and communicate with you. Or how to even get along. Our personalities are so different."

"Is that so bad?" He'd better not be saying their differences were her fault!

"Not bad. But would you mind if we talked to someone about our issues?"

"You think I'm helping at the shelter because of some underlying issue?" Her voice rose and echoed in the night air.

"Don't we all have underlying issues?"

"I guess." His was Laurie. Was he thinking fondly of her? Wishing she was his wife instead of bold, brash Irish?

"You're hot and cold. You love me, and you hate me." He cleared his throat. "Not love, literally. I'm confused about you most of the time." He nodded his chin toward the snow-covered land glowing in the moonlight. "I thought you wanted all this. For us to spend our time training our dogs here. Working on building our kennels and boarding business together."

"I do." Her heart rate accelerated as she tried formulating her words. "We've been married less than a week, but I am thankful for you and the chance you've given me to run the trails with my dogs. To have this much space is amazing! I do hope to build my team in the future."

"But?"

"But I like helping at the shelter, too."

"You don't even have to work if you don't want to."

That answered her question about whether she needed to work. However, her considering not working was one thing. Lake pushing her to quit would be another thing.

"Is this about you wanting to control what I'm doing? Dominate the little wife?" A rush of anger burned through her.

"Of course not. Geesh."

"Because if you're being even the tiniest bit controlling, we need more than a counselor." She jabbed her finger toward him. "Five years? We'll need a divorce lawyer before the month is over!"

"Irish—"

"I mean it. You were upset about my involvement with the shelter from the beginning." Once she started dismantling her thoughts, tempering her skyrocketing emotions was futile. "But it doesn't make sense to me. Why give your money and not your time? You care about the dogs. I know that much about you! Why not do something about that?"

"I did something! I gave a large chunk of my inheritance! I have three dogs. Between us, we have six. We plan to grow our pack. We intend to keep racing, which takes time, energy, and dedication." Lake stood and dumped his coffee onto the ice beside the porch, forming a brown patch. He leaned his backside against the railing and crossed his arms. "You're angry too. Maybe we should wait for this discussion until morning."

"You're the one who started this! Are you afraid of a passionate discussion with me?" She pushed off the chair, leaving Aurora to curl up by herself. "You said we should talk, so talk!" Puffs of air rose in front of her with each word. "I'm listening. What is biting at you?"

His lips twitching showed he fought a chuckle or words he shouldn't say.

Nothing was holding her back from airing her thoughts. "Maybe the eldest North brother, the preacher's prized son, doesn't want the town seeing his wife working in the animal shelter previously run by a sleaze. Is this about your pride? About your place in the community?"

"Irish, honestly, I have no idea where all this is coming from." He adjusted the knit cap on his head. "I want to understand what's driving you to become involved in more than the financial stakes at the shelter. You're passionate about it. Please, help me understand why you want to be the director. Why aren't you equally passionate about staying here and working with our dogs?"

"But I am." Suddenly her resentment, wounded pride, and bad feelings about Lake not wanting her to be the director melted. She felt foolish for taking everything he said so personally. Did she have to fight with him about everything? What was wrong with her? She stepped back and inhaled a long breath of cool evening air. "Are you saying you want to know my thoughts? You're not just trying to regulate my actions since I married you for your money?"

He reeled as if she slugged him.

"What I mean is—"

"I know what you mean," he growled. "Do you want this marriage to work? Are you in this with me for the long haul? If so, we need to work together. Pull together. Attempt to be a couple even when it's difficult."

"What marriage? At this point, we're strangers, business associates, living under the same roof." Her voice sounded sad and distant even to her ears.

"Is that all our relationship is to you? All I am to you? A business arrangement?"

"For now. Although, I honestly hope that changes in the future."

He rubbed his palms over his face. "Would you be willing to chat with a counselor with me?"

"I don't see what good it would do."

"I don't see how it could hurt."

His strained expression and moist eyes seemed to show his internal wounds more clearly tonight. Recalling the way his gaze lit up at the sight of Laurie the day after their wedding, something painful twisted in her middle. Maybe he was the one who wasn't committed to this agreement. Perhaps he'd be out before the month ended.

"When you asked me to marry you, I kissed you, didn't I?" She was grasping for straws. But she'd grab at anything to turn their dark conversation into a lighter vibe. "Didn't that kiss and embrace prove I hoped for more from this marriage than a business partnership?"

Some color returned to his cheeks.

"Maybe. I still think counseling might help us." He reached out and stroked his hands down her arms. "I am attracted to you, Irish. I can't say I love you yet. But I want us to fall for each other. I pray it happens soon."

Gazes locked, they drew closer like magnets forced to meet in the middle. Swirls of breath arced around them in the brisk air. Some kissing might soothe both their troubled hearts. Maybe they'd find love in a passionate embrace—or at least comfort.

No, no, no. Irish stepped back. Jumping into kissing and cuddling with Lake without being on the path toward love wasn't right. Not when they didn't have strong feelings for each other yet.

Glancing at the night sky sprinkled with stars, she sighed. "We'd better work out the animal shelter stuff before we get overly involved in romantic overtures. We don't want anything clouding our judgment. Your kisses have already proven to be—"

"What?"

"A distraction."

"We wouldn't want that to happen, would we?" He winked, then kissed her cheek. "Good night, Irish."

"'Night, Lake."

He left her alone on the porch with Aurora. But his words danced in her thoughts like embers bursting into the air. He was attracted to her. He wanted them to fall for each other. Did he mean he wanted things to move forward in their marriage faster than she did? Before they were in love?

Five years would be a long, lonely stretch without romantic affection between them. Wouldn't those years be better spent if they were sharing their whole lives? Sharing a bedroom?

Yet something held her back from following her husband inside the cabin.

Chapter Thirty-three

Sitting across from Pastor North in a small conference room at the church, Irish wished she hadn't agreed to this meeting. Lake's father being their counselor? What was she thinking?

If her father-in-law took his son's side on everything, she'd be out the door in a flash. She gnawed on her lower lip and twisted her hands in her lap, hoping neither of the two men saw her nervous gestures. She wasn't the anxious type. This counseling session was the culprit. Or else the problem was Smith North sitting across from her like her judge and jury.

Although, that wasn't fair. The man had shown her only kindness. Still, he was a pastor and Lake's father!

Lake said he'd be impartial and discreet and that he understood their unique marriage. However, his attempts to reassure her hadn't resolved her worries. Married one week, and she was already entertaining second thoughts. Why had she been so reckless? She leaped into marriage without genuinely considering what trying to have a real relationship with Lake might be like. And without knowing how much he still cared for his ex!

"Why don't we start with prayer?" Pastor North smiled in her direction. Maybe he would be understanding and compassionate like Lake claimed he would be.

She didn't hear the first part of his prayer, but the ending caught her attention.

"We give our lives, hopes and dreams, and everything to You, Lord Jesus. Make us into the people You want us to be, filled with love and grace for each other. Amen."

Love and grace.

Maybe one day, after a long time and with lots of grace, she'd love Lake and he'd love her like real marriage partners. But first, they needed to learn how to get along and share accommodations. Why was communication between them so difficult? When they were only competitors, she had liked him fine. And she certainly enjoyed kissing him, but sharing the small cabin? Nearly falling over each other to get to the tiny bathroom, make coffee, or wash dishes? It was too close.

Her desire to be the shelter's director, and Lake digging his feet in about it, had caused more turmoil than she knew how to deal with. She'd never been married before. She didn't know how to get along and discuss things with a man. In the past, she would have left the jerk if they didn't get along well. She couldn't do that with her husband, not with Lake.

He stroked his fingers across the back of her hand. Sparks zinged through her nerve endings. Simultaneously, images of him kissing her during their marriage ceremony fluttered in her thoughts. The way his mouth felt against hers. The taste of his minty breath. How he touched her cheek during the kiss. Gulping, she pulled her hand away.

Her gaze met Pastor North's. Did he notice her reaction to Lake's touch? She lifted her chin.

"Irish, how do you feel about marrying Lake?"

"That marriage is foreign to both of us."

"What's bothering you the most about having married him?" Pastor North tilted his head.

"Did I say anything was bothering me?" She didn't like the pastor assuming anything.

He cleared his throat and held up his hands. "My apologies. Lake mentioned you both were struggling to communicate. If that isn't the case—"

"Fine. It is. I'm not used to talking about personal stuff like this with him, you, or anyone. I'm used to making my own decisions. Having to run things by him is difficult, to say the least." She glanced at Lake. His features looked somber and a little strained.

"Is there anything you'd like us to talk about?" Pastor North's tone was gentle, not pushy.

"Dad, maybe now isn't the time."

"Time for what?" Irish asked, suspicious of the undertones she detected between father and son. "What did you tell him about us?"

Both men made almost identical gestures of raking their hands through their hair.

"Well?"

"I told him about the shelter. About your wanting to dive in and my reluctance to upset our barely holding-it-together lifestyle. About us not agreeing on pretty much anything."

Her face flamed. "Then why am I here? If you already explained our problems to your dad, maybe you two should be having this chat and leaving me out of it!" She pushed away from the table and stood.

"Irish—" Lake stood also.

"What?" She glared at him.

"I'm sorry. I needed to talk to someone." He did the hair-raking thing again. "It's not like I've been married before. I've made mistakes already. Please, stay. We need to talk. My dad is willing to assist us."

Irish glanced at her father-in-law.

He shrugged. "It's up to you. If you want to wait until another time, I understand. Or if you'd rather talk to someone else, such as my wife, that's okay."

Liv was nice. But Irish didn't want to talk with her about marital stuff. How could anyone understand the weirdness she felt living in the cabin with Lake? Being attracted to him one minute then distrusting him to stay with her the next? Imagining him thinking about Laurie all the time drove her nuts! She'd rather remain single than for Lake to back out of the relationship after she fell in love with him.

Sighing, she sat down. "I'll stay. Sorry, Pastor North."

"That's all right. And it's Smith. We're family here."

"If Lake and I were here because we are family, I wouldn't talk about our situation with you." She boldly met his gaze. "So, in this session, and if we return for any others, I'll call you Pastor North."

"Okay. No problem."

Lake sat down and exchanged glances with his dad. He slid his palms over his thighs as if wiping his hands free of sweat. "If you'd rather we not do this today—"

"We're here. Let's just get it over with."

"Let me reword my previous question," Pastor North said soothingly. "Is there anything you'd like to discuss that's troubling you today?"

"Other than sitting here with you two expecting me to bare my heart?"

"While I love you as my son and daughter-in-law"—the pastor smiled at her as if trying to convey sympathy or understanding—"I'm here as a pastor. What you say won't go beyond these walls."

"That's good to know." She didn't want Spur and Wilks hearing about this discussion at the dinner table and then blabbing their information around Nelly's. All she needed was for Tiffany to hear about her marital situation. "This arrangement of Lake's and mine is complicated. And private. However, as he already told you, we've had some arguments."

Pastor North folded his hands and nodded.

"How is talking about our marriage going to help? It seems like a waste of time." She shrugged. "We need to work through this in our own time and way."

"Do you also think it's a waste of time?" Pastor North turned toward Lake. "Or will talking about things relieve your concerns? Your stress?"

Was Lake stressed? He faced her, his eyes moist. "We took a giant step into the unknown when we married as we did. I am trusting God to help us and guide us."

"I know."

"I've told you I plan to pursue you, but maybe I haven't convinced you." He breathed out a deep, weighted breath. "I'm probably rushing things. Maybe I've been less than attentive through our first week of marriage. But I want us to move closer to being compatible."

"You don't think we're compatible?"

"We're not talking. Not trying to work things out."

"I barely know you." She shuddered, and the movement went through her whole body. "We hardly talk. You're the one who doesn't want to discuss anything at the dinner table!"

"We can talk. I don't want us fighting at the table." He tipped his head, gazing intently at her as if his father weren't present. "Do you have any suggestions for getting to know each other better?"

"Other than sleeping in the same room?"

His face reddened. Maybe she shouldn't have brought up that intimate detail here.

"Don't mind me." Pastor North raised his hands. "You two need to talk this through. I'm only here to assist. Although, since you brought up a valid point, are you concerned with taking that marital step with Lake?"

"I'm not concerned about us being incompatible in intimacy, if that's what you mean." Irish let a roguish smile cross her mouth. Lake got her into this. He deserved a little discomfort too. "I made sure we were well-suited in the passion department before we married."

"Oh? Is that right?" Pastor North tugged on the neck of his tie as if the knot strangled him.

Lake coughed hard. "It's not what you think."

"Don't underestimate Pastor North's powers of observation. He can sense when a couple can't wait to be in each other's arms."

Both men gawked at her.

"Just kidding. I kissed Lake first, okay?" Some of her humor evaporated at the heated look she found in Lake's gaze. "I wanted to make sure we had passion before I plunged into a marriage that might be—"

"What?" he whispered.

Was she brave enough to finish her thoughts with Lake staring at her like she ripped out his heart and pasted it on his sleeve?

"Stale and lifeless, like most marriages I've observed."

He closed his eyes for a moment.

"What did you discover?" Pastor North stroked his chin.

"Where do I start?" Irish took a fortifying breath. "I discovered his mouth fit mine perfectly. He tasted like mint candy. And I enjoyed his kisses more than any other man's."

"Irish, Irish." Lake shook his head, his cheeks a deep red.

Pastor North covered his mouth with his hand, but his merry-looking eyes said he fought a chuckle.

"His kiss was the best one I've ever experienced." She felt intoxicated with the warmth of Lake's perusal.

"Then we should try it again. And again."

She refrained from laughing, but everything within her balked at the restraint. "I told you that isn't happening until—"

"We love each other. Which is why we're here." He nodded at his dad. "Why we're seeking counseling. To try to jumpstart our caring and love for each other."

"I think you want to circumvent our argument about the shelter so much you're forcing us into a dialogue we're not ready for!" Her warm feelings toward Lake evaporated like rain on a hot summer day.

"We disagree about the shelter. That's the truth."

"What's the big deal about me working there? We'd have a say in how the animals are treated." She tapped the table. "Isn't it valuable for us to make sure the funds you generously gave are being used wisely?"

"Sure." Lake stroked his forehead. "It just isn't the way I pictured it."

"Pictured what?" Pastor North asked.

"Marriage. Sharing my life with a woman."

"How did you picture it? You've observed your mom's and my marriage. Do we always agree?"

"No, sir."

"Do we always see eye to eye?"

"Nope." Lake tossed up his hands. "But you work things out. You talk until you agree. Away from the dinner table!"

"Oh, here we go," Irish grumbled.

"We eventually agreed, but it wasn't always easy. Especially in the early days." Pastor North glanced at his watch. "I made mistakes too. I'm sure your mom still remembers some of those."

"Yet, you still love each other thirty-five years into your marriage. You share the same bedroom. Kiss each other good night." Lake glanced at Irish.

She felt the heat of a blush spread through her. "You doubt we'll ever share those things, right? You think we won't make it as a couple?"

"I didn't say that."

"You don't have to. It's obvious."

"I want this marriage to work!"

"But you can't force a relationship to work." Irish felt the fire of anger building in her again. "You can't force me to be who you want me to be. A weak-willed woman who goes along with everything you say. I am not Laurie!" She hadn't meant to shout the woman's name.

"No, you're not." Lake's shoulders heaved.

"Lake—" Pastor North shook his head.

Pain ricocheted through Irish. "Excuse me. I need a break." She scrambled for the closed door.

She had no one to blame for this wretchedness but herself. They couldn't call it quits and still have the funds for the shelter. Or for Lake to pay off the mortgage, which he already had. They must stay married and share a house for five years. How were they going to do that? She yanked on the doorknob.

"Irish, wait. I didn't mean—"

But she was already marching down the hallway.

Chapter Thirty-four

As soon as Lake reached his property, he checked on the dogs. All of them bayed and howled their greetings. Pal, Ice, and Rambler's howling sounded like they were singing as a trio. He let them out of their kennels to run and sniff the fenced yard. Then he did the same with Irish's dogs. Next, he mucked the yard, doing anything to prolong his time outdoors.

He and Irish hadn't spoken a word on the miserable drive home. A lot of good counseling did for them. Why did he agree with her that she wasn't Laurie? The blunder popped out of his mouth before he silenced it. Of course, she wasn't Laurie! Thank God she wasn't!

He'd loved Laurie. But Irish? He married her! She was his wife. Her fiery passion for living and how she kissed him stirred his blood, heart, and whole being in ways no one else ever had!

When she had left Dad's office, Lake thought she'd use the bathroom or walk around the building, cool down, and return. He'd waited for a few minutes without that happening. It didn't seem like she was coming back to their counseling session, and he was starting to feel antsy about finding her.

"Son, may I offer you a word of advice?" Dad asked.

"Of course." They came to his office for some wisdom and advice.

"If I could give you one thing to take your marriage to a deeper level—"

"Yes?" Lake imagined what he might say. Kiss his wife good night. Never go to bed angry. Bake chocolate chip cookies with her.

"Pray together."

"Huh?"

"That's the best place to start. Every day over the next week, I encourage you to clasp Irish's hand and pray with her about your marriage. Ask for God's help. Then trust Him to be working in your lives together."

"Pray together, huh?"

"That's right."

Lake heaved a sigh. "I'm willing to try anything."

"Good. John G. Lake, the man you were named after, was a man of great faith and prayer."

"I remember." Lake stood quickly. "Sorry to cut this short, but I should probably find my wife."

"Of course." Dad stood also. "I'll be praying for you guys."

"Thanks." Lake shook his father's hand and headed for his truck, where Irish waited inside.

An hour later, her claim that he didn't think they'd make it as a couple still churned in his mind. Had he unintentionally perpetrated the idea that their marriage was temporary? On their wedding day, he told her he'd pursue her. But in the days since then, had he done anything to show her he meant it?

He took a deep breath of cold air and rubbed Pal's chest. A throaty rumble of pleasure coming from the dog made him chuckle. "Let's go, buddy. Back into your kennel. I have important husbandly things to take care of." Pal sauntered into his pen, then curled up in a circle, his nose resting against his tail.

When Lake entered the warm cabin, he slipped off his boots, thankful for the inviting scent of simmering meat that greeted him. "Smells great in here." He appreciated Irish pitching in and doing some of the workload. Every day over the last week, she had jumped in and helped with the dogs, food prep, and keeping the woodstove filled with wood. Had he even thanked her?

"Wash up. It's ready."

"Will do. Thanks for fixing dinner. I appreciate it."

"Uh-huh." She squinted at him like she was surprised to hear him say something positive to her.

He headed for the bathroom, feeling lighter already.

Back in the kitchen, they both dished up meat, fried potatoes, and peas. Once they were seated on the couch and chair, eating casually away from the table, he drummed up the courage to talk with her. Even if it might be an uncomfortable mealtime conversation, he must address what happened earlier.

"I'm sorry for the awkwardness in the meeting today." He pushed the fried potatoes and ketchup back and forth with his fork. "I don't want you thinking I'm not invested in our marriage. I am. Honestly, I am."

"Good to know." She ate a couple of bites without facing him.

"We have a lot to learn about each other. I'm sure that will come with talking and spending time together. Getting comfortable with one another will take effort on both our parts."

She glanced at him but didn't comment.

"My dad loves my mom and all of us guys in the family." He felt the need to explain. "But I didn't want us speaking with him because he's my dad, or because he'd be on my side. He's a pastor with a heart for helping people. We can trust him to be discreet and to do his best to help us."

Irish set her plate on the end table and turned toward him, her eyes moist, her lips parted slightly. He could watch her eyes and lips for hours. Her expressions intrigued him.

"I'm sorry for my response about Laurie, too."

She still didn't say anything.

"Of course, you aren't her. That's a good thing!" He wanted to be completely honest. "She carelessly broke up with me. She hardly even told me why, other than accusing me of having romantic feelings for a friend—which wasn't true! You showed courage when you married me even though you didn't know what you were getting into." A tight smile crossed his mouth. "I like your willingness to take a risk. A beautiful fire in you attracts me to you like crazy!"

Her eyes widened.

"That's right. I am attracted to you, Irish North. I admire your passion and your determination. It makes you want to do right by the animals in the shelter. I like those qualities about you."

"Then why—"

"Why am I being such a clod about your involvement there?" A warmth of embarrassment and the breaking of his pride seeped through him.

"Something along those lines."

"My parents led busy lives but forged a strong team together."

"What does that have to do with us?"

He wet his lips, feeling the dryness. "I'd like to have a sense of teamwork with you. Since we didn't have a courtship, we must work harder at a relationship now."

"Working harder at it doesn't sound very romantic."

"No. But I think it's true." He set his plate down even though he wasn't finished with the food. "If you're at the shelter all the time, and I'm here working with the dogs and building our kennel business, it will be like we're living separate lives. Like we aren't even married!"

"People do it all the time!" Her tone heated up.

"Sure. But we are different, you and me. We haven't—"

"Made love?"

"Not just that. We haven't fallen in love. We haven't gotten closer in the week since our wedding."

"You don't want me to work so we'll be around each other all the time, driving each other mad?" She shook her head, her long red hair swishing over her shoulders. "I have to work! I can't live off your windfall."

"Why not? I'm your husband."

"I plan to pull my share of the weight. That's all!" Quickly, she scooped up her plate and carried it to the sink.

Lake remained seated, pondering what he should say next. Should they talk some more about the shelter? Or keep the discussion centered on their marriage?

Irish returned with two mugs of steaming black coffee and handed him one.

"Thanks."

"You're welcome." Sipping her drink, she sat back in the chair and eyed him. "What do you want out of this marriage?"

Her question surprised him, but he answered, "Everything."

"Seriously?"

"Yes."

"Right now, if I wanted—" She glanced toward her open bedroom door.

"I'd want that too. You're a beautiful woman." He sucked in a breath. "But it's right for us to wait for intimacy and work on our relationship first."

"There you go saying 'work' again. What about fun? Romance?" She sipped her hot coffee, her cheeks revealing some embarrassment over the topic.

Reaching across the gap between them, he clasped her free hand. "I want fun and romance with you. I look forward to all the benefits of married love, but I want it to be right for both of us. What about you? What do you want?"

She tugged her hand free. "I gave up on the idea of a perfect love long ago."

"I'm sad to hear that."

"I saw the harm my mother went through because she always needed a man to make her happy. One guy barely walked out the door before she contacted someone else." Irish became more animated. "I'm independent and self-reliant. Sorry if it bursts your bubble, but I don't need a man to make me happy. Although, a little romance sounds nice." She winced like she was reluctant to admit that.

"What about love? Do you hope for love between us?"

"I won't hold my breath, but it's the dream." She sighed, and the sound vibrated between them like the aching chords of a melancholy song. "You're a nice guy, Lake. A great kisser. I can work with those things."

She winked, probably trying to lighten the mood. But he wasn't ready to go there.

"That isn't enough for me." He set down his coffee cup on the end table.

"You don't get to choose how I feel about you!"

"Not just about me. About us."

"Okay, then. You don't get to decide how I feel about us. Your negative attitude about me being the director at the animal shelter has been a bad start."

"I'm sorry. I could have approached that topic a dozen better ways."

"Yes, you could have."

He ran his hand over his scruffy chin, which he hadn't shaved in a few days. "I still feel strongly about working together here and training our dogs. Starting a kennel and boarding business like the team we talked about being."

"I guess I shouldn't have jumped into directing the shelter without discussing my wishes with you first. Even if it goes against my grain!" She cleared her throat. "I'm not used to running things by anyone else."

"I understand. We'll have to learn to do better at communicating with each other." He clutched his hands loosely around one knee. "I need to run my decisions by you too."

"Thank you. I'd still like to pitch in at the shelter, even if the job isn't permanent."

Recalling his dad's suggestion, Lake asked, "Do you mind if we pray about it?"

"Well, I, uh—" She stared at him. "Is that what you usually do?"

"I try to remember to pray. If I had talked to God before I barked at you about the shelter, I might have spoken kinder and been wiser in choosing my words. Sorry about that."

"I should have thought more before speaking too. It's a bad habit."

"Are you okay with this?" He held out his hands, palms up. "My dad suggested that we pray together daily for a week."

"Why?"

"So we're trusting the Lord for His help in our marriage. And being humble about it."

"All right." She rested her palms lightly over his.

He closed his eyes. "Lord, thank You for blessing us with this marriage we are sharing. You know our hearts and how we're trying to figure out a relationship between us." He took a slow breath. "Help us to make good decisions that will bring us closer toward a real marriage and loving each other for the rest of our lives. In Jesus's name."

"Amen," Irish whispered and pulled her hands back. "Now what?"

"We talked. We prayed. Is there anything you'd like to say or bring up before we do our chores?"

"About the shelter?" She gnawed on her lower lip, bringing his attention to her soft mouth. "Do you mind if I work there for a while longer?"

"I don't mind. I'm sure the business needs help with the animals. There's no one better than you who could look after them."

"Thanks." Her whole face transformed, her eyes widened, and a beautiful smile crossed her lips. "I didn't expect you to agree so quickly."

"Thought I'd keep fighting about it, huh?" He chuckled lightly. "There's a lot about me you don't know. Besides my being a great kisser, I am a nice guy who normally wouldn't keep his wife from doing what she wants to do."

"How often are you going to remind me I said you are a great kisser?"

"Is every day enough for you to know I'm looking forward to kissing you again?"

"Lake North, you surprise me!"

"Sweetheart, I hope I keep surprising you for a long time."

Chapter Thirty-five

Irish experienced a few hectic days juggling schedules and working two jobs. She'd given notice at the diner, but Brenda had begged her to finish the week. That meant double duty, working a shift at the restaurant and then one at the shelter.

Between the two positions, she was exhausted. Determined to show Lake she could accomplish everything she set out to do and not fall apart, she worked too many long hours.

When she wound up in town at ten p.m. on Thursday night, Lake told her she shouldn't be driving out to the cabin in her exhausted state and arranged for her to stay at his grandmother's house. His caring about her and making the sleepover arrangement was thoughtful, especially at such a late hour. Maybe his feelings were getting deeper for her already.

Although she'd noticed a tightness in his voice a few times when speaking on the phone over the last couple of days. In her absence, he was taking care of her dogs, too. Dropping her workload on him wasn't fair. And she missed North Star, Aurora, and Pleiades.

Whenever she worked with one of the shelter dogs, she ached to be spending time with her own dogs.

Another race was coming up, but she hadn't prepared for it like usual. How could she when she spent most of her days in town?

As she settled down to sleep at Trish's house, she missed her bed in the little cabin. She missed drinking coffee or tea with Lake and even praying with him like they'd been doing lately. She closed her eyes in the unfamiliar room, imagining them holding hands, then she prayed silently for their marriage as if her husband were right here with her. She fell asleep picturing Lake kissing her cheek.

The following morning when she woke up, it took a few seconds for her to remember where she was and why she'd slept in Trish's living room on a fold-up couch.

"Good morning, dear." Trish walked through the living room in her long mint-colored robe.

"Thanks for letting me crash here," Irish said groggily.

"Any time. Since the boys are grown, no one camps out here with me anymore."

"Did Lake used to stay overnight a lot?"

"He did. Hud, too. When Smith built this house for me, the boys took turns staying over," Trish said wistfully. "We had fun escapades. Reading. Cooking. Telling stories. Building forts. I miss those days."

"I loved spending weekends with my grandmother when she was alive too."

"How long has she been gone?"

"Ten years." Irish sat up and stretched.

"I'm sorry." Trish gave her a sympathetic smile. "What would you like for breakfast, dear?"

"I'm not really—"

"Will scrambled eggs and toast suffice? I can still make those. Lake says you're busy. But that I should insist you eat a healthy breakfast before leaving for work."

Lake, Lake, Lake. "Scrambled eggs will be fine."

"Coffee's ready."

"Excellent." Irish folded the bed, then headed for the shower. After she cleaned up and dressed, she grabbed some coffee and sat at a table for two in the kitchen and living room combo.

"Lord, be with us today," Trish prayed. "Bless Irish in all the tasks she must do. Thank You for the good things You are bringing our way. Be with my family. I thank you for every one of them. Please touch Stone's heart and remind him of Your love." She went on for a while, talking to God like He was her dearest friend.

"Amen," Irish said when Trish finished praying. Then she dug into her food which smelled fantastic. "Thanks for preparing this for me."

"Certainly. I'm honored to have you sitting at my table. My first grandchild's wife. I am blessed, indeed."

Everything about Trish seemed welcoming and encouraging, which put Irish more at ease.

"Can I ask you a personal question?" Here was one of the people who knew Lake the best. Why not ask a few questions?

"You may." The older woman sipped her tea.

"When you heard Lake was marrying me, what did you think?"

Trish set down her teacup. She closed her eyes briefly as if praying or seeking wisdom before meeting Irish's gaze. "Do you mean since I'd never met you before?"

"Yes. Did you hate the idea of Lake marrying me?"

A soft smile spread across Trish's lips. Her white hair nearly glowed beneath the overhead lighting. "I worried about Lake proposing so soon after his breakup with Laurie."

"Oh, right." Laurie. Would she ever escape the woman's name?

"However, I trust him to make his own decisions and to follow the Lord's leading. He's a good man with a tender heart like his father. He's his mother's son, too. Liv was a wonderful mama to those boys." She chuckled as if recalling a fond memory. "After helping her and Smith raise nine boys, nothing surprises me. Those boys kept us laughing and pulling our hair out."

"I can't imagine nine boys in the same house."

"We called mealtimes 'blessed chaos!' That was the reason Liv never allowed bickering at the table. She wanted peace while her family ate."

"That makes sense." It gave Irish some clarity about why Lake didn't want them discussing negative things at the dinner table.

"After being an only child without a single cousin, Smith dreamed of having a big family." Trish ate a bite of her eggs. "Liv and the Lord's blessing fulfilled his dream."

Irish tugged off the edge of the crust on the toast, not as hungry as before. "And me? What about Lake asking me to marry him?" She needed an answer about that.

"I knew he cared for you. It wasn't all about the money."

"Oh, he doesn't—"

"Yes, he does. Otherwise, he would have waited for love. The money wouldn't have mattered to him. It never did."

Trish spoke so confidently Irish could only stare into the older woman's moist seafoam eyes.

"You doubt, don't you?"

"Sort of. Our marriage isn't a love match." Irish laughed nervously. "He and I get along most of the time. I'm headstrong. He's determined. We're both independent, but we're trying. We're praying together now. That's something."

"Oh, sweetie. I'm thrilled to hear you're praying together. Prayer changes everything." Trish smiled affectionately. "May I give you a small suggestion?"

"Why not?" Irish steeled herself.

"Accept your husband."

"What do you mean?"

"Accept Lake as the man God planned for you. Accept this marriage as a perfect answer for both of you." Trish clasped her hand gently. "Dear one, your beginning may not be the dreamy stuff you wished for as a little girl. But it can become so much more in the future. A beginning is simply a beginning. The rest of the days and years together and what you do with them is what matters."

Irish swallowed the dryness in her throat.

"Goodness." Trish released her hand. "I didn't mean to sound like a know-it-all. I wasn't even married long myself."

"You sound wise and honest. I appreciate that."

"I want the best for you and Lake. I love you both. You've done my heart good by sharing with me this morning." Trish waved her hand slowly toward the small space. "Come by anytime you want to talk."

"Thank you."

They finished their breakfasts. Irish helped Trish with cleaning up the dishes. Then she had to hurry to get to the diner. Trish's words stayed in her thoughts throughout her shift. *"Accept Lake as the man God has planned for you."*

If God meant Lake for her, did He plan her for Lake, too?

Chapter Thirty-six

The windy, moist air hit Lake's cheeks with icy precision as he sped down the trail between the partially snow-laden trees. In this section of the forest, he'd gained speed during previous races.

Up ahead, Irish would be making her break toward the finish line. Even though she hadn't been practicing and running her dogs much in the last week, she still wanted to compete this weekend. She'd done well in yesterday's races. Their posted times were close. With her being ahead of him now, she must be up for the challenge of a strong finish.

"Go, Pal! Let's go, Ice!" Lake called to his huskies. "We'll catch up to her. You can do it!"

As the trail opened up to a snowy meadow, he saw Irish's team wasn't as far ahead of him as he initially thought. His heart pounded at the possibility of passing her on the straightaway. He'd tried it before and never held his lead. Maybe he could do it this time.

"Let's go, Pal. Run hard, Ice!" Lake skied powerfully down the slight slope into the flat land. His leg muscles felt strong. The dogs were maintaining their speed. "Let's go, guys!"

Lake

He had some time to make up if he was going to beat Irish's two-day tally. Snow fell lightly, making the groomed trail a bit slower. But he liked these conditions. He squinted to see through the mist of falling flakes.

Irish must have heard him. She veered her dogs to the right side of the trail, her legs moving powerfully too. "Gee! Keep going, Aurora! You've got this, Star!" She made her yips.

Lake knew Irish and her team's movements because he'd followed behind her enough times. But something seemed different now. Perhaps her dogs had slowed down. Or else his dogs were primed for this passing and couldn't wait to do it.

"Passing!" he shouted the warning. "Haw! Let's go, boys!" Lake's breathing came hard as he skied across the packed snow, digging and pulling with his ski poles, working his thighs, and directing his team to the left for the pass. "On by! On by!"

"Hold steady, Star!" Irish shouted.

Their two teams skied and ran beside each other in a broad section of the trail. Lake glanced at Irish, but she didn't meet his gaze. He lost a tad of his momentum. Her dogs pulled ahead. No longer beside her, Lake focused strongly on skiing and getting ahead of Irish.

Here on the trail, they were competitors. He couldn't let go of his drive to win. She wasn't letting go of hers, not even meeting his gaze for a second.

Heart pounding, thighs burning, eyes stinging with icy snow pelting them, Lake skied with one consuming desire—to safely reach the finish line first! Digging his poles into the hardpack, he yelled, "Let's go, boys! On by!" His dogs charged ahead of Irish's duo by half a head. "That's it! You're doing it!"

"Yip-yip-yip!" Her shrill yelping sounded loud. Her dogs lunged forward, taking the lead. It appeared their battle would be a close match to the finish.

"Come on, Pal! Let's go, Ice!"

"Go fast, Aurora! Take us home, Star!"

Suddenly, Irish's dogs got a last-second burst of energy or drive. In Lake's peripheral vision, he saw his wife's legs working, her poles digging in like an Olympic skier on steroids. Where had such powerful strides and last-minute momentum come from?

Something ignited within him, too. He wanted to win this race! His huskies were strong athletes and equal to Irish's pointers. Lake's legs burned and worked as hard, if not harder, than Irish's. "Go, Ice! Run, Pal!"

The finish line in sight, he skied relentlessly, digging and pushing off the firm snow with each powerful stride of his skis and poles.

Their teams ran side by side again, bound for the finish at a fast pace. Lake and Irish shouted praise and encouragement to their dogs, cheering them on.

The two-day combined scores favored Irish's team, but all Lake could think about was pulling off this win! Even if he didn't stand a chance of leading in the two-day event, he wanted to finish first today!

Up ahead, the crowd cheered wildly!

With adrenaline pounding through his system, Lake skied past Irish, and Pal and Ice took the lead ahead of her dogs. Amid the cheers from spectators, his team crossed the finish line first. Yes! He pulsed his right ski pole in the air.

He and his dogs were well past the onlookers when he brought Ice and Pal to a stop. "Good job, guys!" He petted them both enthusiastically. "Excellent run!"

"You did it!" Spur ran up to Lake and clapped him on the back. "You beat her!" He bent over and petted the dogs, too. "I knew you'd do it one day. I'm so proud of you guys."

A hush came over the spectators.

Where were Irish and her dogs? Lake glanced back.

Oh, no! Twenty feet before the finish line, Irish knelt on the packed snow, leaning over Aurora's russet body. The dog wiggled, showing she was alive, but she must have been injured.

"I'd better—"

"Go!" Spur grabbed hold of the dogs' harnesses. "I've got this!"

Lake unclipped Ice and Pal from his belt. Then, despite his shaking legs tanking after his intense race, he jogged back along the trail to assist Irish in any way he could.

Chapter Thirty-seven

While Irish and her team skied and ran beside Lake and his dogs, she felt the exhilaration of the race and the competition charging up between them. She always had last-minute energy. She could still win, even with Lake's team moving powerfully next to hers. She had a faster ski time yesterday, which meant her combined scores would be better than his.

Of course, Lake wanted to win. He had told her enough times he'd beat her someday. Even the remembrance of his threat made her heart beat faster. She held the skijoring title Lake desired, and she wanted to keep it. That driving force would push her across the finish line ahead of him!

But then Aurora limped. *Limped!*

"Whoa. Whoa." Irish immediately brought her dogs and her skis to a stop.

Aurora dropped to the ground, panting and licking her right front foot. Fearful of a bad injury, Irish knelt beside her. "Are you okay, baby? What's wrong with your leg?"

Due to her hectic schedule, she hadn't taken the dogs out on the trails daily like usual in preparation for a race. Did she warm them up enough this morning? They ate a race-day breakfast. She didn't think she pushed them any more than she would have in the final leg of any other race. But what if she did because she couldn't bear to concede the win to Lake? No, she would never do that! Her dogs' safety and well-being always came first.

"Sweet baby." She nuzzled Aurora's neck with her face. "I'm so sorry for whatever happened. You're going to be okay."

Irish heard the cheers as Lake won. Another team passed her. She stayed on the packed snow, checking Aurora's front ankles. Were they swollen? Was it her paw? Maybe she stepped on some sharp ice. Did her previous injury cause this to happen?

One of the officials jogged over to her. "Everything okay here?"

"She just started limping." Aurora wagged her tail and squirmed like she loved all the attention. "I'll bring her to the vet's tent in a minute."

"All right. Let me know if you need assistance." The guy strode back to the finish line, talking into his cell phone.

Aurora stood up next to North Star, looking as if nothing was bothering her now.

"You okay, baby?" Irish kissed the top of Aurora's head. "You scared me."

Lake ran up to her and squatted beside her. "Is she okay?"

"I think so. She limped, so I stopped."

"I'm so sorry." He hugged her and then petted Aurora. "How are you, girl?"

His caring tone and his hug were comforting. Irish silenced any competitive comments about Aurora's injury being the only reason he won. "We were going at full speed until the moment she limped."

"Want me to carry her over to the vet for you?"

"Thanks, but I'll manage."

"What can I do to help?" he asked softly.

"Would you mind getting Star back to my stake-out area and keeping an eye on her?"

"Not at all." He unclipped Star. Holding onto her harness, he patted her with his other hand. "Good girl. You did a great job."

A couple of racers and their dogs zipped past them.

"I'll take your skis too."

Irish handed them to him while holding onto Aurora, who didn't appear to be limping now. "Thanks, Lake."

"Sure. Let me know how it goes." With his hands full of her skis in one arm and gripping Star's harness with his other hand, he said, "It'll be okay, Irish."

"Thanks. I hope so."

She scooped up Aurora and headed toward the vet's tent. The dog wasn't terribly heavy, but she squirmed in Irish's arms, trying to get down and making it difficult to hold her.

Doctor Cochrane checked Aurora's leg and foot. "There's some swelling in her paw." He held Aurora's foot up so Irish could see the slight bump. "Must have stepped on ice or something hard. Keep her resting as much as possible. She should be fine in a day or two."

"Thank you, Doctor. That's a relief."

"Follow up with your vet if anything changes or the swelling worsens."

"Will do."

Thankfully, Aurora's leg wasn't broken or sprained. Irish carried her back to her parking area and found Lake sitting in a chair by a glowing fire with Star leaning against his knee. He held her harness with one hand and petted her with the other. It was an inviting, tranquil scene.

"You're back."

"I didn't mean you had to stay here." Irish clipped Aurora to the hitch line.

Lake did the same with Star. Both dogs licked and smelled each other.

"I didn't want to leave North Star until you got back. Spur is with my dogs."

"Still, you're in your racing garb." No wonder he was huddling near the fire.

"I'm okay. How's Aurora?"

Lake followed Irish to the car, where she grabbed some healthy after-racing treats.

"There's some swelling. She must have stepped on a piece of jagged ice, or a frozen branch, or something." Irish released a long breath. "Maybe it was due to her previous injury."

"I'm glad it wasn't worse."

"Me too."

Aurora whimpered and wiggled as Irish brought her snacks over to her.

"Here you go, baby. You earned this."

Aurora gobbled up the food.

Lake held Star back, petting her.

"Here you go, Star." Irish offered her a treat. "You did great today!"

"Yeah, she did," Lake agreed. "You okay?"

"Frazzled and worried. But better now." She petted both dogs. "I've never experienced one of my babies getting injured during a race."

"Scary, huh?"

"A freaky experience I hope never happens again." She shuddered. Her adrenaline was nosediving, leaving her with shivers trembling through her body. "I'm going to get my coat." She hurried to the car and grabbed her winter jacket and a thick hat. Once she put on the outerwear, she felt some relief.

Back at the fire, Lake fed the flames with more wood.

"You should get a coat on, too." Seeing his grin, she asked, "What?"

"For a second, you sounded wifely."

"I suppose I did." She sighed, feeling a release of tightly wound emotions in the aftermath of Aurora's emergency and the high of the race. "Someone better look after the guy who might not be thinking straight following such an unexpected win."

"Unexpected?" His thick eyebrows quirked. "You said you didn't pull up until the end."

"That's right."

"But you thought you'd win?"

"Of course I did!" Fire shot through her system. "You caught a stroke of luck today."

Lake dared to laugh!

"What's so funny?"

"I still had energy and willpower left."

"My girls and I had plenty of energy and willpower left too."

"I am sorry Aurora got hurt," he said softly. "I would never want to win at the expense of a dog's injury."

She gulped. "Me either."

He brushed his cool lips across her hot cheeks. "I'm glad Aurora is okay. Good race, North."

A snapshot of Lake rushing to help her and Aurora, acting tender and caring, flashed through her thoughts. His asking if he could carry Aurora to the vet's tent was considerate, too. Not that she needed his help. She could manage her team herself. But it was comforting to have someone standing beside her in a crisis. Someone she could lean on if she wanted to.

The way he kissed her cheek and gazed into her eyes just now was also sweet. He had a tender spirit. She liked the gentle side of Lake North.

As he strolled toward his parking area, her gaze trailed him. And her heart warmed a little more toward her husband.

Chapter Thirty-eight

Three days after the race, Lake and Irish were finishing preparations for a lasagna dinner for his parents. Lake planned to give them the repayment check tonight. He'd included an additional thank-you gift in the envelope and couldn't wait to see their reaction to it!

Irish had finished her duties at the diner, easing her schedule. But Lake still wished she'd hire a manager for the shelter and be done with that full-time responsibility. Far be it from him to quash her dreams if she truly had her heart set on working there. Somehow they'd figure out the details of owning their own kennels and racing teams, too. Wasn't working things out together what husbands and wives did all the time?

He still needed to nail down his ideas for constructing the new house and kennels. His inheritance would help fulfill those dreams. Each day he felt more confident about his decision to agree to the terms of the will and marrying Irish. The more they got along, the more peaceful he felt about their marriage. Their praying together at night was helping as well.

Two weeks had passed since he accepted the inheritance, and he hadn't spoken with Hud since then. Was Hud still angry about it? Did he still think of him as a traitor? Lake needed to reach out and have a discussion with the brother he'd been the closest to growing up. Even Gran called earlier in the week, encouraging him to call Hud. She mentioned having a strong sense about their relationship during her prayer time.

"You know what God wants you to do, Lake. 'Love covers over a multitude of sins,'" Gran had quoted. If he didn't call Hud, she'd surely call and ask him about it again.

He chuckled.

"What's so funny?" Irish placed a steaming foil bag of garlic bread on a plate.

"My grandmother still gives me advice as if I'm ten."

"You're lucky that you still have her." She set the plate in the middle of the small table that barely held four place settings. "I miss my grandmother."

He waited for her to explain and reveal more of her past. When she didn't, he asked, "What about the rest of your family?"

"Dad and I text each other. He was against me coming north. After I told him about our impromptu wedding, I got the silent treatment."

"I'm sorry." Although he could relate, considering how Hud took the news.

"Me too." She moved a couple of plates, making more room. "On a weird note, my mom sent me an email peppered with questions about the financial aspects of our marriage. I'm nervous about that."

"Like she may want a cut?"

"Something like that." Irish grimaced.

The sound of a car pulling into the driveway announced his parents' arrival, so Lake didn't pursue the topic. While he planned to be generous with his legacy, he didn't want family members expecting or demanding that he and Irish give them money. Thankfully, that hadn't happened so far.

At the dinner table, Dad said grace, and then they passed the food around.

"Everything smells wonderful. I can't wait to try the lasagna." Mom glanced between Irish and Lake as if wondering who cooked.

"We both worked on dinner," Lake explained.

"Perfect. I always enjoy it when Dad and I bake together." Mom clasped Dad's hand. "He and I had some of our best romantic moments while baking."

Dad kissed Mom's cheek. "Those times hold fond memories for me, too, Livvy."

A look passed between his parents. Lake was familiar with them acting like they were still young and crazy in love. If only he and Irish could find such love and affection between them, he'd be the most blessed man on earth! How long would that take? Years? Something hurt in his chest.

"Has Lake told you how Smith and I met?" Liv glanced toward Irish.

"Bits and pieces. I know he respects you both and his grandmother."

Dad clapped Lake on the shoulder. "And we're honored to have him as our son."

Lake appreciated the bond he felt with Dad too.

"And the rest of the brood?" Irish cracked a grin. "How did you manage nine boys and hold a marriage together?"

"It wasn't easy," Mom said in a light tone. "But Smith and I found love, we believed in Jesus, and we had Granny Trish to help with the boys. Going on at least one date a month was our saving grace."

"Our monthly anniversary. We're still celebrating it too!" Dad winked at Mom.

"That's right. I'm so thankful for how our lives turned out together." Mom stroked Dad's cheek with her fingertips. "I'm thankful for our family of boys. And now, Irish is our first daughter-in-law." She reached over and clasped her hand. "I'm thankful for you too, sweetie."

"Aw, thanks," Irish murmured.

While they ate lasagna, salad, and French bread, Mom shared family stories. She told Irish about Hud bringing a stray dog home and cleaning him with whipped cream because he couldn't find a bar of soap that wouldn't sting the pup's eyes. She spoke of Lake swimming out to rescue Stone from being swept away in a current, only to have Stone lunge at him and hold him underwater. They wrestled and dunked each other back to shore. Then she talked about them adopting Finn as a newborn, and how meaningful it was when he joined their family.

So many memories. Would Lake and Irish have those kinds of shared stories and memories to tell their kids someday? If they ever had kids? A longing went through him. An aching to have a real marriage and family with Irish. Their gazes met. Was it possible she was thinking of the same thing? Wishing for more between them?

Eventually, with dinner over and homemade fudge brownies eaten, Lake grabbed the envelope he had prepared. He passed it to Dad. "I want to give this to you and Mom."

"What is it?"

"The repayment for the money you loaned me."

"Son, I told you not to worry about that until you've settled everything. Your mom and I are in a good place financially." Dad held out the envelope toward him.

Lake lifted his hands outward. "I appreciate what you both sacrificed to help me buy my land. I can't thank you enough. I want you to have this."

"Do you feel good about receiving the inheritance? I mean, you took it under unexpected circumstances." Mom smiled kindly at Irish. "You have a beautiful bride who is most welcome in our family. But the money is—"

"Liv." Dad shook his head slightly.

"It's a sore subject, I know. It was your decision to make." Mom patted Lake's hand. "Has Hud spoken with you recently?" Her voice went soft.

"No. But he already expressed his opinion about my accepting Grandfather's money."

"Money is just … money. A means of provision. The good part is it opened a door for you and Irish to meet and plan a life together." Mom glanced back and forth between them.

Lake wished she hadn't mentioned this since he and Irish weren't on stable footing yet. Hopefully, his wife wasn't embarrassed by it.

"I'm sorry if I said too much." Mom shrugged. "It was sweet of you to return the funds to us so quickly."

Dad opened the envelope and silently read the card. His eyes moistened.

Lake and Irish exchanged a glance. She knew what he was giving his folks. Did she want to do something nice for her parents too?

Mom stared at the card with wide eyes. "A cruise? You got tickets for us to take a cruise? What perfect timing!"

"You guys deserve a nice trip for your thirty-fifth anniversary."

"My father wouldn't appreciate the irony." Mom turned toward Irish. "He kicked me out of his life when he found out I was expecting Lake. But I'm glad you and Lake are doing something meaningful with the money, both with the animal shelter and your generosity toward us." She stood and hugged Lake, then Irish. "Thank you, both. It's the sweetest gift."

The evening ended with Irish serving them hot chocolate. At Mom's prompting, she shared about her three dogs and how she got into racing with Aurora and North Star. Her eyes lit up with the telling of adding Pleiades to the family. She explained about Aurora's recent injury and how thankful she was that she was mending well.

Overall, it was a great evening.

On the porch, as they waved good night to his parents in the chilly air, Lake settled his arm over Irish's shoulder and pulled her close against his side. It was cold out, plus he was trying to act more like a husband and be more affectionate with her.

As soon as Dad pulled out of the driveway, Irish shoved away and glared at him.

"What's wrong?"

"You know what's wrong!" She stomped inside.

No, he didn't. But this must mean they were about to have an argument.

Lord, help us.

Chapter Thirty-nine

Irish plunged dirty dishes into soapy water, and her skin crawled with the remembrance of Lake putting his arm over her shoulder and tugging her to his side. How dare he act cuddly for his parents' benefit! She hated subterfuge. Faking a romance was the worst deception! If he wasn't feeling something tender and sweet toward her, she didn't want him acting like he did!

Oh, sure. She had gone along with the pretense in front of Spur and Wilks the morning after their wedding. That was different. They deserved a payback prank. Liv and Smith did not! She did not deserve to be pulled into such prank-pulling either!

"What's wrong?" Lake scooped up dessert plates off the table. "You said I know what's wrong, but I don't. Unless you hate me touching you so much that you'll be angry whenever I do."

Growling out a guttural sound, she spun around with a pile of soap suds in her right hand, and before thinking it through, she hurled them at him. He ducked like she threw a snowball instead of frothy bubbles. Some white foam stuck to his sweater.

Wide-eyed, he demanded, "What's this about?" He flicked off the suds and glowered at her.

"I don't want you playacting as if you care for me! You did that at our wedding." Her voice accelerated in volume and speed alongside her rising temperature. "You acted like we're closer than we are tonight. I'm not pretending we love each other for your parents' benefit!"

"But, Irish, I do care for you."

"Not like that, you don't." She jabbed her finger at him, soapy water dripping off her hand and puddling on the floor. "Unless Laurie walks into the room, and you have to prove to her that you and I are together, keep your hands to yourself." Fury pounded through her temples, and adrenaline shot up and down her middle. No man, not even her husband, was messing with her emotions for a fake reason!

"I didn't know you felt so strongly about this."

"Well, I do!"

He set the dishes on the small counter to the left of her. Then stepped back quickly as if afraid she might throw an object other than soap at him next time. "I didn't mean to offend you by putting my arm over your shoulder. Good grief. We are married, Irish."

She glared at him. "So, you think every time your parents or one of your million brothers come around, you can play the role of the doting husband?"

"It wasn't like that! I wasn't playing any role."

"No? You weren't trying to make your parents assume something else would happen after they left?" She stared hard into his gaze. "Be honest!"

"I am being honest. And you're wrong." He stuffed his hands into the back pockets of his jeans. "However, I may have wanted them to leave with a good impression of us. I don't want my mom worrying."

She gritted her teeth and had to concede his point. "Okay. So you're a nice son who doesn't want his mother to worry."

"It had nothing to do with making them think we would be intimate." He gulped.

"They're probably already hoping for grandchildren."

"They'll be disappointed, then." He let out a soft huff. "Look. How you and I live our lives is our business. If we never have, uh, marital bliss, it's for our knowledge only. Okay?"

"Fine!" Some of her anger melted like the bubbles on the floor. Grabbing a dish towel, she bent down and wiped up the soapy mess. She stood slowly and faced him, heat rushing up her face. "If you're playing a role at my expense, that drives me nuts!" Especially since she'd started having deeper feelings for him after the race a few days ago. She could barely look into his eyes without remembering their previous kisses and wanting to taste his lips again.

Not now, though. She did not feel that way toward him tonight!

"I'm sorry. I really am, Irish." He pointed toward the dishes. "Can I dry?"

"Yes." Sighing, she washed four plates before speaking again. "Is that the way you want it?"

"What are we talking about now?"

"Us never having 'marital bliss?'"

He made a smirky sound. "You want to discuss our love life, or lack thereof, after fighting with me?"

"Maybe." She flicked some bubbles at him. "Do you regret marrying me outside of love?"

"Sometimes." He smiled tightly.

Pain shot through her emotional center, but she'd wanted to marry an honest man. It seemed she had.

Lake scooped the bubbles off his sweater and tossed them back at her. Some foam landed in her hair.

The next thing she knew, his hands rested gently on her shoulders, and he turned her toward him. Her wet hands landed on the chest of his sweater for balance.

They stared into each other's gazes for several heartbeats. She gulped, mentally reliving their wedding kiss two weeks ago.

He smoothed his fingers down her hair, removing bubbles. Then he stroked her cheek lightly. "No one is watching us now. And this isn't for show."

She peered into his dark, intense irises.

He didn't close the gap between them—neither did she. His gaze traveled slowly down her nose, lingering on her lips, then down to her chin before lifting to meet her gaze again.

"What do you want?" she whispered.

"Oh, Irish—" He took a shaky breath. "That's a dangerous question to ask a new bridegroom."

"About the other—"

"I promise you, I wasn't trying to prove anything was going to happen between us." He stepped back and leaned his hip against the counter. "I'm in this marriage for good. I'll wait however long it takes for us to feel comfortable with each other and fall for one another. Didn't I give you my word?"

"Yes. But I thought you were just saying that."

"I was serious then. I am serious now. It will take some time for us, that's all." He reached out and stroked a clump of hair off her shoulder, his fingertips brushing against her neck. "Let's call it a night, hmm?"

Did he mean together? She frowned at him.

"In separate rooms, Irish." He groaned softly. "When are you going to trust me?"

"I don't know."

"Look. I'm not going to push for anything you don't want. After the way you bit my head off a few minutes ago, you've stated your feelings on the subject quite well." He strode to the door and checked the lock. Then he walked to his bedroom door. "Good night," he said without kissing her cheek or suggesting they pray together.

"Lake?"

"Hmm?"

"I'm sorry for jumping to conclusions. Good night."

How was she supposed to know when he said, "Let's call it a night," he didn't mean for them to share a bedroom? Her romantic sensors were haywire. One minute she pictured herself kissing him madly, and the next, she didn't want him touching her. Why was she so sensitive about Lake acting affectionately with her, anyway? Was that so bad?

Only if he was faking it!

Chapter Forty

On Sunday afternoon, after Lake and Irish attended their first morning worship together as a married couple, Lake couldn't stop thinking about the conflict between him and Hud. Was the Lord speaking to his heart to make things right with his brother? Or was this about more guilt settling inside him? Between Gran and Mom, he wouldn't hear the end of it if he didn't reach out to him. But he was having a hard enough time keeping things even-keeled with him and Irish. Now he was supposed to mend fences with Hud?

Yeah, he should try.

Still, he hesitated to make the call. He prepped a cup of coffee and spent a few minutes praying for God's help and intervention. He prayed for Hud's heart to soften toward reconciliation between them. And he confessed his pride to the Lord.

Distracted, his thoughts wandered to his dogs. Sipping his drink, he gazed out the back window at Pal and Ice running around the freshly-cleaned enclosed yard. They'd probably like a skijoring run on the trails this afternoon like Irish was doing with North Star. Lake would like that too.

Yesterday, he used his rundown four-wheeler and grooming tool to clear the paths of fresh snow, so the conditions should be almost perfect. Now that he had money in the bank, he ought to invest in a few equipment upgrades around here. A heavy-duty snowblower for the driveway and a four wheeler with a snowplow to clear the trails would make his tasks more manageable.

Enough stalling.

He sat on the small couch and took a few more sips of coffee. Then he tapped his brother's name on his cell phone screen.

"Yeah?" Hud answered in a long-suffering tone.

"Got a minute?"

"About that much." The sound of Hud's hand moving over the phone and his voice speaking to someone else in muffled tones reached Lake. "Sorry. Things are a bit chaotic."

"Even on a Sunday?"

"Even then." Hud sighed.

"How's Alaska?"

"Raining cats and dogs like usual."

"What's the draw for you to stay there?" Lake asked, seeking a nonemotional topic for them to discuss before launching into something heavier. "Other than getting as far away from the family drama as possible?"

"I'd say she's five-foot-three." Hud's tone deepened. "Has strikingly dark hair. Sparks of purple in her deep indigo eyes. Need I say more?"

"You have a girlfriend?"

"No, unfortunately, I don't." Hud cleared his throat. "Don't mention this to Mom or Gran, either."

"I won't. What's to tell?"

"Nothing. I don't want them bugging me."

"You and me both." Lake sipped his lukewarm coffee, then set the mug on the end table. At least Hud hadn't gotten angry with him yet.

"What's up? I have a call to make to an investor."

"Still staking your claim to wealth?"

"Some of us must work for a living."

Lake let the dig pass. "I thought we should talk and clear the air."

Silence.

"Hud?"

"Listening."

"I did the thing we agreed neither of us would do." He hardly knew where to go from there. He'd made the call, but he didn't have a plan about what to say to try to fix things between them. "I realize that was a breach of our pact. Your trust. I'm sorry. But—"

"Don't add the 'but,' Lake. It ruins everything."

"Sorry." If only he could sit across from Hud, they'd have a better chance of talking this out. Trying to have a gut-honest discussion over the phone was weird. "Any chance you're heading this way soon?"

"Nope. I'm up to my eyeballs in business problems."

"Sounds rough."

"Not your concern."

Another silence fell between them.

"I want to say I'm sorry," Lake said sincerely.

"Did Gran put you up to this? Too bad she didn't stop you from making the worst mistake of your life."

"Which is?"

"Marrying outside of love."

A sword pierced his heart, but Lake tried not to react negatively. "I thought you would say taking the money from our grandfather's estate was the worst mistake."

"That too." The sound of rustling paper came through the phone. Then a long sigh. "However, I admit I understand the temptation to grab the money and run with it better than I did three weeks ago."

"Things are that bad, huh?"

"Pie-in-the-face bad. I've invested up to my gills. If things don't—" Hud coughed loudly. "Never mind. I've got to make this short."

"If there's anything I can do—"

"You'll split your half of Granddad's payout? No thanks."

"Hud, when I said I was sorry, I meant it. I don't want this to be a thing between us."

"Too late. It's already there. Your choice. Not mine."

"Your choice too. The money's there for you to take if you act fast."

"Say hi to Mom and Gran for me." Hud ended the call.

Lake set the edge of the cell phone against his forehead. The memory of Hud's question before Lake and Irish's wedding churned in his thoughts. *"How can you reconcile our grandfather's betrayal of Mom by taking the inheritance he denied her?"* Doing good with the money had seemed like a noble reason. And Mom didn't act upset about his decision to accept the legacy. But Hud sure did. What now? More prayer?

Lord, please help Hud. Whatever situation he's in, help him find You in it. Help us find our way back to a brotherly relationship again. I'm sorry for my part in the conflict.

Lake was glad that praying and trusting the Lord in his troubles and that of his family was coming more naturally to him again. Maybe the Lord was already healing him of some of his internal wounds from Laurie. If so, thank God!

Still, Hud's harsh assessment of Lake being at fault for marrying a woman he didn't love and taking their grandfather's money roiled inside him. Was he wrong on both accounts? Acting impulsively, did he go against God's will? He hoped not. He wanted to be sensitive to the Lord's leading and trust in Him for direction. And he honestly wanted to be helpful with the funds.

Lord, help me to make the right choices. If I've made some decisions that hurt my brothers or choices that weren't in Your will for my life, I'm sorry.

He spent a few more minutes praying about his relationship with Hud and his other brothers. Were some of them still disgruntled because he took Richard Dupont's inheritance?

After the uncomfortable conversation with Hud, he couldn't imagine discussions with his other brothers going any better. He didn't want to even think about what Stone might say. He'd probably curse and tell him to go live on the equator. Or somewhere much hotter.

He wished Coe were here. He was the brother who pressed into God and looked at the world through spiritual eyes more like Dad did. Lake would do well to follow his example and try finding out what the Lord wanted to do in his life right now. Wasn't that what Coe had encouraged him to do?

Lord Jesus, is there something You are trying to show me? What else should I be doing?

Immediately, he thought of Irish. His bride. The woman he'd promised to pursue. The woman he wanted to fall in love with. Had he started falling in love with her even a little bit yet? What was she feeling toward him?

He spent a few minutes praying for her and asking God to help him be a better husband. And that soon, they'd both fall in love with each other.

Chapter Forty-one

It was mid-morning on Monday and Irish hadn't grabbed a cup of coffee or taken a bathroom break since arriving at the shelter three hours ago. A blue-eyed husky stray someone recently turned in had gone into labor. After calling the vet, Irish sat with the mama-to-be who she called Bright Eyes, petting her and saying soothing things to her, until Doctor Cooper arrived.

Since the older gentleman had difficulty remaining on his knees, Irish knelt and followed the instructions he gave her. Mostly they observed Bright Eyes delivering the first three pups and then cleaning them. Irish had never assisted with or watched the birthing of puppies before. The whole experience was awe-inspiring! And the puppies were so cute and soft!

The mama dog licked her babies and put them to nursing like a pro. Then nothing happened for an hour. Impatient for the other puppies to be born, Irish checked the clock on the wall every few minutes. She was supposed to be meeting Lake and the contractor this morning to talk about their home. What if she had to cancel?

Would Lake understand that the puppy delivery took priority over their appointment?

She thought of his plans to build a gigantic house and groaned. Something larger than the cabin was understandable. But why did he want to make a colossal home for the two of them? Was that what he and Laurie had planned?

Irish preferred minimalistic living. Hadn't she told Lake that from the start? More square footage than the cabin would be nice so the dogs could sleep inside, but not some castle!

Thinking of a cozy house where they might live as husband and wife, sharing everything, including a bedroom, made warmth flood her cheeks. A slight smile played on her lips as she leaned against the wall, waiting for puppy number four to be born and picturing herself spending time with Lake as a truly married couple. The man she'd married was a handsome guy. A fantastic cook and baker. A superb kisser. Most of the time, he was friendly and polite. And sometimes, when he gazed into her eyes with his tender look, she could hardly breathe.

He'd made it obvious he wanted them to pursue a relationship with all the benefits of marital love. How could he want that when he didn't love her? Of course, she didn't love him either. But did she even know what love was? Did he?

Bright Eyes moaned, signaling the start of another delivery.

Doctor Cooper squatted down near the mama's hindquarters. A small sack began its descent from the adult dog's body. Watching the miracle of babies four and five entering the world and helping as needed, Irish felt a strange yearning for motherhood, for holding a baby of her own someday.

Lake would probably scoff at her. They weren't even being intimate, and she was imagining having their child? Hadn't she told him she was fine without bringing a mini-Irish into the world? Her family was dysfunctional enough without adding to the woes of the world. Lake's parents had populated the planet enough on their own! Still, some warm, unexpected, motherly feelings stirred inside her this morning.

Shelley rushed into the room of kennels, igniting a chorus of barking from the other dozen caged dogs.

Irish had been trying to keep all the animals calm during the birthing. Scurrying out of Bright Eyes's pen, where she had just watched baby number six be born, she gave Shelley an exasperated look. Then she quieted the other dogs. "We must keep things as calm as possible for the mama and pups."

"I know, but it's Lake," Shelley stage whispered and held up a phone. "He says he's been calling your cell, and you haven't answered. I told him about the puppies. He still wants to talk with you."

"Okay, fine. You help Doc if he needs anything. I'll be right back."

"Wait!" Giving her a jaw-dropped look, Shelley huffed. "You don't pay me enough to ruin my clothes doing that stuff!"

Irish gritted her teeth. "Just help for a minute, will you? It won't kill you to pitch in if the doctor needs something! There's an apron on the wall hook. Use that to protect your clothes."

Grabbing the phone, she strode down the corridor of kennels before exiting into the office area. She needed an assistant who wasn't averse to working with animals.

"Lake?" Anticipating he might be upset with her tardiness, she spoke tensely.

"Sounds like you're in an emergency there." His soft voice calmed some of her unease.

"That's right. A husky has delivered six babies so far."

"Did you get to help?"

"I did. It was amazing! Exhilarating!"

"I bet. Hey, did you, uh, forget about our meeting with the contractor?"

"I didn't forget." Tension rose quickly within her again. "I stayed to help Doc Cooper. I'm sorry about the timing."

"I understand, but this is important to me." A hint of hurt edged his voice.

"Are you still at the contractor's office now?"

"Yeah. Dillan and I are duking it out over some ideas. Vaulted ceilings or not." He chuckled in a humorless way.

Vaulted ceilings? There went her daydreams about a cozy little house.

"Do you have time to join us? Time for—" He groaned softly.

What? Time for him?

"Give me ten minutes. I'll check on Bright Eyes and talk to the vet. Then I'll run over."

"Thanks, Irish."

After the call ended, she sighed. This struggle of compromising and trying to keep the doors of communication open between them was more arduous than she realized it would be. Right now, she preferred doing what she wanted—staying with Bright Eyes and her puppies. Leaving the mama dog with Shelley conflicted with her desire to give the animals the best care possible.

But she had to meet her husband halfway.

She strode back into the kennel area. "How's it going?"

"She's a trooper. All seven pups are healthy!" Doctor Cooper loaded his medical tools back into his black bag.

"Is she done delivering?"

"She's finished and resting. I'll check in on the litter later. I don't anticipate any problems."

"What a relief!" Irish glanced at Shelley, who looked exasperated, but she didn't appear to have done anything to help with the dogs. "Listen. Will you watch Bright Eyes and the puppies for thirty minutes while I run over for a quick meeting with Lake? I was supposed to be at the contractor's office forty-five minutes ago."

"I told you I don't do this stuff!" Shelley grimaced. "I wouldn't even know what to do if something happened."

"Bright Eyes is taking care of the puppies." Dr. Cooper nodded toward the mama dog. "If anything goes wrong, or if she shoves any pups away, give me a call. My office isn't far."

"Thanks, Doc." Irish stared intensely at Shelley. "Please?"

"Oh, all right! We should hire an aide to do this stuff. I'm a receptionist. And I don't scoop doggie-doo!" She crossed her arms, emphasizing her displeasure.

"I appreciate all you've done to keep things running here." Irish wiped some slimy stuff off the thighs of her jeans. "You're right. We should have more help. Why don't you put an ad on the door for a part-time assistant?"

"Finally! I will do that immediately."

Even though Lake wanted her to hire a manager, she'd put off the task. Maybe hiring a part-time worker would prime the pump for her eventually leaving this post. Although nothing about the idea appealed to her. She liked caring for the animals. Helping with the puppies this morning made her want to work here even more. Was there anything wrong with that?

Chapter Forty-two

When Irish entered the office where Lake was meeting with the contractor, she wanted to rush right back to the shelter. That was probably why the first words out of her mouth sounded as tense as she felt. "Sorry for the delay. Tell me the important stuff, then I've got to get back to the shelter."

Lake glanced up from where he stood beside a table with drawings and printouts spread over the surface. "Are the puppies having problems?"

"No."

"The mom?"

"No! I just need to be there."

Their gazes clashed.

This wasn't how she imagined talking to him a while ago. She'd been waiting for the puppies to be born and picturing how handsome her husband was. Thinking of how she enjoyed gazing into his eyes and hoping for a cozy house where they would genuinely begin loving each other. Where were all those good feelings now?

"We've been waiting for a while, so please give us a few minutes. Unless there is another emergency—"

"No, there isn't. I'm just stressed with the delivery and all." She pressed her lower lip tightly between her upper and lower teeth.

"I understand. This is my wife, Irish." He waved his hand toward her, then toward the other man. "This is Dillan Frazier, our contractor."

"Hey." She shook hands with the man who appeared to be in his early fifties. "Sorry I'm late," she said more sincerely.

"No problem." Dillan pushed his black glasses up his nose.

Irish smiled, but the pleasant look she hoped for felt clumsy and tired. She took a deep breath, held it, and slowly let it go as Lake leaned over some sample pictures of houses.

"What do you think about this one?" He tapped his index finger on a photograph of a prominent two-story structure. "Something similar. Not logs. Board and batten. Maybe some stonework on the lower part." He met her gaze, his eyes wide. He seemed eager to hear her optimistic viewpoint.

"It's nice. A little too nice, perhaps." She lifted her chin.

"Did you want more of a cabin aesthetic?" Dillan ran his hand over his dark hair sprinkled with gray.

"Not necessarily. I'm not into fancy things. Lake knows I'm outdoorsy, and this house is—" Irish groaned, not wanting to blast his ideas to shreds.

Lake stood to his full height. "If you have something to say, say it."

Did she dare? She took a breath. "All right. Why do we need this castle?"

"It's five bedrooms and an office. Hardly a castle."

"It's hard to imagine us ever needing five bedrooms. Maybe something cozier and less grand would be better. At least, preferable for my taste." Her voice rose along with her temper. "But you expect everything to go your way, don't you?"

"Hold on. Where's this coming from?"

"Just because you say, 'heel,' don't expect me to go along with it!"

"What?"

A flush of heat rushed up her face. Ugh. She opened her mouth, and out popped a barrel of frustrations toward Lake in front of his professional acquaintance. She was embarrassing him and herself! She should have stayed at the shelter where she wanted to be. Not come here acting defensive about the house he and Laurie had planned.

"I'm sorry. Maybe we should have discussed this more before now." She eyed Lake, hoping he agreed.

"Obviously. But you haven't been especially communicative."

No, she hadn't been. Not that she'd admit that to him! And not in front of the contractor.

"Shall I give you two the room?" Dillan asked in a cautious tone.

"That would be great," Irish said.

"That's unnecessary," Lake said at the same time.

Irish squinted at him. Couldn't he see they needed to discuss this privately?

Dillan lifted his hands and shrugged. "Shall we continue, then?"

"What kind of house do you foresee us having, Irish?" Lake asked in an agitated tone.

"A place less castle-like."

"I don't see a castle in any of these pictures." He bent over the drawing, peering at it, then at her. "What's the problem?"

Did he mean, what was her problem? Like the tension between them was all her fault?

"There are better ways to spend your money without building a fortress for two people to tromp around in." She captured her lower lip between her teeth again. "Can we talk about this some more later, alone?"

"Sure. But I want to make some preliminary decisions so Dillan and his crew can get the drawings prepared. Tell me what you want in a house, and we'll shave it down to the basics."

"The basics?" She fluttered her hands over the prints. "With all this grandeur?"

"Yes. Tell me what you want." Sighing, Lake dropped onto a chair and nodded toward an empty chair for her. "Dillan's time is valuable. You and I can address the other issues later. But please, let's look at the sample blueprints he prepared."

"Fine." Dillan was a professional who'd made a presentation for them. She got here late and had a chip on her shoulder. Sitting down stiffly, she met Dillan's gaze. "Again, I'm sorry for my tardiness and for holding things up."

"That's all right." Dillan pulled out some other sketches for her to peruse. He pointed at the blueprint on the table, enumerating changes to accommodate their mutual wishes. He assured her the house was reducible, but he needed to know their desired square footage before drawing up more plans.

"Is there anything about this house you like?" Lake asked like he was grasping for the last straw.

"I like the open spaces for the dogs on the first floor." She tapped the drawing. "In a smaller footprint, would two bedrooms work for upstairs?"

"Yes," Dillan answered. "Two bedrooms and an en suite. Maybe a guest bath?"

"Can we call and let you know?"

"Absolutely." Dillan exchanged a look with Lake.

"Is there something else I should know?" She glanced between the two men.

"Spring is a busy time for me. Lake suggested I prioritize his project." Dillan chuckled nervously. "That works for me only if I get started immediately."

His project. Irish tensed. "I see."

"He meant 'our' project." Lake's cheeks flushed.

Right. Dillan didn't mean anything personal. Then why was she taking offense? Standing, she pointed at another drawing of the proposed kennels. "I like this outbuilding and the dogs' play yard."

Lake nodded. "Our animals come first with us."

"The animals at the shelter, too." She felt a need to say. "Maybe instead of putting so much money into a grand house, we could modernize the shelter and improve the grounds."

"Irish—"

"When you've invested as much into a cause as we have, you can't just walk away from it."

"Well, I wouldn't say—"

He stopped abruptly, but she guessed what he almost said. Plenty of wealthy people gave their money to charities without contributing their time. But that wasn't how she wanted to live her life. She couldn't live her life that way.

They were invested in their dogs. Could they care any less for the well-being of the dogs they provided for financially? Especially when she and Lake had gone to all the trouble to get married to protect them?

Chapter Forty-three

After they finished the roast beef dinner Lake had cooked, he went outside to feed the dogs and check their kennels one last time before nightfall. His thoughts returned to their meeting with Dillan earlier. Everything had gone great until Irish showed up. If she hadn't arrived when she did, and with the negative attitude that she carried with her like a flag, he would have signed the contractor's proposal. He loved the plans! He fully approved of the luxurious style of the five-bedroom house.

With all the zeroes on the inheritance allotment, what was wrong with building a lovely home for him and Irish and any kids they might have? He wanted a couple of guest rooms and a big enough dining room to fit them, his eight brothers, their future families, and Mom, Dad, and Gran. That meant a lot of potential space!

But his signing the contract alone would have been a grave error. Especially considering Irish's wishes for a more modest home. After living in a cramped household of twelve, then staying in the tiny cabin, he was ready to spread out and enjoy some bigger space. If only they had discussed the project at length before he arranged the appointment with the contractor, then he wouldn't have been blindsided by Irish's comments.

Dillan needed an answer by tomorrow. That meant Lake and Irish had to have a serious discussion tonight. One he wasn't looking forward to.

Why did she oppose everything he said? What did she mean about him calling "heel" and her not obeying? He'd never acted controlling or treated her like she must obey him. But he had a right to his opinion too.

He strolled past Aurora's empty kennel. Irish must be letting her sleep in the cabin again, which irked him. She probably wanted to keep an eye on her. But if it wasn't Aurora, she would have brought in Pleiades. Two humans and a big dog in the cabin were too much. Wasn't that reason enough for them to build a large house?

Lake stopped at Pal's kennel. He leaned down and rubbed his dog's neck. "How are you doing, buddy? You ready for a long winter's nap?"

Pal whined and wiggled.

"I bet you'd like to sleep in the house, too."

Pal panted and wagged his fluffy tail furiously.

"When we get into our new house, you, Ice, and Rambler can take turns coming inside too."

Pal woofed like he agreed with the promise.

"Good boy." Lake patted his head and stood. "Sleep well. We'll take a run tomorrow, weather permitting."

He'd lingered in the kennels long enough. Time to face the music with Irish. But as he strode toward the back steps, he heard a noisy vehicle pull into the driveway in front. Was it Spur's?

The dogs howled and bayed their greetings. They obviously recognized the visitor's vehicle.

Lake walked around the cabin and found his brother's dilapidated truck parked in the driveway.

"Hey, Lake!" Spur tromped up the path. "Thought I'd drop by with some news."

"That right?" Lake pulsed his thumb toward the cabin. "Come in and have some coffee. I made apple pie. How about pie a' la mode?"

"Sounds great!" Spur caught up to him and clapped him over the shoulders. "Have you ever known me to turn down pie and ice cream?"

"Never." Lake led the way to the door. "So, what's this news?"

"If I tell you now, you might not give me the pie." Spur shrugged sheepishly.

"Is something wrong?" Lake opened the door and stepped inside the warm cabin.

Spur followed, not answering. "Hello, Irish."

"Hey, Spur." Irish sat on their loveseat with a steaming cup in her hands, and Aurora curled up beside her. The dog thumped her tail but didn't stand up. "What brings you out here?"

"I smelled Lake's pie from town!"

"No doubt."

"And he has news." Lake met Irish's gaze and shrugged.

"Not bad news, I hope. Is everyone okay?"

"The folks and Gran are fine, but"—Spur tugged at the neck of his sweatshirt—"I've got to quit being your dog handler. I'm turning in my official notice."

"Really?" A glug settled in Lake's gut. Despite Spur's bachelor-night prank, he was a great asset to his team. "I'm sorry to hear that."

"I'm off on an adventure, or so Dad calls it."

"Dad?" Lake nodded toward a chair. "Sit. Tell us what's going on. Want some coffee?"

"Sure. And a big helping of pie!" Spur melted onto the chair, his legs and arms spread out.

Lake cut two pieces of pie. He already had one helping after dinner, but Spur shouldn't eat pie alone. "Want another piece, Irish?"

"No, thanks." She sipped her coffee.

Lake put ice cream on both pieces of pie, then delivered the dessert and a steaming cup of coffee to Spur.

"Thanks." He wolfed down a couple of bites like he was starving. "You are the best pie maker in the family. I will miss this!"

"Thanks for that. Now, explain." Lake grabbed his plate piled with pie and ice cream and sat down. "Where is this adventure taking you? And why?"

Spur set his elbows on his knees. "You know how Dad has always tried to get us to be more spiritual or service minded? Like Charles Spurgeon or someone of strong faith?"

"Sure. He's told me stories about John G. Lake since I was in diapers. Gran too. But I haven't done anything remarkable like him. I have my own life to live. You do too!"

"I know. Still—"

"What's this about?" Irish set her cup on the end table and glanced between Lake and Spur.

"It's about our names." Lake stuffed his final bite of ice cream into his mouth and set his plate beside Irish's cup. "The folks chose our names based on men of faith or people who did extraordinary things for God. They wanted us to have godly characters like these men to look up to while we were growing up."

"Ah. Kind of like how I hope Aurora will glow like the northern lights"—she petted her dog—"and North Star will lead the way in my races?"

"Exactly." Lake enjoyed seeing Irish smiling and acting more relaxed. That boded well for the conversation they still needed to have. He turned toward his brother. "So what does Dad want you to do instead of helping me with my dogs and the new kennel I'm going to build this spring?"

"I forgot about the kennels." Spur smacked his palm against his forehead. "I want to see them built!"

"The job's still yours."

"Yeah, but we're talking about Hawaii!"

"You're going to Hawaii?" Irish asked.

"Yep. Dad's been bugging me to go over and help his buddy. The guy is starting a soup kitchen and homeless shelter." Spur flopped back against the chair. "Since I'm almost thirty and still don't have a career, Dad says I need some direction. He might be right."

That was the most serious monologue Lake had ever heard Spur express. Maybe he was looking at his life more genuinely, which was good. But it had to be his decision.

"You've lived the way you wanted to, right?"

"Yeah, but you, Hud, and Coe knew what you wanted to do with your lives for a long time. You wanted to work with dogs. Hud was gung-ho about building specialty houses. Coe has his humanitarian work." Spur moaned. "Stone? Who knows what he wanted to do? Get in trouble, probably."

"No one sets out to get in trouble. Not even Stone."

"Gran told me I should follow in Dad's footsteps." Spur thrust both hands over his hair like the idea frustrated him.

"It's still up to you. Why not go back to college and get a degree in history like you were planning to do?"

"Don't throw my failure in my face!" Spur jumped up and paced over to the door.

"I wasn't trying to—"

"College didn't work out for me." The room was small, so it didn't take long for him to walk back and forth a couple of times. "Since then, I haven't done much besides helping you with the dogs and mooching off the folks."

"Do you want to go to Hawaii?" Irish asked.

"Who wouldn't want to lay on the beaches? Maybe find a Hawaiian babe."

"Is that why you're going?" Lake needed to talk some sense into this brother. "Because if you plan to lay on the beach and gawk at women when Dad's pal expects honest work from you, there will be consequences."

Groaning, Spur dropped back into the chair and covered his face. "I don't know what I want."

"Whatever you decide, I support you. But it'll be tough here without you."

"You can always hire Wilks." Lowering his hands, Spur winked. "Let him work with Irish's dogs."

"What's this?" Irish glanced between them. "Did I miss something?"

"Wilks hates dogs." Lake enunciated the words strongly. "Seriously hates them."

"Then why would—" She moaned. "Ah. Another prank?"

"Something like that." Spur jumped back up and held out his hand to Lake. "No hard feelings?"

"Of course not." Lake stood and shook his hand. "Thanks for coming out here and telling me what's going on. Let's get coffee or a meal this week." He walked out on the porch with Spur. "You've been a big help with my skijoring team. Thank you."

"You're welcome." Spur glanced back at Irish. "Maybe this will help you two work things out."

What did he mean by that? "Uh, sure. Thanks for caring, bro."

Now, Lake was even more eager to talk with Spur alone.

Chapter Forty-four

"Can we talk?" Lake asked as they cleared breakfast dishes off the table the following day.

His request didn't surprise Irish. Ever since they had gotten home yesterday, he'd acted cool toward her, like he was internalizing something. She'd certainly felt tense toward him following their discussion at Dillan's office. The visit from Spur last night didn't help either of their moods.

"Sure. What do you want to discuss?"

"Our house plans." Lake poured another splash of coffee into his mug and then held the carafe out to her in invitation.

"No, thanks. I've had enough." She walked a few feet to the short couch and plopped down.

She didn't want to argue with him anymore. They'd done enough of that lately. But how could they discuss the house plans and find common ground when they had such opposing views? She could give in and let him have his way about the size of the house. Right. When had she ever given in to anyone else's wishes without expressing her opinion?

Lake dropped onto the chair. "What can we agree on about the plans? Dillan needs an answer today."

She drew in a breath and released it before speaking. "Honestly, I don't know if we can agree."

"Why is a five-bedroom house so wrong for us? After living in a house with twelve people, a bigger house sounds fantastic to me."

"But it's like a mausoleum. I prefer something cozy. If we aren't going to have kids, I don't see why—"

"Wait. You don't ever plan to have kids?" He shuffled on the chair, leaning his elbows against the nearly bare arms of the furniture, and stared hard at her. "We said we'd wait. That's different than never planning to."

"All right. I agree with that." A brief thought of her maternal feelings on the day of the puppies' birth came to mind. Maybe someday she would want to be a mom. "I thought you chose rural living to escape your big loud family. That you didn't want that lifestyle for yourself."

Lake took a deep breath as if the topic hurt. "That, and other things. Like having a place to start a kennel and training area of my own. Of our own, I mean."

"I know I wasn't a part of your original plans. You were going to do this grand project with Laurie." She couldn't seem to dispose of her negative feelings toward his ex.

"Yeah, well, things changed."

"You still care for her, though, right?" She watched him intently. This was something she had to know. Did he still love Laurie?

"Care, yes." He lifted an eyebrow. "Where's this going?"

"It's been less than three months since you guys broke up. Not nearly enough time to get over someone. Yet you married me."

"Look." He set his mug down on the end table with a thud. "I'm not daydreaming about her and me, if that's what you're implying."

"I'm not." *Liar!* She'd spent too much time wondering about his thoughts and feelings about Laurie. "Do you still think warmly of her?" She avoided using the word "love."

"Warmly?" A smile crossed his lips, sieving some of the tension from the room. "I think warmly about you most of the time."

What did he mean by "most" of the time?

"You mean to tell me you haven't thought about your ex in terms of what marriage to her might have been like compared to how it's turned out between us?" She nodded toward the back of the cabin. "Our sleeping in separate bedrooms?"

"Nope." He leaned against the chair and stared at the ceiling. "Can we drop this? We were supposed to be talking about the house design. About how we can compromise on building a house that works for both of us."

"You're the one who said you thought warmly about me." The heat of a blush swept up her face.

"So I did." He pushed away from his chair and landed beside her on the loveseat in one languid move. He put his arm over the back of the couch, the fabric of his sweatshirt brushing against her neck, sending tingles dancing up her skin. His gaze meshed with hers. "I warned you that I was going to pursue you."

"Lake. Be serious." But the words didn't come out as strongly as she intended.

"I am being serious, sweetheart." His warm breath brushed her cheek. Followed by his fingers lightly stroking the same spot. "I really like you, Irish. It's as if I'm intoxicated with you. I want to breathe you in. Kiss you and … kiss you."

"Lake—" If she didn't know better, she'd think her mouth hung open and she was panting like a dog for a treat. The treat would be a massive kissing session with Lake, ending with them walking into the bedroom together.

But one thing other than their disagreement about the house kept her from meeting his lips in an all-consuming, all-or-nothing, tender exchange of kissing her husband. She feared where this would go if they had intimacy but never fell in love. She pulled back from what she knew would happen in the next second if she didn't.

"You don't want me to kiss you?" he asked in a hoarse whisper.

"No," she forced herself to whisper back, even though the word was hard to say. "Because we don't love each other."

"We didn't love each other when you kissed me before we were engaged. Or when I kissed you at our wedding." He stroked her cheeks with ultimate gentleness, his gaze still tangling with hers. "Are you waiting for us to be in love with each other before we are intimate?"

"Aren't you waiting for that?"

He pulled his hands back from touching her face and then raked his fingers through his longish hair. "Not really. I mean, caring, yes. Feeling close, sure. I believe we'll fall in love in time. But the other stuff?" He blew out a long breath. The few inches he scooted away from her felt like a mile. "Do you even like me, Irish?"

"As a seventh grader likes her first crush?"

"No, more like someone you can barely tolerate."

"I can tolerate you, Lake. You're a nice person." She smoothed her fingers down the side of his arm, wanting some physical contact between them. "You gave a huge financial gift to the animal shelter. You gave your parents a special gift of a cruise. And you helped me when Aurora got hurt. Doing those things showed me how great of a person you are." By the way his head shook, she wasn't saying what he wanted to hear. She clasped her hands in her lap. "What?"

"I not only like you, but I plan to fall in love with you." He gently set his hands over her clasped ones. "I hope you'll fall for me too. Until we are emotionally closer, we are legally and morally married. We can do whatever we want."

"And you're fine with intimacy outside of love?"

"I'm fine with it inside of marriage. I'm attracted to you. I care about you. You're my wife. And I plan to stay married to you. So, yes," he spoke softly.

She pulled her hands free of his touch. "I'd rather wait for us to be closer to loving each other." And for her to absolutely know he didn't have strong feelings for Laurie.

He let out a long, low sigh. His eyes shuttered partially closed.

"Admittedly"—she said with a catch in her voice—"I'd like to take your hand in mine and lead you back to my room."

His gaze met hers with sparks of lightning-like glints.

"I look forward to the day we kiss as two people who have fallen for each other. We have a marriage license, but until—"

"Your expectations are met. I get it." He groaned and rubbed his forehead.

"Not met. But this will have to be enough until we care deeply for one another as more than housemates." She scooted to the edge of the cushion and huffed. "Just go ahead and build your house however you'd like it!"

"That's not the way it works, Irish. It's your house too." His tense expression eased. He stroked her arm with his palm. "We'll work on the footprint together, or not build a house at all."

She was surprised by his words. Touched by them too. "Are you sure?"

"I'm not sure about anything." His sigh sounded like he released a heavy burden. "But I'm determined to try my best. I'm asking you to do the same."

"Okay." She couldn't argue with that. "Um. Would you like us to pray together about it?"

"Well, sure, I guess." He seemed startled by her suggestion.

She was surprised by it too. But she wouldn't back down. Tentatively, she clasped his hands and closed her eyes. "Uh, Lord, you see the mess we've made of things ..."

Before Lake's dad suggested that they pray together, Irish had never prayed aloud with someone listening. But after two weeks of praying with Lake, she found she enjoyed holding his hand while they took turns speaking to God. She liked them asking for good things to happen in their marriage. Now, his saying that he liked her, and even his comment about wanting intimacy between them, gave her hope for their future as a married couple.

Only later, as they were discussing house plans, did she recall her question about Laurie. Lake said he didn't think about what their marriage would have been like. Did he mean he didn't have any feelings for his ex? Or had he stuffed them inside himself so deeply he didn't know they existed?

Chapter Forty-five

Irish felt awkward sitting across from her mother-in-law at Nelly's Diner. Not only was she in the workplace from which she had resigned, but she had asked for this private meeting with Liv.

After Lake's and her conversation about the house plans, Laurie, and what he thought about taking their relationship further two days ago, it felt like an emotional wall had been erected between them. She spent as much time as possible at the animal shelter, and spent the rest giving her dogs some needed attention and staying out of the cabin. Thankfully, Aurora's paw had healed and she could go on short skijoring runs.

Irish also spent some quiet time on the back porch last night, contemplating her life and her choices up to this point. She always jumped into things without counting the cost, like when she loaded her car and moved to Thunder Ridge. Like when she agreed to Lake's proposal. And the way she dived into the managerial position at the shelter.

Usually, she jumped at the first opportunity that presented itself. So why wasn't she leaping into Lake's arms?

She remembered the prayer he prayed for them during breakfast yesterday. His tender voice imploring God to work in their lives together as a couple had touched her heart. His words made her ponder their relationship more seriously too. And it's partly why she texted Liv and asked her to meet with her at Nelly's.

"How are you doing?" Liv asked. "Are you okay?"

"I'm okay. But I—" Irish groaned softly. "I think I made a mistake."

"Not about marrying Lake, I hope."

"Not that. Or maybe it is. I probably shouldn't have asked you to meet me here. It's like a betrayal."

"Oh, dear." Liv took a quick sip of her coffee. "I promise not to ask any prying questions. If you want to say something or need some advice, go right ahead and say it. However, I'll wink a few times if it's too private. After thirty-five years of marriage, Smith and I have some secrets too." She winked a couple of times as if making her point.

Irish giggled. She appreciated having an understanding mother-in-law. Maybe because Liv had married Smith in an irregular union, Irish sensed a rapport with her.

Breakfasts ordered, and casual topics discussed, Irish met her mother-in-law's gaze. "How did you do it?"

"Do what, sweetie?" Liv's tone sounded kind and understanding, like Trish's.

"Marry a man you didn't love, manage to fall in love with him, stay together for thirty-five years, and raise nine boys?" The sentence came out in one breath.

"Put like that, it doesn't seem possible!" Liv reached across the table and clasped Irish's hand for a moment. "God was right there helping us every day. Smith made it obvious from the beginning that we would get through the awkward parts and eventually fall in love. And we did! Praise God!"

"There wasn't the slightest doubt?"

Their food arrived, and the conversation stopped until the server set their plates down and walked away. The scrambled eggs and toast Irish ordered looked great, but her appetite had diminished. She waited for Liv to resume the discussion.

"I can't say there wasn't *ever* any doubt." Liv cut a sausage link into three pieces. "When we married, Smith wasn't over someone else. I was adjusting to marrying a man I liked as a friend but didn't love as a husband." She leaned forward, keeping her voice low. "I understand what you're going through more than you may realize."

"That's why I wanted to talk with you."

"How are you doing with God?" Liv gave her a motherly look. "I don't mean to pry. But are you trusting in Jesus to help you through this time that must be a bit uncomfortable for you and Lake?"

"A bit?" Irish's slight laugh turned into a cough. "I believe in Jesus. I pray, although not as much as I should. I went to Sunday school as a kid. Then my folks broke up. Things were tough as my mom went from one man to another seeking … whatever." She heaved a sigh that hurt.

"That sounds like it was hard. But I'm glad your heart is open to our Savior." Liv patted her hand. "I'm thankful you and Lake share a belief in Him. He will be an anchor throughout your lives. I'll pray for you to trust in Him more every day, too."

"Thank you. Lake and I have been praying together."

"That's wonderful!"

"Pastor North, er, Smith, suggested it."

Their praying together had been a spiritual reset for Irish. Praying in front of Lake still felt awkward. But it seemed like he felt emotionally vulnerable about it too, which made her more comfortable exposing her thoughts. She would have felt inferior from the start if he had prayed like a spiritual powerhouse. Instead, they were finding their way back to God together.

"I really do want things to work out between Lake and me." Irish rarely got teary-eyed. But with Liv's loving attitude and tender words, it was easier for her to become emotional. "Thank you for talking with me. For letting me share what's going on."

"Oh, honey, any time."

They ate their meals, the sounds of the diner filling the space around them. But Irish still had a burning question she wanted to ask Liv.

"Did you ever have—" How could she phrase the question without embarrassing herself or her mother-in-law?

"Have what, sweetie?"

"Um, intimacy. Before you were in love, I mean."

"Oh. Well. Irish—" Liv stuffed a bite of pancake in her mouth and coughed as if she was nearly choking. She winked rapidly. "Will this winter weather ever turn into spring?"

"I guess." Irish ate a few bites of her eggs, then pushed her plate aside. "Thanks for meeting with me. I'm sorry if my question was too uncomfortable."

"Not the question. My answer might have been." Liv smiled tenderly. "Irish, my eldest son is a good man. He was a kindhearted boy for all his growing-up years. I'm as proud of him as any mama can be."

"Do I hear a 'but' coming?"

"You can trust him with your heart. He would never intentionally make you feel bad." Liv glanced away before resuming the topic. "But he has been deeply hurt himself."

"Laurie." Irish said the woman's name with some animosity.

"Until he lets go of that, he may be—"

"Difficult? Unreasonable?"

"I was going to say he might need reassurance from you." Liv winked like this was another topic she wouldn't get too deeply into. Yet she brought it up!

"Reassurance in what way?"

Liv's face turned rosy. "Lake married you. He chose you, and you chose him—each for your own reasons." Her voice thickened with emotion. "Due to his broken engagement, he might need assurance that you won't bolt as his ex-fiancée did."

Lake needed assurance from her? Irish was worried about him caring for Laurie. Was it possible he had doubts about her, too?

"He says he's going to pursue me."

"I'm sure he will." Liv smiled.

"But you still think he needs me to say I won't dump him?"

"I would say it differently, but yes. Whether you express yourself through talking or kissing him in such a way that he no longer doubts your devotion, that's up to you." Liv winked a couple of times.

Her suggestion gave Irish plenty to think about.

Outside the diner, Liv hugged her. "I hope we can do this again soon."

"Even if I ask embarrassing questions?"

"Even then." Liv patted her shoulder. "God loves you, sweetie. Smith, Trish, and I love you. You're part of our family now. Trish is praying for you and Lake. When she prays, things change!"

A warmth spread through Irish. She appreciated being part of this family much more now than when she married Lake three weeks ago.

Was Liv right about him needing reassurance from her? How was she supposed to assure him of her devotion when she wasn't sure of her feelings toward him? Or of his toward her?

Chapter Forty-six

Lake had just put on his cross-country skis when he heard a loud vehicle pull into the driveway. It sounded like Dad's ancient Neon. When would he turn the decrepit vehicle in for a newer model?

"Good morning!" Dad rounded the cabin and lifted a pair of skis in the air. "How about skiing and a chat?"

"Perfect timing."

What did his father come all this way to discuss?

Dad sat on the bench near the kennels. "Hey, fellas," he called to the dogs barking at his arrival. "It's nice to be greeted with such enthusiasm."

"They are anticipating a ski run. But they're also thrilled to see you."

"Sorry, guys." Dad attached his boots to the skis, then stood. "I ruined their fun by showing up now."

"No problem." Lake had planned to take the dogs out one at a time and work with them, but he'd do that later.

They skied about half a mile before Dad asked, "How are things going with you and Irish?"

Lake glanced over his shoulder between digging his poles into the snow and pulling his left ski forward. "Why?"

"With her asking your mom out for breakfast this morning, I thought you might also need someone to talk to. Did I assume wrong?"

Lake brought his forward motion to a halt. "Irish asked to speak with Mom?" Did his wife think their problems were so bad she had to speak with his mom about it?

Dad's face darkened. "You weren't aware of their outing?"

"Not at all." Lake gritted his teeth.

"I'm so sorry. I've gone and stuck my boot in my mouth." Dad wiped the back of his thick glove across his nose. "I pride myself on being discreet. Now I blabbed—"

"It's all right. But I didn't know." Lake took off skiing again, needing to work off some angst.

"It irritates you, doesn't it?"

"How's that?" Lake made his thighs work harder, driving his poles into the ice and snow.

"Irish seeking your mom's counsel annoys you. It's written all over your face."

"Wouldn't it bother you?" Lake brought his skis to a quick stop. But Dad was skiing too close and rammed into the back of his skis. Hands flailing to catch themselves, both toppled into the snow, almost on top of each other. "Dad! Are you okay?" Lake scooted away from him.

"Been better." Dad sat up and unclipped his skis from his boots. He touched his right ankle and moaned. "Why didn't you warn me you were going to stop suddenly?"

"Why were you skiing so close to me?" Lake checked his ski equipment and stood.

"Just trying to hear what you were saying."

"Are you going to be able to ski back to the cabin?" Lake helped Dad stand up.

"My ankle twisted, but I doubt it's a serious injury." He attached the skis and boots again. "I'm not trying to butt into your marriage, son. If you want to talk, I'm here. I'm sorry for mentioning our wives chatting. I honestly thought you knew."

Some of Lake's inner turmoil eased at his dad's humble-sounding words.

"Thanks, Dad. The whole part about marrying and not being in love is weird. You saw how badly our counseling session went. Trying to figure out how to have a real relationship with Irish when we're almost strangers is sometimes difficult and discouraging." Lake blew out a breath of air that steamed in front of his mouth. "She wants her way. I want mine. But we've still been praying together. Sometimes that's awkward too."

"I'm sure it is. I'm praying for both of you." Dad rocked on his skis, testing his ankle. "Look at your mom and me. Despite our initial uncertainties, we've been blessed with love and closeness for a lot of years."

"I know." Lake had heard all this before. "We should head back. Get your ankle iced."

"I'd say it's getting iced right now. But all right."

They skied back the way they came, slower this time, and kept some distance between them. When they reached the cabin's backyard, amid the barking of six dogs, they unclipped their boots. Dad hobbled toward the back door. His ankle must be swelling. Good thing Lake insisted they return.

"Hush, guys! It's okay," he called to the dogs. It took some coaxing to get them settled down again.

Inside the cabin, Dad sat on the loveseat with his leg elevated and a bag of frozen peas resting against his ankle. Lake fixed them coffee and pie. Dad didn't refuse either.

"So, why did Irish call Mom?" Lake decided to bring up the subject again.

"She didn't say. Just asked me to pray like we usually do for each other." Dad took a couple of bites of apple pie. "This is great. What does Irish think of your cooking?"

"She likes it. Eats it." Lake heard his disgruntled tone but didn't alter it.

"Your mom and I found cooking together to be extremely romantic."

"TMI." Lake pointed his fork tines in the air. "Please don't tell me anything else about Mom's and your romantic experiences, okay?"

"Sorry. If there's anything I can do to help you and Irish, please let me know."

"All right. But we have to work it out by ourselves."

"And with the Lord's help, right?" Dad nodded solemnly.

"That's right. With His daily help."

"Amen."

They finished their pie in silence.

"There is another topic I've been wanting to mention." Lake set his empty plate on the end table. "Why are you pushing Spur to go to Hawaii when I need him here?"

Dad cringed. "I'm sorry if his leaving affects you adversely."

"It does. I thought he would help me with the new kennels in the spring. Continue being a part of my team."

"Sorry, son." Dad sat up straighter on the cushions. "I didn't decide for him. But I have been praying about this opportunity for him."

"You don't mean the Charles Spurgeon thing, do you?"

"I may have mentioned that to him." Dad's face turned ruddy. "I never tried to push any of you into doing things my way. Yes, we named you after men of faith. But I accept and love you and your brothers just as you are."

"Even Stone?" Lake asked lightly.

"Even Stone." Dad gazed out the window as if picturing his fourth son. "God is working in him too. I'm proud of all my boys."

Hearing Dad say that stirred something heartwarming in Lake's spirit. "I appreciate that. But back to my question, why are you pushing Spur to go to Hawaii?"

"Not pushing. Nudging, perhaps." Dad set his cup down, then adjusted his frozen vegetable bag over his ankle. "It's his choice."

"So, if he stayed here and continued working with me, you'd be fine with his decision?"

"Absolutely. But working with dogs has always been your dream. Is it Spur's?" Dad's forehead wrinkled. "Why don't you ask Wilks to help you?"

"Wilks hasn't liked dogs since the Mayfields' Doberman bit him."

"It doesn't hurt to ask him." Wincing, Dad stood. "Honestly, I'm not trying to direct any of your lives. After all the years of being a father and coach, it's hard to sit back and not say anything."

"We all love and respect you, Dad. Even Stone." Lake stood too. "But we have to live our own lives."

"Of course." Dad heaved a sigh. "Thanks for the pie and chat. I'm going to head home and rest my leg." He hobbled toward the door.

"Can you drive?"

"You bet."

"I'm sorry you got hurt. Maybe you should see a doctor."

"Eh. It's sprained. Nothing a day of rest won't cure. Love you." He reached the door but didn't open it. "Talk to Spur if you feel strongly about him staying in Thunder Ridge. I don't want him to travel to Hawaii because I consider the mission noble. I'd rather he felt passionate here than dispassionate somewhere else." Dad limped out of the cabin and closed the door.

For a few minutes, Lake contemplated what his dad had said about being proud of all his sons and accepting them as they were, and allowing them to make their own decisions. The image of God as a loving father trying to lead His kids in the right direction came to mind. A caring, merciful, grace-filled Father who was wooing and guiding His children closer to Him, even while they sometimes made foolish mistakes. Just like Lake had made plenty of blunders.

Dad wasn't a perfect father. He'd made his share of mistakes too. But if Lake ever had the chance to be a parent, he hoped he would turn out as loving and kind as him.

Right then, he felt proud to be one of the preacher's sons.

Chapter Forty-seven

Irish spent the next day taking care of the puppies, working on the shelter's books, and mulling over Liv's words about Lake needing reassurance from her. Liv mentioned Irish kissing him. That's all she meant, right? Surely, she wasn't implying taking things further before Irish and Lake had deeper feelings for each other.

But what if she did? What would happen if Irish asked Lake to—

No, she couldn't. Kissing him, yes. But that was all. And she'd been reluctant to kiss him lately for fear of where it would lead.

Lord? Help me. I want to find true love in my marriage to Lake. I think he wants that too. But there's this thing between us. Rather, this person. Can You please heal Lake's heart where Laurie is concerned? I want to be the only woman he loves.

Sitting on a blanket in Bright Eyes's kennel, she cuddled her favorite of the tiny husky puppies. She appreciated the new aide Shelley had hired. Benson, a twenty-something short-haired guy, did a fantastic job of keeping the kennels clean and the animals fed. He had a cheerful disposition and seemed gentle and caring with all the creatures. However, Irish preferred looking after this little one herself.

She nuzzled the puppy's ear with her nose. He was so cute. If she wasn't careful, she'd lose her heart to him. Perhaps she already had. Maybe she'd pick a name for him. Something to do with the constellations—Orion, Ursa Major, Big Dipper. When Lake built the kennels at their property, they'd add more dogs to their teams. She couldn't wait for that to happen! But he probably wouldn't appreciate her bringing home a puppy to live in the small cabin with them. Still, she wanted this guy for herself.

"You're still cuddling that dog?" Shelley flicked a dangling earring back and forth, staring down at her.

"I can't help myself. I want to hold him all day." Irish inhaled the sweet scent of puppy breath. "But I have an appointment in a few minutes, so I'd better get ready to go." She kissed the top of the puppy's head. "Be safe and well, Little Dipper."

"You already named him?"

"Just testing it out."

"The way you are with these dogs, you might want the whole litter."

"Don't tempt me!" Irish settled the sleepy pup next to its mama and siblings. She stood and watched the dog family for a few minutes, enjoying the peacefulness of them all full of milk and cutely piled up next to each other sleeping. The beauty of motherhood filled her with unusual longings again.

"A call came in," Shelley said tightly.

"Oh? Who was it?" Not a problem that would detain her from meeting up with Lake and Dillan, she hoped. She had assured Lake she'd be on time.

"A bill collector." Shelley swiftly marched back toward the receptionist's desk.

"I thought all the past bills were paid in full." Frowning, Irish followed her until only the desk remained between them.

"Most were. The caller says the shelter, er, Mac, owes a large debt."

"Why haven't we heard about this before now?"

"I'm sorry, but I may have turned a blind eye to it." Shelley fidgeted with a paperclip, not meeting Irish's gaze.

"You purposefully overlooked a bill?"

"I set it aside, that's all."

Irish felt herself getting riled. "You knew about this debt and didn't show me when we were gathering the bills and paying them off?"

"Mac is a good guy." Shelly's penciled-in brows scrunched up on her forehead. "He doesn't deserve to be treated like a pariah! Cast out like garbage!"

"What are you talking about? He quit! Apparently, he's still causing the shelter financial trouble, and you're covering for him?"

"What's the big deal? You had the money to bail out the place!" Shelley grabbed a nail file and scraped it against the ends of her fuchsia-colored fingernails. "Why couldn't you let Mac manage the shelter on his terms and leave with his dignity?"

"What dignity?"

Why was Shelley being so defensive about Mac? What did any of this have to do with an unpaid bill?

"Was your donation so precious that you had to ruin a good man's reputation?" Shelley suddenly dropped onto her chair, covered her hands over her face, and wept noisily.

What in the world?

"Why did you overlook the bill?" Irish persisted despite Shelley's emotional breakdown. Whatever this business was about, she needed to get to the bottom of it and then rush over to Dillan's office.

Shelley wiped her face with a tissue, leaving streaks of black mascara beneath her eyes. "I suppose you'll be wanting my resignation, too."

"Maybe I will! Right now, I want the truth. What is this mystery bill you hid?"

Shelley blew her nose. "Mac asked me not to mention it. But I couldn't keep quiet any longer."

"Yet you still deem him trustworthy?"

"Yes. He's a little lost, but he's a good man. He said he'd resolve everything with the bank."

"The bank? What was the debt? Tell me, or so help me, I will fire you!"

Shelley whimpered.

Irish yanked her cell out of her back pocket. She shot Lake a text. *Emergency at the shelter. I will be there as soon as I can.* She hated doing this to him again.

She faced Shelley with the fiercest boss persona she could muster. "Explain the bill. Now!"

"It's for overdue payments for a small parcel of land." Shelley's lower lip trembled. "Mac wanted to set up a business to funnel funds into the shelter. He had the best intentions."

Sure, he did. "What kind of business was this?"

"Doggie daycare. Overnight care for pets."

That sounded a lot like the business Lake hoped to start. But something smelled fishy about Mac's plan. And about Shelley covering up the debt for him.

"Whose funding did he use?"

"The shelter's," Shelley said in a weepy tone.

"That's why the place was broke? And you both hid it?"

"He made some bad financial decisions."

"No kidding! You didn't think the board should know about it? You conspired to defraud this organization, didn't you?"

"No." Shelley wrung her hands together. "I wasn't conspiring about anything. But until the call came in about the foreclosure—"

"Foreclosure? Not this building! So help me, it better not be this building."

"No. Just the land for the kennels."

"You lied. Kept vital information from the board and me." Proverbial steam was billowing out of Irish's ears. She had never fired anyone before. "Clean out your drawer! Leave the keys to the building on the desk."

"You're firing me?"

"Yes. You're fired! I'll decide about pressing charges after I speak to a lawyer."

"Can't you overlook this one error on my part?" Shelley cried as she dropped her keys on the desk and scooped her belongings out of the bottom drawer.

"If I can't trust you, I don't want you working here."

"I'm sorry." Shoulders hunched, head down, Shelley shuffled out the front door. She didn't glance back.

Irish checked her phone. There were three messages from Lake.

Are you okay?
We're waiting for you to get here to make the final changes.
Irish?

Frustrated with Shelley and the latest problem for the shelter, she left Benson a note, locked the door, and ran to her car.

Chapter Forty-eight

Sitting alone in the contractor's office, Lake raked his fingers through his hair. Was Irish even going to make it to this appointment? Didn't she realize how important this meeting was to him and their future? She mentioned an emergency at the shelter. Would there always be some crisis there keeping her from meeting with him or being on time?

Dillan had gone into another room to take a call. Sighing, Lake crossed and uncrossed his arms. Then he pressed his fingers against his temples and groaned. If he had to postpone making final arrangements about the house plans, it was going to set the construction schedule back further. Why couldn't Irish just show up and—

The door opened and she rushed in. "I'm sorry. I didn't mean for this to happen again. I apologize for making you wait."

He appreciated her leading with an apology. Even though his first instinct was to tell her how he felt about her lack of priorities, he asked, "Are you all right?"

"I'm fine." She dropped into the chair across from him. "Well, not fine. Some stuff happened at the shelter. But we can talk about that later. Where's Dillan?"

"Taking a call. He has other clients, you know." He didn't subdue his frustration like he probably should have. "The time he reserved for us is nearly over. Time is valuable in the real world, Irish."

"I said I'm sorry." She glared at him.

"Is your work at the shelter always going to be more important than our plans? Than our marriage?"

"That's not fair."

No, it probably wasn't. Yet irritation still churned in him. If Irish didn't even value their marriage—

Dillan strode into the office. "Sorry about the call. With spring on the way, things are revving up."

"No problem." Lake met Irish's cold glance. He should have interacted with her more peaceably. He had been asking God to help him be a better husband, and he was failing already. He'd have to watch what he said in the next few minutes, or they would be arguing in front of Dillan. "This is the plan Dillan proposes to compromise on our semi-minimalistic home."

"Semi?" She barely glanced at the blueprints. "Thanks for your extra work, Dillan."

"Sure. I changed this part right here." With his index finger, Dillan circled a section on the drawing of the upper floor. "Where there were four bedrooms upstairs, there are three. A smaller bathroom, per your request." He spoke tentatively, no doubt sensing the tightrope of emotions twisting between them.

"Irish?" Lake asked.

"Oh, what? Sorry. I have some things on my mind." She seemed to focus on the drawings. "This is better. However, two rooms upstairs would have been enough for us." She tapped her finger against the drawing of a room on the lower floor. "What's this?"

"A mudroom and laundry," Dillan answered. "A place for the dogs to get toweled off, or whatever."

"That's good. Did the lower floor's square footage decrease, as we discussed?"

"Yes. We reduced the size of the primary bedroom. Although the dining room remained the same."

"And the garage?"

"Two doors instead of three." Dillan met Lake's gaze and raised his eyebrows.

"What do you think about this?" Lake hoped for a quick agreement so they could move forward with the plans.

Irish's shoulders rose and fell. "It still seems like a large house to me."

Lake rubbed the back of his neck where tension tightened his muscles. "I'm trying to compromise with you, but I've planned for a lodge-style home since I bought the land with my folks. The kennels. The business. Everything."

"Right. Back when you were making those plans with someone else."

A sword pierced his heart. How many times was she going to bring up Laurie?

"Your ex would have probably said, 'Oh, Lake, these are perfect,' even if she hated them."

"Let's talk about this later," he said through gritted teeth. "Alone."

"No!" Irish stood suddenly, glaring down at him. "Let's discuss this now."

Dillan gathered his blueprints protectively.

"Fine!" Lake shot to his feet. "I planned to build a bigger house from the get-go. Not to irk you. You want your room to be minimalistic? No problem." His voice increased in volume right alongside his building anger. "We can put a hammock and a cardboard box in your room for clothes. Do you prefer a compost toilet in your bathroom? I'll get you one. But we aren't going smaller with the house than this!"

"Why? Because the mighty Lake North has spoken?"

"Because we have to move forward, and someone must make a decision."

"My point exactly!"

They glared at each other, both breathing heavily.

Dillan hovered next to the wall, his rolled-up blueprints clutched in his hands.

"Please. Look at these plans." Lake lowered his voice. They were in Dillan's office, and their argument must sound petty and self-centered. "Tell me what's so intolerable about them to you."

"What's the fourth bedroom for?" She squinted at him, obviously not taking any cues from him lowering his voice. "You have a room. I have a room. One is for a guest room. What's the fourth bedroom for?"

"I'm just going to—" Dillan rushed out of the room.

Lake moaned. "Now he knows all our private business. And we've embarrassed him."

"I doubt we're the first couple to argue about house plans in front of him!"

"You want Dillan to hear all about our marriage in name only? About us having our own rooms?" He paced across the few feet of the conference room, controlling the urge to march out of the building and head straight to the District Court office. This marriage was a farce. Hadn't Hud warned him it would turn out like this?

As quickly as his temper rose, Lake felt sick with how far his thoughts had traveled. How tempted he was to throw in the towel. All because Irish was late to their meeting and didn't want the house to be as big as he did? He felt utterly foolish. Expelling a noisy sigh, he turned back toward her. "Do you want this to be over?" The question in his mouth felt like gravel swirled over his tongue.

"This disagreement?"

"Our marriage. This arrangement. Do you want us to end it?"

"Because I don't like wasting money on a gigantic house, you want to give up on us?" She thrust out her hands in an exaggerated gesture. "Seriously? You want out because things aren't going your way? Because we haven't shared a bedroom yet?"

"Don't bring our lack of intimacy into this. It has nothing to do with that."

"I think it does."

Anger and humiliation prickled heat up his chest and neck. With the table separating them, he clutched the edges. "Just tell me what has a burr under your saddle about the house. Why are you so against it?"

"You planned it with Laurie!" She pegged him with a steely look. "You and her. The couple with the L names who were meant to be. That's the reason I don't like these plans! They reek of her!"

"You're jealous because you think I made this house plan with another woman?" He unclenched his hands from the table and took a step backward.

She tightened her right fist like she was digging her nails into her palm or getting ready to sock him. "I agreed to marry you, but one thing I won't do is play second fiddle to anyone. It's you and me—or nothing!"

Or nothing, repeated in his brain like a hammer.

"You still pine for Laurie? I'll give you time to get over that." She pointed toward the door Dillan went through and her voice rose. "But when it comes to the house you and I are going to live in, when it comes to the life Lake and Irish North *might* one day enjoy, I will never take second place! Not in building a home. Not in a business. Not in intimacy."

Lake gulped and gulped again.

Irish strode around the table until she stood two feet in front of him. He was shocked and awed by the temperamental and irrational spewing of words and emotions between them. But he was also extremely attracted to his wife. She thought of herself as second best to Laurie? Heavens! Where did she get such a notion?

Laurie had no ambition. Irish was a Viking queen, fearless and awe-inspiring.

The electrical powerhouse of emotion simmering between him and her stirred his blood. Stirred his desire to take her home and—

"Are you hearing me?" Irish's gaze pinned him to the spot where he stood.

"I hear you." He swallowed with difficulty. "What do you want, Irish?"

"Your heart, for starters."

If she were a Viking queen, she might mean on a stake.

"My heart is yours for the taking." He spoke the words with as much meaning and passion as possible. "But I meant about the house. It's not fair for us to leave Dillan hanging on a project when he has other landowners hounding him for his time. If we must start over—"

"That's not necessary." Her shoulders heaved with her sigh. "I want an outbuilding of my own. You can give me that, can't you?"

"Sure." He could buy her anything she wanted. But an outbuilding? Was she planning to live in a shed?

"I'd like one thing on your land to be mine. A small building with a woodstove will be sufficient. A place where I can bring my dogs and relax." Her lips formed a faint smile. "Something you and Laurie didn't plan or dream over."

"You've got it." He stepped closer but didn't touch her. "For the record, she and I never discussed house plans."

"Really?" Irish made a sound of disbelief.

"She said it could be however I wanted."

"That will never happen between you and me. I will always have an opinion!"

"Good! I've shown you the plans and asked for your input. This house has your name written all through it." He smiled then, releasing a whale of tension. "What about the hammock? You want one of those in your room, too?"

"I'm minimalistic, but I like my comfort. A soft bed will do." She moved away from him, heading for the door. "Can you apologize to Dillan for me?" She paused. "And my name written all through your house? That suits me fine." A beautiful smile crossed her lips.

Lake let the stagnant air in his lungs expel. He and Irish had a long way to go to find love. But passion? Man, oh, man. He experienced unexpected passion between them today.

Somewhere, he would make sure he wrote her name on the wall of his house. On the wall of his heart, too.

Chapter Forty-nine

Early the next day, Irish left the house before Lake woke up, knowing she had a full day of work ahead of her. She scraped six inches of fresh snow off her vehicle before leaving the yard. It seemed winter was here to stay for a while longer. That was good news for getting to practice more skijoring with Aurora and North Star. Not so good when it came to driving conditions between Lake's property and Thunder Ridge.

After their explosive conversation yesterday, they both tiptoed around each other during dinner. Then she tackled some dog-related chores, avoiding having another awkward discussion with him before bedtime. Unfortunately, that meant they didn't pray together, nor did Lake kiss her good night.

Back at the animal shelter, without Shelley answering phones and keeping up with the paperwork, an even greater workload awaited Irish. She'd call a temp agency and get someone to handle the phones and scheduling as soon as possible. Talking with Benson about working full time, including caring for the puppies, was also high on her to-do list. For her well-being, and to avoid another debate with

Lake, she'd have to stay clear of Little Dipper. Otherwise, she'd bring him home the moment he turned six weeks old.

She had been working at the desk for an hour when the front door opened. Lake sauntered in, shaking snow off his hat and shoulders. She immediately tensed. But when she noticed he carried a couple of to-go cups of coffee, her mouth watered at the prospect of a possible vanilla latte. "What are you doing here?"

"I came to find out where my lovely wife went in such an all-fired hurry this morning." He dropped into the chair across from her and handed her one of the warm cups, his cool fingers brushing against hers. "Vanilla latte?"

"Yes. Thank you." She sipped the drink. "Mmm. It hits the spot."

"I thought you'd like that. We never talked about the emergency here yesterday."

"Oh, right."

His dark eyes blinked slowly at her. "Want to tell me about it now? I'm here to chat."

She should have told him about firing Shelley last night, but things were weird between them, so she had kept it bottled up. "I fired Shelley. That leaves me with lots to do today to cover all the bases—scheduling, ordering, filing, and answering the phone."

"You fired her? Why?"

"It's a long story. We may need more funding." She cringed.

"Why's that?"

"It appears Mac bought some local property in the shelter's name. I don't know the board's financial obligation concerning it."

"Land? How could that happen?" Lake shook his head, and more snowflakes descended.

"The bank is foreclosing on the property."

"Oh, man. Do we need to talk to a lawyer?"

"Would you mind? I hate to ask since you have enough to do with the dogs and the house. Still, would you call your lawyer?"

"Sure. I'll help wherever you need me, Irish. I'm always here for you." He dropped his chin to his chest and sighed. "I'm sorry things have been awkward between us with the house plans. I'm sorry for my part in the disagreements. I got pretty worked up yesterday, and I shouldn't have. If you want, we can keep discussing our ideas for the house and kennels. I meant for us to keep praying together, too."

At his humble admission, the feeling of something being tightly bound around her chest eased. She sighed. "Me too. I'm sorry for being so tense and outspoken. We need to figure out how to talk about stuff, even when we disagree."

"You're right." He met her gaze with a tender look. "Do you mind if we pray together now? Sort of make up for what we didn't do last night?"

"I'm okay with that."

Had he come all this way on a snowy morning to talk with her and pray together? A warm sense of his caring for her and their belonging together filled her. Maybe it was the beginning of love. Perhaps the butterflies of hope and tenderness were already dancing in her heart.

Lake set his cup on the edge of her desk and clasped her hands. Feeling his hands surrounding hers, she felt languid and peaceful.

"Lord, you see our failings and efforts to do better," Lake prayed quietly. "Help us find our way to being closer in our relationship. Please give us wisdom in everything we do. In Jesus's name."

Lake held her hands without speaking, his thumbs brushing ticklish strokes against her palms. Then he cleared his throat as if working through some deep emotion. "I'm honored to get to pray with you, Irish. For you to be my wife. I mean that."

"Thanks. I feel that way about you, too."

She squeezed his hands lightly before releasing them. For a second, she was tempted to lean over the desk and kiss him like a wife who was attracted to her husband. She didn't. But that strong urge to kiss Lake was in her thoughts, just like it had been the day she brazenly tested out his kissing abilities.

"I guess I should take care of this now." He pulled out his cell phone and tapped the screen. "Hey, Michael. This is Lake North. When you get this message, call me." He put the phone back into his jacket pocket. "Now, how was Shelley involved?" He grabbed his to-go cup again and settled back against his chair.

Focusing on yesterday's events, Irish explained what the ex-receptionist had told her.

"Mac doing that seems bizarre." Lake scratched his jaw and frowned.

"I know. And Shelley was involved! I can't have someone around me who I don't trust."

Lake squeezed his eyes nearly shut and heaved a sigh. Did he assume she included him in the statement? She hadn't meant it that way but didn't refute the idea either.

"Are you going to hire a replacement?"

"For Shelley? Yes. I'll get someone in here as soon as I can."

The door opened, and Benson breezed in, stomping his feet and dusting snowflakes off his coat. "It's freezing out there."

"Hey, Benson. This is my husband, Lake."

"Hello, sir." He stomped his boots a couple more times.

"Good morning."

There was no time like the present to take care of business, even with Lake sitting here. Irish stood. "I want to ask if you'll consider working full time starting today."

"Really?" Benson pulled off his knit hat and grinned. "I'd be glad to. Does this mean my probationary period is over?"

"It sure does. You are one of the team now." She stuck her hand out to shake his, and he reciprocated. "For now, it's you and me, but I'll hire others." She glanced at Lake. His eyebrows rose. Was he surprised by her take-charge attitude? Or by her making it sound like she was sticking around here indefinitely?

"Thank you, Mrs. North. I appreciate the job. I love working with the animals."

"I can tell. Keep up the good work." She sat back down. "We'll figure out your schedule and a raise later."

"Awesome! Nice to meet you." He nodded at Lake, then hurried into the next room.

"He's a good worker. Hopefully, he has the fortitude to do what a full-time job here requires." Irish spoke fast, feeling nervous with Lake observing her acting like a boss.

"Sometimes being thrown into the deep end makes you learn to swim." A soft-looking smile crossed his lips. "You're doing a great job, Irish."

His unexpected praise brought a flush to her cheeks and warmth to her emotions. "Have you and I jumped into the deep end with our marriage?"

"I guess we have."

Their gazes met and held. She smiled at him, hoping he felt the emotional stirrings she was feeling toward him. In different circumstances, she might flirt with him. Maybe kiss him like she imagined doing a few minutes ago.

"Do you want to go out with me tonight? I'd like to spend some time alone with you. Maybe stir up some romance with my wife." He winked at her.

Some romance sounded intriguing, and she was ready to put their recent conflicts behind them. "I could dress up in a nice pair of slacks and eat a steak."

"That's my girl." Lake pushed up from the chair. "I'll let you know how my discussion with Michael goes. Best case scenario, he takes care of the whole thing."

"That would be great. Thanks for everything, Lake."

"Sure. I'm looking forward to our date."

"So am I." In fact, she couldn't take her gaze off him as he strolled across the room and walked out the door.

Chapter Fifty

After talking with Irish, Lake set up a makeshift office in the corner of Nelly's Diner. He'd done this a few times over the last year of owning property too far from town to dash home and make a phone call. The loud environment made hearing difficult, but the engine of his truck would have been noisy if he made the call from inside his running vehicle, too.

He texted Spur, letting him know he was at Nelly's if he wanted to stop by and have breakfast. Lake was still hoping to discuss his brother's trip to Hawaii.

The call from the lawyer took longer than he wished. Spur arrived during the call, and Lake waved him toward the chair on the opposite side of the table. While he answered Michael's questions and asked a few of his own, he observed Spur chatting with a server. She was a younger woman who blushed a lot. Did they already like each other? Or was Spur just flirting and teasing her?

Michael agreed to call the bank and try to negotiate a settlement. Lake told him he'd buy the property if the bank was willing to work with him. That would get the shelter off the hook. Maybe the land would come in handy for something—an investment, if nothing else.

After the call ended, he quickly texted Irish, updating her on what Michael had said. He asked her to forward his comments to the board members. They needed to keep them apprised of the steps they were taking to ensure all the legalities were followed after Mac's poor business decisions.

By the time he set down his phone, his coffee was cold and Spur's breakfast plate sat partially eaten in front of him. "Sorry about that."

"What's this? You invite me to meet you for breakfast, then talk on your phone the whole time?"

"I didn't expect the call to go that long. And I had to send a text to Irish."

"Yeah, yeah."

Lake held up his coffee cup to a passing server. The older woman smiled and poured the black brew. "Thanks."

"So, what did you want to see me about?" Spur stuffed a thick bite of his triple stack of pancakes dripping syrup into his mouth.

"Can't brothers meet without ulterior motives?"

"Not likely." Spur barked out a laugh and then coughed hard like his food went down wrong.

"Are you okay?" The server he chatted with before leaned down beside him. "Do you need help, Spur?" She nearly purred his name.

"He's fine." Lake waved off the woman. "You should stay back. He has a rare condition."

"Oh? Is that right?" The woman's eyes widened.

Spur kicked him under the table.

Lake groaned. "Uh, yeah. It's not contagious or anything."

Another kick.

"If I can be of service, let me know." The woman spun around and left their table as if someone were chasing her.

"Thanks a lot!" Spur scowled.

Lake burst out laughing. "I can still give as good as I get."

"I might have deserved that."

"After what you did to Irish and me, that's for sure." Lake sipped his hot drink. "So, are you still planning to head off to Hawaii?"

"Yep."

"You sure about such a move?"

"Why wouldn't I be?" Spur dropped his fork onto the plate. "Why are you so hot under the collar about me having a bit of fun in my life?"

"What do you mean?"

"You're the one who races with your dogs, owns land, and has the big bucks. Not to mention the girl." Spur tapped the table with each point. "Why shouldn't I have a little adventure? Maybe I'll find a girl for myself, too."

"I didn't know you felt like that." Some of the big brotherly sway Lake thought he'd have evaporated. "I wouldn't want you to miss out on anything important in your life."

"But?"

"Who mentioned a but?"

"Your eyelids shutter to half-mast whenever you keep back a rude comment or unwanted advice. You might as well spit it out!"

Lake clenched his jaw. "I wish you the best. You've been a great help with my dogs. I hoped you and I would continue working together. But I respect your decision to move on to something else."

"Okay. Thanks." Spur's somber expression changed into a grin. "It's hard to explain being a professional pooper-scooper to a woman."

"You were always more than that to my dogs and me."

"Canine babysitter, then."

"Canine uncle." Lake snorted.

Spur laughed and then folded a long piece of bacon into his mouth. "Which of the younger brothers will you get to work for you next?"

"I don't know."

"I still say you should ask Wilks!"

"Right."

While Spur finished his breakfast, Lake checked his phone. Michael hadn't contacted him yet.

"What about you?" Spur pushed his plate to the edge of the table.

"What about me?" Lake set down his phone.

"How do you plan to win the fair maiden's heart?" Spur's grin nearly reached the width of his face.

Irish's words about wanting his heart came to mind.

"You think I'm desperate enough to talk to you about my love life?"

"Maybe."

"Well, I'm not."

"Fine." Spur held up his hands, palm out. "I accidentally overheard Gran and Mom praying for you and Irish. I got the gist of the situation."

"You eavesdropped on their prayer time?"

"Did I say eavesdropped? I was upstairs and overheard them." Spur stroked his whiskered chin. "Although, when we were kids, Wilks and I used to listen in on Gran praying."

"Spur!"

"No one told us, middle kids, anything." He fidgeted around in his seat like he couldn't sit still. "Wilks and I found out family secrets in our own way."

"You'd better confess that to God. Then Gran!"

"To God, maybe. Not to Gran." Spur crossed his arms. "I'd get sermonized for the next ten years!"

"And deserve every minute of it. Here you're about to become a ministry assistant, and you aren't clearing your conscience first?"

"Your big brotherly snobbery is hilarious." Spur wadded up his napkin and pelted it at Lake.

"Where is this negativity coming from?" Lake set the projectile napkin on the table.

"What about clearing your conscience? You're the one who broke the pact. Things will never be the same between us guys because of it!"

Lake felt stabbed by Spur's cruel-sounding yet possibly honest words.

"Got you!" Spur guffawed and jabbed Lake's shoulder.

"You're joking?"

"What else?" Grinning widely, Spur stood. "I have a Zoom meeting with Dad and Perry Banyan, the guy in Hawaii, in fifteen minutes."

"I'm going to miss you, despite your biting humor." Lake stood and shook his brother's hand.

Lake paid for Spur's breakfast and headed out to his truck, but his brother's comments stuck with him. Even if Spur was razzing him, did Lake alter their sibling relationship by accepting the inheritance and marrying Irish? If so, was there anything he could do to rectify it?

Chapter Fifty-one

Irish rarely wore dresses—and never red ones! The outdated color rule had been ingrained in her brain since she was a kid that redheads don't wear red! Yet, as soon as she saw the dress in the shop and felt its butter-like softness, she loved it. When she tried it on and experienced how the fabric caressed her body like it was made for her, she had to have it!

Now, she cringed, staring at herself in her bedroom mirror and pondering the price tag. Before marrying Lake, she wouldn't have considered buying an expensive dress like this. What would he think of the mid-thigh, slim-fitting dress? Would he say it was worth the cost? She'd spent her own tip money on it. Of course, she wouldn't use Lake's funds. Not even with him being a billionaire and telling her to use their joint debit card for whatever she needed. She was too independent for that.

She wore clear gloss over red lipstick, dark blue eye shadow, and thick mascara, leaving her long hair cascading naturally over her shoulders. She turned one way and the other, critiquing her reflection in the mirror. Maybe she'd feel better about her appearance if the dress were black. Or if she removed some makeup. Perhaps it came down to wishing things were different between her and Lake. Better, somehow. That had to be it because she couldn't regret buying this dress!

She picked up her long sweater and a slim black purse, and her comment about wanting Lake's heart replayed in her mind. Why was she so bold? And what did he mean when he said his heart was hers for the taking? Seriously? As if she could walk up to him, kiss him for five minutes, and he'd fall at her feet? Nice thought, though.

"Irish?" Lake tapped on the door. "Are you ready to go?"

"Yes, I am."

Any worry over how she looked in her red dress or what Lake's reaction might be, vanished the instant she stepped into the living room and his eyes lit up.

"Wow, Irish! You look amazing. Just darling in that dress."

"Thanks. I usually avoid this color." She fiddled with the sweater hanging over her arm.

"Why? It's gorgeous on you. I mean, you're gorgeous in it."

A soft laugh escaped her. "Okay, thanks. You look handsome, too."

Her gaze wandered over his tan sports coat resting over a baby-blue shirt open at the neck. His crisp black jeans looked new. He wore a smidge of shadowy whiskers over his lower face. She wanted to smooth her palms across his cheeks and feel the sandpaper roughness. His hair was tamed back, inviting her fingers to wander through the strands.

"Can I help you?" He stepped closer with his hands outstretched toward her sweater.

"Sure."

He smelled of musk and spice. She wanted to lean in, fake a trip so she'd fall against his chest, and inhale his scent to her heart's content. But since she didn't like faking anything, she resisted.

She enjoyed the feeling of Lake's hands brushing against her as he snugged the thick sweater around her. He gently set his arm over her shoulders, tugging her closer to his side, which was nice too. A second and third whiff of his cologne spun her thoughts into imagining herself kissing him for the rest of the night.

To an outsider, they'd surely look like a real couple, smiling and gazing at each other. Perhaps they appeared as newlyweds who were enjoying happily-ever-after bliss. *If only!*

"I don't want you to be cold, so I'll keep you warm tonight. Is that okay?"

The rumble of his husky voice sent shockwaves through her emotionally sensitive system. His breath smelled of mint, making her want to move close enough to taste his lips.

"With you nearby, I'm sure I won't be anything but warm." She gave him a flirty smile.

With a heated look, his gaze zeroed in on her glossed lips. "We should get going. Don't want to lose our reservation."

"No. We wouldn't want that."

Or maybe she did! Perhaps she wanted to turn in his arms and kiss him like she did the day he asked her to marry him. She could tell him to forget the reservations. Why not stay here and get better acquainted?

He lowered his arm from her shoulder and opened the door. "It's chilly out. Let's hurry. I have the truck running already."

"You do?"

"Mmhmm." Clasping her hand, he drew her into the frigid air.

"Whoa." Her teeth chattered as she braced against the windy night that chilled her romantic feelings. Holding Lake's hand, she hoped she didn't fall on her face on the icy trail thanks to the stupid heels she wore. Why had she worn this dress? Thick pants and boots would have been smarter! And much warmer.

As they approached Lake's pickup, steaming from the engine running, Irish was grateful he had started it in advance. He opened her door. Now, how was she supposed to slide into the truck gracefully?

Lake averted his gaze. Quickly, she climbed into the truck like she would have if she had worn pants. "Ready."

He closed the door and hustled around to his side. They were on the road in a minute, listening to a country tune on the radio.

Irish glanced at her escort several times in the dark. The lights from the dash illuminated his manly face and attractive soft lips. Her thoughts about hungrily kissing him crashed through her mind like an unleashed dog in a china shop. Would she get to kiss Lake and find out how he felt about her tonight? His gaze met hers, and he smiled like he knew what she was thinking.

She'd have to be careful, or she would kiss him and tell him what she thought of being married to such a handsome man. She wouldn't let any concerns about their first twenty-six days of marriage bother her. Tonight she wanted to be Lake's date and get to know her husband better.

The miles flew by as they chatted about the dogs, their future kennels, and something funny Spur had told him. They even discussed some ideas about a smaller house without either of them getting riled up. She avoided discussing the animal shelter, Mac's horrible leadership, or her lack of recruiting a manager yet. She tabled those topics for another time.

Lake let the valet drive his rig to the parking lot at the restaurant. He was the perfect gentleman, offering Irish his arm to hold, opening the big glass door, and letting her go first, then holding her hand lightly as the maître d' led them to a table. Irish could adapt to this kind of attention from him. Not that she felt needy or desperate for a man's notice. But romantic gestures? Tender glances and Lake's arm brushing against her side? Those were excellent benefits of being married to him that she didn't mind at all!

After they ordered their meals—a steak and caramelized onion entrée for her, a salmon filet and baked potato for him—they sipped hot tea and made small talk. Gazing at Lake across a candlelit table and having his undivided attention centered on her felt amazing. What girl wouldn't be smitten with his good looks, charm, and politeness?

Several people strolled past and greeted Lake. It seemed he was known and liked in the community. When Irish was a server, she had heard some customers saying things about "those preacher's sons" like they had insider information about them. Now that she was part of the North family, hearing her husband and his brothers discussed as if the people in town had some input in their lives felt weird. Did they think they might have a say about Lake's wife, too?

"Final race of the winter season is coming up." He sounded eager.

Was this another topic she should avoid? They had been competitors before they were spouses, so this was probably a safe conversation.

"After her injury, I'm worried about racing with Aurora."

"Has she been limping during practice?"

"No. But I'd hate for anything to happen to her in a future race."

"You're not thinking of withdrawing from this one, are you?" Frown lines encircled his eyes, making him look older than thirty-five.

"Maybe. I've been so busy. I haven't had time to prepare my team like usual." She sighed, hating to admit she might have to withdraw from the race. She'd never canceled a racing event before.

"If you weren't there, it would be a shame." He met her gaze over the candlelight, and she read the sincerity in his expression. It felt like he truly had compassion for her and her dogs.

She wanted to reach across the table and clasp his hand. "Are you saying you'd miss me?"

A lopsided grin spread across his mouth. "I'd miss you and then some."

"What would more than missing me be like?" Smiling widely, she touched the tip of her tongue against the corner of her mouth. She was blatantly flirting with him now.

He made a fist over his heart. "A sweeter longing to be with you." He lowered his hand and picked up his cup. Slowly, he brought it to his lips, watching her the whole time.

His smoldering gaze left her speechless. Either this man was sincere in his desire to pursue and be devoted to her, or he'd make a fantastic actor. Right this minute, she believed Lake's intentions toward her were honest and passionate and that he planned for them to stay married for the rest of their lives. And that he wasn't thinking one thought about his ex!

Irish picked up her cup and sipped her drink, not breaking the visual ties binding them. Only when the server set their plates of food down did they glance away from each other.

The warm scent of grilled steak reached her senses. "Mmm. The food smells fantastic."

"I hope you enjoy it. I'll be right back with more hot water." The server hurried away.

Irish glanced between her plate and Lake's dish of salmon and potato. "Yours looks great too. Have you eaten here before?"

"Uh, sure. A few times."

"Ohhh. With her?" She choppily sliced a chunk of steak with her knife. "Sorry. I shouldn't have asked." She stuffed the piece of meat in her mouth.

"Irish, if you're curious about my previous relationship, I don't mind you asking. As long as you're nice about it."

"Nice, huh?" Her romantic mood seeped away. She stuffed another bite of meat into her mouth. After she chewed and swallowed, she said, "Okay. Did you bring Miss I'm-Too-Good-For-You to this restaurant where you've now brought your wife?"

Lake's lips wobbled. He was fighting a grin! "Yes. She and I dined here several times. Also, my family came here recently for our parents' thirty-fifth wedding anniversary."

"Thirty-five years sounds like forever." Sighing, she let herself get distracted from thinking about the other woman.

"Did I mention my parents celebrate every monthly anniversary?"

"You did."

Lake squeezed a lemon slice over his salmon. "This month will be their four-hundred-and-twenty-first monthly celebration."

"That's impressive."

"They honored their marriage like that even when they hadn't fallen in love yet." His warm gaze met hers like he was communicating something to her. Was he saying they hadn't fallen in love yet, but he planned to fall in love with her? Or maybe they should celebrate like his parents did, too? "Dad wanted Mom to know he was serious about their relationship from the beginning, or so the story goes."

"Sounds like he's a romantic. If we survive until our first anniversary, we'll have something to throw a party about!"

Lake's fork stopped midair with a piece of potato and sour cream on it. "You doubt we'll make it a year?"

"No one can be certain of a long marriage."

"But you're not planning on us failing, are you?"

"Planning?" Their nice dinner would be nothing but a bad memory with no kissing afterward if she let this discussion spiral out of control. She took a deep breath, settling her emotions and her thoughts down. "Let's enjoy what we have now. A great meal. Great company. Almost four weeks of marriage without one of us giving up. Why should we worry about what will be happening between us in a year?"

Lake put the forkful of food in his mouth and chewed slowly, staring at his plate like he was in deep thought.

Goodness. Had she ruined everything with her remark?

Five minutes of silence passed between them.

"Did I tell you about the time Hud came inside the house slathered in mud?" Lake finally asked.

"No. Tell me." Relief pulsed through her. The awkward silence had been maddening.

He told a humorous story of Hud scrambling through the house, dropping chunks of mud from the back door to the bathroom. "His reasoning? He was digging for gold! But the bees liked the mud so much they stung him a dozen times before he reached the house." Lake chuckled. "Gran got the shower going, shouting at anyone who'd listen to get into the living room and clean up the mud because she wasn't living in a pigsty."

"Did you clean the mess?"

"Coe and I did. But I'll never forget Hud slinking out of the bathroom speckled with stings." He tapped his face and neck in several spots. "The moral of the story? Never pan for gold in a muddy backyard in northern Idaho!"

Thankfully, Lake's storytelling broke the tension between them. Would he let her comment about what their relationship might be like a year from now slide for the rest of the evening? Or would he bring it up again later?

Chapter Fifty-two

For the last five miles along the country highway toward their cabin, the truck's interior sparked with tension. Fireworks ignited in Lake's thoughts whenever he imagined the flirtatious exchanges he and Irish experienced tonight. From how she came out of her room, swaying in the sexy red dress, to her snuggling against him as they walked out to his truck, to her gaze shining at him across the restaurant table, all evening he wanted to kiss her.

One mile from his property, his heart galloped across the barren fields of his nonexistent romantic life since he and Laurie broke up. Was he ready to give his heart to another woman? To his wife?

He wouldn't push for anything outside of Irish's comfort zone. But was she prepared for them to move their relationship to a deeper level like he was? Not staying in the same bedroom yet, but kissing and acting more romantic with each other?

He swallowed and tried focusing on driving.

Irish's comment about what their relationship might be like in a year still bugged him. Imagining things not working out between them had the power to stifle all his romantic feelings. He'd better compartmentalize the what-ifs and focus on what they had going for them now, as she suggested. Besides, wasn't he trusting God to be working in their lives together? Wasn't having faith about hoping for the best in all situations, even when the road before them wasn't easy or clear?

He pulled his truck into their driveway and quickly shut off the engine. The stillness in the cab hummed. Should he kiss her right here? Maybe he'd wait until they got inside the cabin and he banked the fire in the woodstove. Or until the mood was right.

"Guess I'll have to run to keep ahead of the cold," Irish spoke softly. "These heels might be dangerous."

"I could always carry you."

"That would keep me warm." A mischievous grin crossed her face in the semi-dark interior. "However, both of us falling on our faces would create a bigger problem."

"I'd have you in my arms sooner." His heart pounded out a rock band beat.

"Is that what you want? To have me in your arms?"

"Yes," he whispered.

"For a chaste, good night kiss?" She touched her tongue to the corner of her lips, reminding him of when she did the same thing earlier. And it drove him crazy.

"I wouldn't call what I'm picturing exactly chaste."

"So, you've been imagining kissing me?" Her words were barely audible.

"Sure have." He went to reach for her.

Giggling and squirming away, she grabbed hold of the door handle and hopped out of the truck before he released his seatbelt.

"Hey. Wait up." He exited the vehicle and followed her along the trail. How in the world was she able to stay upright in those heels? Women's footwear was a mystery to him as much as the female personality intrigued him. He caught up to Irish as she opened the front door.

"Beat you," she whispered.

"Yes, you did."

As soon as they crossed the threshold and shut the door, he took her in his arms. He leaned her back slightly, and their gazes tangled. His mouth two inches from hers, he paused, their breathing mingling.

"Is this okay with you?"

"It's okay if—"

His lips met hers in a hungry, desperate-feeling kiss that turned out just as passionate as when she kissed him the first time. She wrapped her arms around his shoulders, leaning into his chest, seemingly getting as close to him as possible with his coat and her sweater still on. The kiss went from fiery hot to a slow burn, then back to fiery.

Dazed, besotted, and attempting to catch his breath, Lake stepped back, reluctantly letting go of her. Irish's foggy gaze met his with a questioning look. Like she couldn't believe he had stopped kissing her. He could barely believe it either.

"I should, uh, stoke the fire."

She chuckled lightly. "I think you already did that quite well."

"The house." He cleared his throat. "I meant the room."

"Us," she whispered.

He gulped. "If we're not going to move this into the other room, we should slow down. Talk and have coffee. Or tea. Maybe chamomile tea. I'll just—" He nodded toward the woodstove.

Still moved by their kissing and proximity, he wanted to keep kissing her. To embrace his wife and everything a sweet married life allowed and fulfilled. But he wouldn't push her into doing anything before she was ready.

In front of the woodstove, he fanned the glowing embers left from his previous fire. The task helped him concentrate on getting the room prepared for the night. And kept his thoughts off the idea of following Irish into the bedroom she'd gone into. Her closed door would keep him out as much as her saying she wanted them to be in love before intimacy would.

He couldn't say he loved her yet. But like a chocolate lover longing for fudge, he was attracted to his wife and wanted to be with her.

After fifteen minutes without Irish leaving her bedroom, Lake entered the guest room and removed his dressy clothes. Once he put on blue checkered pajama bottoms and a white thermal shirt with a sweatshirt over the top, he sat on his bed and sighed. Crossing the small space between their bedrooms was a strong temptation. A good night kiss might be too enticing. Maybe he'd read for a while.

The quiet knock at his door set his heart to pounding again.

"Yeah?"

"I'm going to put on some water for tea. Want some?"

"Uh, sure." The hesitancy in his voice had to be obvious.

The pattering of Irish's slippers shuffling away reached him. Hopefully, she wore her parka, thick sweatpants, and her long hair stuffed into her racing hat. Anything to keep him from thinking of her as a beautiful and desirable woman who happened to be his wedded wife.

* * * *

Irish prepared hot peppermint tea and had their cups resting on the table before Lake strolled out of his bedroom. Was he avoiding her after their kisses?

His passion had equaled hers. She liked that about him. Yet he gallantly put on the brakes. She might not have had the courage or the tenacity to do so tonight.

With all their flirting at the restaurant and in the truck, she anticipated he might push for them to take the next marital step tonight. He hadn't. She respected him and trusted him more because of it. She was a lucky woman to have married an honorable man like Lake North.

"The tea is ready."

"Good." The one huskily spoken word reminded her of what his lips felt like when they kissed. How he smelled of musk and spice and everything nice!

She glanced at his pjs and sweatshirt. He looked prepared to hibernate for the winter instead of luring her into his den. She'd put pajama bottoms and a flannel shirt over leggings and a long-sleeved Henley—plenty of modest coverage. Her bedroom was cold at night, and she'd probably fall asleep with the door shut. Too bad she hadn't taken the time to run out to the kennels and bring Pleiades inside. She would have kept her feet warm tonight.

She met Lake's gaze as they sat across from each other at the table, gripping their teacups.

"Smells good," he said.

"Something warm before bed."

His eyes sparkled in her direction.

Maybe she shouldn't have mentioned bed. Or warmth.

"I enjoyed tonight. Thanks for going out with me." He sipped from his cup, his big hands encircling the small pottery cup, his shining gaze still on her.

"Sure. I enjoyed it too. And I liked what happened afterward." She wasn't going to avoid the topic of their kissing because they weren't taking their relationship any further yet.

"Me too." He smiled at her tenderly.

Everything within her wanted to leap up, charge around the table, sit on his lap, and continue kissing him until she knew he loved her. Or at least until she knew he wasn't thinking about Laurie anymore.

Instead, she sipped her minty drink. They needed to talk about his ex. But after their lovely date, she didn't want to discuss the taboo subject. What if Laurie continued to be a problem between them? Liv's suggestion came to mind. Had tonight's kisses given Lake the assurance he needed about Irish planning to stay with him and wanting their marriage to work?

Or did her comment about their first anniversary make him worry even more?

Chapter Fifty-three

Early the next morning, Lake discovered he'd missed an email the previous afternoon. Michael wrote that he negotiated a fair purchase of the land for him. And that the local bank was glad to have the situation resolved without the hassles of foreclosure or a stigma being placed on the animal shelter. This meant Lake and Irish were the owners of a small commercial property in town. He didn't have any idea about what to do with the land. But he'd make it a matter of prayer for a future venture.

With a lot on his mind and eager to clear a space for his kennel business on his land, Lake texted Wilks at six a.m. to ask if he wanted to help with removing brush. Per his usual morning routine, he fed the dogs first and then drove the truck slowly out of the driveway, hoping not to awaken Irish with the noise.

Throughout his tasks, his thoughts weren't far from last night's date, their kissing, and the conversation that followed. Moments of exhilaration and frustration peppered the evening, especially when Irish brought up Laurie. Why did she insist on mentioning her? He wasn't married to Laurie! He'd married Irish. He wanted to stay married to her. Hadn't he made that clear?

Maybe not as clear as he thought. Especially with how she seemed to doubt that they'd be together in a year. But he was trying to leave that with God and not worry about it. What good did worrying do, anyway?

A half-hour after he began trimming away bushes and several small trees with a chainsaw, Wilks pulled up in his noisy pickup. The muffler belched out a plume of black smoke.

Lake shut off the chainsaw.

"Ho!" Wilks shouted. "Started without me, did you?"

"Did you even answer my text?"

"I thought so. I'm here now."

Lake swallowed a disgruntled groan. Thankfully, his brother made the journey safely in his rattletrap. "Isn't it about time you got a new rig?"

"For that to happen, I'd need a wealthy relative to endow me with an inheritance. Too bad I can't claim Hud's share." He was singing a different tune today. Wilks stomped through a foot of snow to reach where Lake worked. "So this is where you and Irish are going to build your happily ever after, huh?" He peered around the flat piece of land with its condensed blanket of white as if trying to see into their future. "Not much to look at, is it?"

"It has potential." The same as their marriage did. Why did everyone assume he and Irish weren't happy? Or that their marriage wouldn't last? "Are you here to help, or what?"

"Is this a paying gig?" Wilks pulled on thick work gloves. "Because if you want brotherly help, I'll work leisurely. If you're paying me, I'll be inclined to work faster."

"I must have a few extra bucks lying around to pay you." He let out an exaggerated sigh.

"Spur warned me that you're a cheapskate." Wilks stomped over to some tree limbs Lake had cut off. "Where do you want the burn pile to be?"

"Over there." Lake pointed to the center of the clearing, but he couldn't let his brother's comment slide. "Why does he say I'm a cheapskate?"

"You've always been stingy with your money." Wilks scooped up a stack of evergreen boughs. "Everyone knows that!"

"That's because I was saving for this." He lifted his chin toward the land still hidden by snow.

"Whatever." Wilks carried his load to the middle area and flung it down.

Lake started up the chainsaw again. He worked at clearing the perimeter while Wilks added tree branches and bushes to the growing pile. His brother wasn't a slouch at working, which would be a benefit if Lake hired him. His verbal jabs and attitude were another thing.

After they'd worked for a while, Lake retrieved a thermos of coffee and some pastries from his truck.

"You brought homemade snacks?" Wilks's eyes lit up like he'd never seen food before.

"Bakery fresh yesterday."

"That'll do." Wilks sat down on a chopped log. "We miss your cooking at Mom and Dad's. Even Gran mentioned she missed your tarts and pies."

"Gran is a fine cook."

"She's not baking much these days due to arthritis."

"That's too bad." Lake hadn't heard his grandmother complaining about the ailment. He poured a cup of steaming black coffee, then passed it to Wilks before fixing himself one. "I'll have everyone out for dinner when my house is finished."

"How long until your mansion gets built?"

"Five or six months." Lake dropped onto a second log. "Don't call it a mansion around Irish."

"Why not?"

"She likes things to be more minimalistic." Lake subdued any negative attitude about Irish's viewpoint. He was compromising on his wishes about the house's size, but so was she.

"You two sure are opposites."

"You know what they say about opposites attracting." Lake pictured their kisses last night. So, she liked fewer things in a house, while he liked more material goods after living in a frugal pastorate. They would work it out together like a married couple. His heart warmed at the thought of him and Irish becoming an honest-to-goodness married couple who shared everything.

"Just don't let it kill the other stuff." Wilks gave him a rarely-seen serious look.

"What other stuff might that be?"

"The family stuff. Come on, Lake. Open your eyes. Our family is falling apart. And you're so busy with—" He turned away sharply and sipped his drink.

"Who's falling apart? What's happened?" Concern raced through Lake.

Wilks took a giant bite of a bear claw pastry. "Don't be obtuse for your whole newlywed year, okay? Especially with someone like her."

"Knock it off!" Lake glowered at him.

"What?" Wilks chewed his food fast like he was starving.

"Don't say rude things about my wife."

"Cool the jets." Wilks wiped the back of his hand against his mouth. "We all know your marriage isn't real. You have to live with her for five years to get the cash. You're stuck. But why not enjoy it, huh?" He rocked his eyebrows. "She's a beauty even if you don't love her."

"Shut up!" Lake grabbed his brother by the front of his work coat and shook him, dumping his coffee on the ground. "Don't ever say anything so stupid and rude about Irish again. I mean it! She is my wife. My *real* wife."

"Okay, okay. You're trying to make do with a bad situation. That's admirable." Wilks's smile disappeared. "Let go of my jacket, will you? I think I spilled my coffee down the side of your coat."

"What?" Lake released him and shoved him backward. Feeling the wetness of the coffee dripping down his jeans, he groaned. "For your information, not that it's any of your business, Irish and I have feelings for each other. I'm not splitting with her in five years, either." He punctuated the air with his finger. "I value God's plan for marriage. Dad and Mom taught us that was important. So don't bad-mouth my wife or our attempts at a fulfilling marriage ever again!" He picked up his cup and splashed more coffee from the thermos into it, not offering Wilks anymore.

"Maybe I had it wrong."

"Maybe you did!"

Wilks slurped whatever scant amount of coffee remained in his cup. "It's not just me. It's what the whole family assumes."

The hairs stood up on the back of Lake's neck. "How would you know what everyone assumes?" Mom, Dad, and Gran would never openly talk about his relationship with Irish.

"You're out of the loop, but the other brothers keep in touch." Wilks pulled his gloves back on. "Your ears would be burning if you heard what Hud says about your marriage."

"You've spoken to Hud about Irish and me?"

"Since you're busy getting rich, Coe is out of the country, and no one knows where Stone is, Hud's talking to Spur and me. It's about time, too!"

"If Hud has something to say about me, he should speak with me. Not you! And not Spur!" Lake grabbed the empty pastry bag, cups, and thermos in jerky movements. "Furthermore—"

"Got your goat, didn't I?" Wilks's mouth spread so wide that a small Frisbee would almost fit.

"You're joking about all this?"

"Got you good!" Wilks cackled, folding his arms over his middle and rocking back and forth like he had pulled the funniest prank ever.

"Everything you said—" He fell for one of his brothers' jokes again?

"You trip over emotional hogwash so easily. What's wrong with you?"

Lake grabbed a handful of pebbled ice and hurled it at Wilks. He ducked, but some of the particles cascaded over him. "Did Hud call and complain about me?"

"Call him and find out yourself." Wilks pretended to zip his lips shut. "I don't disclose secrets."

"Sure, you don't." Lake jerked his gloves back on. He was sick and tired of his brothers doing this to him. "Let's go. We still have work to do."

"You're the one who called a snack break. I'm still on the clock."

"What do you need money for besides buying a new truck?" Lake asked, letting his peevish mood come out in his tone.

"To escape my poverty."

"Your poverty is your fault! Get a job!" With Wilks's stunts, Lake didn't want to hire him. He trudged back toward the clearing they were working on.

"I did find a job I like."

"What's that? Making prank phone calls?" Lake picked up his chainsaw and fiddled with the starter.

"I'm a barista."

"You make coffee?" Lake laughed mockingly.

An ice-packed snowball hit him square between the shoulders. "Hey!"

"I happen to make good coffee."

"I'll believe that when I taste it." Lake started up the noisy woodcutter.

A couple of hours later, while they were heading toward their rigs, Wilks said, "Stop by the coffee shop in Thunder Ridge any day this week. You can even bring her."

"My wife's name is Irish."

"Fine. Bring Irish by and find out whether I make a good cup of coffee."

"Maybe I will." Lake took out his wallet and handed Wilks a stack of twenties. "Thanks for the help. You did good work." He grabbed one of the bills back and waved it in the air. "Minus the mouthing off and the prank comments."

"Hey."

"Gotcha!" Lake tossed the bill back at him.

"Thanks for this." Wilks stuffed the money into his pants pocket. "See. I'm not the slouch you think I am."

"Did I say you were a slouch?"

"You didn't ask me to take Spur's place as your assistant."

"You don't like dogs."

"No, I don't. But I might be a good racing assistant."

"Do you want to work with me?"

"A week ago, I was desperate enough to say yes. But as I said, I found a job I love. Someday I'm going to own the joint." Wilks jumped into his beat-up truck and started the noisy contraption. Stinky black smoke filled the air.

Coughing, Lake fanned his hand in front of him. Would a salary as a barista even be enough for his younger brother to buy a new rig? He thought of the commercial property he was getting. Was there anything he could do with it that might benefit his family? Maybe even help Wilks?

Chapter Fifty-four

Two days later, Lake sat in the small coffee shop where Wilks worked, waiting for Irish to join him. He counted ten tables filled with customers. Between folks standing in line to order and the lineup of cars in the drive-through, the place hummed with busyness. Maybe Wilks would make enough money in tips over the next few years to purchase a newer truck. Perhaps even get his own apartment and move out of Mom and Dad's house. At twenty-seven, it was about time!

His brother worked behind some coffee-making machinery, but occasionally Lake saw him grinning at a customer or a coworker. Hopefully he didn't spend too much time flirting and goofing off.

As Lake waited for Irish, he made a mental list comparing his two youngest brothers to decide which might be a more responsible assistant for him. Sunday loved sports. Finn was into theater. Would either like to work with his dogs and help on race days?

A familiar perfume hit his nostrils just before someone sat at his table. "Laurie?" He sat up straighter and clenched his hands against the tabletop, tension darting up his spine and neck. "I didn't expect—"

"Hey, Lake." Her long blond hair fell over both shoulders, framing her slender face. Her big blue eyes gazed at him. "Mind if I sit here for a minute?"

"No problem." Unless Irish walked in and saw her sitting across from him, then it might be a problem.

"You look good."

"Uh, thanks." Awkward. "How are you?"

"I'm fine. Enjoying a visit with my family." She shrugged like she didn't want to talk about that. "Not having your usual black coffee?"

"Not yet. I'm waiting for—"

"Your wife. You and her already, huh?"

Did she expect an explanation? He didn't owe her one, but he didn't want to hurt her feelings. He shrugged and glanced back toward the door.

"I hope she won't get the wrong impression with me sitting here."

Lake hoped she didn't, either.

Suddenly, Laurie clasped his hands between hers. "I have to talk with you, Lake."

"About what?" He pulled his fingers free of her grasp.

After a three-month absence, seeing her again stirred up old feelings within him. Not attraction. More like turmoil and resentment. He had loved this woman for two years. While they were together, he cared deeply for her. However, the way she broke things off with him left a bad taste in his mouth. Seeing her sit across from him as if she still belonged at his table filled him with angst and worry. What would Irish say about this unexpected meeting?

"The rumor around town is that your marriage is fake." Laurie said the last word in a whisper. "That it's all for the money. I didn't think you'd go through with getting your inheritance. You were so conflicted about it. But Lake—"

"Hey, honey!" Irish stood beside him and smoothed her hand gently over his shoulder.

He hadn't heard her walk over to him. How much of Laurie's comments did she hear?

"Irish. Have a seat."

"I've missed you so much." She embraced him enthusiastically.

He patted her back. Laurie's gaze, maybe everyone's in the coffee shop, turned toward them.

Irish leaned back, her eyes glistening at him. She smiled and blinked slowly like she was sending him a message. When her lips brushed against his tentatively, then with more passion, he kissed her back like she was his lifesaver, and he needed her breath to survive. For those few seconds, her kissing and affection freed him from Laurie's scrutiny and assessment of their marriage being fake and from his lingering feelings toward his ex, good or bad.

Irish broke away first and turned toward Laurie. "Hey, there. It's nice to see you again. Laurie, isn't it?"

"Uh, yes." Laurie glanced between Lake and Irish with a shocked expression. "I should get going. We'll talk later, hmm?" She eyed Lake.

He didn't answer, shrug, or anything.

"Don't let me intrude." Irish nodded toward the counter where Wilks took orders. "I'll get our usual, okay, sweet lips?"

"Sure." He didn't know what to make of her calling him cutesy names. But his heart still pounded hard after her kiss, even if the romantic display was mostly for Laurie's benefit.

Irish hurried over to the ordering line.

"I guess all the rumors weren't true," Laurie murmured. "When I saw you in here alone, looking handsome and possibly available, I thought maybe—"

"What? That you and I might get back together?" Confidence surged through him, which had much to do with Irish and his feelings toward her. He needed to let any lingering emotions and thoughts about Laurie go. He was already married to the woman he wanted to be with!

"I made a terrible mistake when I broke things off with you. Especially since you went through with the inheritance." Laurie made a pouty expression he used to think was cute. Now, the look seemed manipulative. "Can you find it in your heart to forgive me? We could pick up where we left off. Start fresh."

Was she joking? Her words shocked him. And gave him clarity.

"We aren't getting back together, Laurie. I'm married." He pointed at his wedding ring. "You said my marriage is fake, but you're wrong. This discussion is because of the money I received, isn't it?"

"I'm surprised, is all. You never cared about money. Marrying a girl you don't love to get it? I guess you aren't the man I thought you were."

"I don't suppose I am." He took a deep breath and met Irish's gaze across the room. Her smile sent his heart into overdrive again. She rocked her eyebrows like she was reminding him of their kiss. And, boy, was he remembering! He smiled back at her, thinking of the intoxicating passion he experienced with her.

He felt like a new man. This conversation with Laurie needed to end. But he was curious about something. "Did you ever love me? Was anything real between us?"

"After the obscene way that woman kissed you, and the way you kissed her back"—she nearly snarled at him—"I doubt what we had was anything close to real. You never kissed me so passionately."

"I respected your boundaries."

"What boundaries were those, sweet lips?" Irish dropped into the chair next to him.

"Never mind." Laurie stood. "It was nice seeing you, Lake. This concludes my desire to ever speak with you again." She pivoted away and stomped toward the door.

"Well, well," Irish said.

Lake exhaled. That was over. He kissed his wife's cheek. "Thank you. What you did helped me through a tough situation."

"Kissing you? Any time. Does she want you back?"

"Thanks to you, not anymore."

"I'm glad to hear it."

"I wonder who's been filling her head with stories about us." He peered toward his brother working behind the serving counter.

"Wilks? No doubt, it was one of his gags."

"I feel like gagging him, all right."

The brother in question dropped Irish's vanilla latte in front of her and Lake's black coffee in front of him. "My ears are burning."

"As they should be." Lake was tempted to grab his work shirt like he had his coat the other day. "What did you tell Laurie about Irish and me? Did she ask about the inheritance?"

Wilks held out his hands in an innocent gesture. "Why would I talk about what everyone in town already knows?" He sent Irish a mischievous grin. "I may have mentioned that your hot wife was all caught up in the money."

"Wilks!"

"Enjoy your drinks." Whistling, he strode back to the work counter.

Lake groaned. "Sorry about that."

Irish brushed her warm finger down his cheek. "Your brother said I'm hot. I wonder what my handsome husband thinks of me."

"I'd like the chance to tell you."

"Yeah?"

Their gazes caught and held. If they were at the cabin, even in the truck, Lake would take Irish in his arms and show her what he thought of her. He was ready to pursue his wife without any regrets.

"About your ex, do we need to discuss that?"

"Nope. My 'hot' wife took care of the situation." He pulled her to him for a brief kiss. Then he settled his arm over her shoulder, and she rested against his side as they sipped their drinks. His coffee tasted surprisingly good, but whether that was due to Wilks's coffee-making skills or his own contentment with the woman sitting beside him, he was uncertain.

After how she kissed him in front of Laurie and how close they were sitting together now, if Wilks or anyone in town still thought they had a fake marriage, they were blind!

Chapter Fifty-five

Irish arrived at the animal shelter after her coffee date with Lake and was surprised to hear two male voices shouting back in the kennel room. The dogs sounded worked up too. What in the world?

"I am authorized to take four of these dogs!" a man yelled in a deep husky tone.

"Over my dead body!" Benson said emphatically.

"You can't stop me from doing my job!"

"Yes, I can. Get out of here! Or I'll make you leave!"

Irish ran into the room where a dozen dogs barked frantically. Bright Eyes and a couple other dogs snarled toward a large, fiftyish man dressed in a stained gray winter onesie that sported a dirty nametag of "Walter." "What are you doing here?" Irish marched right over to stand beside Benson, who stood like a sentinel between the guy and the puppies.

"I'm here to pick up the dogs who are on my list to be euthanized." The guy raised his clipboard and thumped it with his thick finger.

"None of these animals are on a kill list!" Benson's face was deep red, and his eyes bulged.

"I am taking the four dogs—all older or aggressive animals. I have my orders!"

"I'm in charge here." Irish pointed at herself. "Show me this work order."

"Who are you? Where's Mac?"

"Mac agreed to this disgusting practice?" She glared at the worker with disdain.

"We have a standing agreement. I pick up the animals on the list once a month."

Irish gaped at him, unable to believe such a cruel practice existed. And Mac condoned it? He was a worse manager than the weasel she had previously judged him to be.

"It can't be true!" Benson held up his clenched fist like he'd punch the guy.

"No, it certainly can't be. I'm Irish North, the manager of this animal shelter. And that's what it is—a protective shelter!" She squinted harshly at the man she'd like to see thrown behind bars. "Your company's association with this facility ends this minute. If I had the power to stop you from making any more pickups across the state or the region, I would." She pulsed her finger toward the door. "Leave now. And never come back here. Or so help me—"

"You won't get away with this," Walter muttered, his lips flattening. "I have a contract for the year."

"The person you made that contract with is gone. Your filthy, slimy agreement with him is null and void. You have me to deal with now. And deal with me, you shall!"

"And me." Benson glowered.

"Fine. But I'm within my legal rights." Walter shot Irish and Benson dirty looks. "You will be hearing from my attorney."

"Good! I have one too." Irish stood taller. "Whatever legal rights you think you have won't stand up against the fight we'll give you. You're trespassing. Leave now!"

Walter's face turned so wine-colored he looked about to implode. He alternated between spitting and cussing all the way to the door. Casting one last sneer in her direction, he stomped out and slammed the door.

"Good riddance!" A blast of cold air hit Irish, but it felt soothing against her hot cheeks and livid temper.

"Wow. Mrs. North, you were amazing!" Benson shook her hand like he might have done if she had saved his life. "I'll never let anyone say anything bad about you again."

"Who's saying bad stuff about me?"

"Never mind. Thank you for standing up to the jerk. I thought I was going to have to belt him!"

"So I noticed. Thanks for feeling so strongly about protecting the animals here." She lifted her chin. "Now, let's get busy. Take extra care with Bright Eyes and her pups. Mama dog is riled."

"I will. I promise."

Over the last few days, Irish had avoided spending time with Little Dipper. But feeling unsettled and wanting to calm down Bright Eyes, she petted her and the puppies, and then cuddled Little Dipper. The special way the puppy sagged in her arms and the sweet scent of his warm breath on her face made him irresistible. Maybe she'd return and spend more time holding him this afternoon.

She went into her office to call Lake and explain what happened. He sounded concerned and prompted her to call Michael herself. So she gathered information from Mac's archaic filing system and called their lawyer. Michael promised to investigate the situation and deal with it promptly. She thanked him, and mentally thanked Lake for having enough money to afford a lawyer they could turn to in a crisis.

After the phone call, Irish faced the pile of paperwork on her desk with greater confidence and pride in her work as a manager.

A couple of hours later, the outer door creaked open. Following the last encounter, Irish tensed, wishing she'd locked up for the day.

"Hello?" a woman called.

"Be right there." Irish saved the spreadsheet she was working on, then strode into the reception area.

A mid-thirties woman with short black hair smiled. "Hello. I'm Jazzy Martin."

"How can I help you?"

"My mom and your mother-in-law have been friends for many years." She strode forward until only the receptionist counter separated them. "I'm sorry to barge in like this, but Liv mentioned to Mom that you might need a receptionist-slash-secretary."

"She did?" Lake must have told his mom about her firing Shelley. "I do need someone."

"I'm available." Jazzy spread out her arms. "I'd love to apply for the job. I get along well with dogs and cats."

"Do you have any office experience?"

"Sure do. I was a receptionist at a dentist's office in Sandpoint."

Irish opened a notebook and jotted down Jazzy's name. "Which dentist?"

"Dr. Arlison. I left on good terms. My maternity leave turned into a longer thing because I wanted more time with my daughter."

"How old is your child?"

"Six months. It's time to find another job and leave my grandmother's house. She used to be Pastor North's secretary. Marla Scarlett."

"She's an acquaintance of my father-in-law?"

"That's right." Jazzy smoothed her hands over the countertop. "They've known each other since he came to Thunder Ridge to be our pastor over thirty years ago."

"Do you know Lake?"

"Only all my life! I was shocked to hear he married on the sly." She grinned and winked. "I think he got the better deal with you than Laurie."

"How's that?" Irish underlined Jazzy Martin's name twice on her sheet of paper.

"Laurie is sweet as honey when she wants to be. But they didn't have—" She shrugged, and her cheeks darkened. "Honestly, they were boring together."

"Is that right?" Irish liked Jazzy more by the second.

"Lake and I were only ever friends. He was like my brother." She stared intensely at Irish. "You never have to worry about him and me or anything."

"Why should I worry?"

"Laurie did." Jazzy heaved a sigh. "She accused me of going after her boyfriend. It was nonsense jealousy."

Irish swallowed hard. "She didn't believe you weren't romantically involved?"

"Nope. But growing up, Lake was my buddy. My twin sister and I felt part of his gang of brothers." She tapped her thumb against her chest. "I know more about the mischief those North boys got into than their parents do. But Lake and I were pals and skiing buddies. Nothing else!"

So, this woman had personal information on Lake and his brothers? That might come in handy!

"When can you start?" Irish pulled out a job application from the file drawer. "I'll double-check your references. But otherwise?"

"Tomorrow. Or whenever." Jazzy grinned.

"Great." Irish slid the application across the desk. "Have a seat and fill this out. I hope we'll make a good team."

"Sounds wonderful."

Later, Irish called Smith. "Hey, this is Irish."

"I'm glad to hear from my favorite daughter-in-law."

"Your only daughter-in-law."

"Moot point. How can I help you?" His tone changed from fatherly to more pastoral.

"I have a Jazzy Martin applying for a receptionist job at the animal shelter. She used you as a reference. Says her grandmother worked for you."

"That's right. Mrs. Scarlett was an outstanding secretary. I officiated at Jazzy and her sister's dedication," he said with a proud tone. "They were involved in our Sunday school program and youth group through the years."

"Regarding work ethic, would you recommend her as a receptionist at the shelter?"

"Absolutely. If she's half the worker Mrs. Scarlett was, you'll have a gem of an employee."

"Any reason you know of for me not hiring her?"

Was there the slightest pause? "Not a one." Smith sighed like he might have something else on his mind, but he didn't say what, and Irish didn't inquire about it.

They talked about the dogs, then she ended the call. After checking with Jazzy's previous employer and receiving a glowing report, she called and offered her the job. Jazzy Martin would start tomorrow.

With the task accomplished, some of Irish's work-related burdens were lifted. Her crew now included one kennel worker and a receptionist. Things were looking up! The employee list would be complete if she hired one more person to assist with the dogs and take care of the grounds. She was putting off the task of finding a permanent manager. And praying about it, too.

Her cell phone buzzed, and Lake's name crossed the screen.

"Hey, beautiful."

His soft voice stirred up delicious sensations within her. Between that kiss she gave him at the coffee shop and the memory of their date-night kissing, thoughts of lip-locking with him kept circling in her brain.

"How's it going?" she asked a little breathlessly.

"I told my mom about you needing a receptionist. I thought she might spread the word."

"Oh, she did! Your friend Jazzy came by. I checked her employment record. Then hired her."

"You did? Why didn't you call me? I would have vouched for her."

"She didn't list you as a reference." Why was he so interested in her mundane tasks at the animal shelter, anyway? As quickly as the troublesome thought crossed her mind, she remembered how he purchased the land, which could have caused the shelter and her a lot of grief. And how he urged her to call the lawyer earlier. He was trying to help her, which was sweet, kind, and so like him. "She mentioned you were *only* friends."

"That's right. We grew up in the same Sunday school classes. Same grade in school."

"Did you know Laurie doubted your platonic relationship?"

Lake went silent. Had she pushed a sore button?

He huffed out a breath that sounded more like a moan. "Laurie was insanely jealous of her. She doubted a male-female friendship existed without ending in kisses and doing other things."

"That never happened between you and Jazzy?"

"No!"

"Okay. I believe you," she spoke quietly so Benson wouldn't hear her. "Here's the deal. All your stuff with Laurie and you is in the past. Now, there's you and me. That's what we need to focus on."

"Sounds good to me. Just us and six dogs."

Seven, if she got her wish. But she wouldn't mention it now.

"Your past love life doesn't affect me unless the person in question gets in my face."

"Like Laurie did in the coffee shop?"

"That's right."

"Then you have to stake your claim?"

"And stake it well." Some heat flooded her face.

"Sweetheart, you can stake your claim on me whenever you want," he said huskily.

Her heart pounded in her ears.

"Did you hear me?"

"Oh, I heard." In her thoughts, her lips were already meeting his.

"Are you going to give him a try?"

"Huh?" What did she miss? "I must have fogged out what you said."

He chuckled like he guessed what she was thinking about. "I asked Finn to work with our dogs on a trial basis. Sunday might be available as a part-time worker at the shelter."

"Sure. Right. Sunday." Her brain felt muddled with her thoughts and feelings toward Lake. "I'll shoot him a text."

"Great. Maybe I can pitch in with painting the building when the weather warms up."

"Really?"

Was he taking her suggestion to heart about giving more of himself to the animal shelter? Or was he volunteering because he cared for her and what she cared about? Either way, his offer was endearing.

"Perhaps we could work on it together," he said as if he'd asked her on a date.

"I'd like that a lot."

"Good. Maybe we could hire a landscape company to spruce up the grounds, too."

"That would be great. Thanks, Lake."

"Of course. Want me to fix dinner tonight?"

"Do I ever not want you to fix dinner?"

"I'm pretty sure you like my cooking." It sounded like he grinned.

"That and a few other things." She ended the call before he said anything else, or before she made promises she might not want to keep later.

Nevertheless, something was happening between them. Every conversation felt laced with undercurrents of romance and flirtation. Or marital love? Whatever it was, she felt on the edge of taking the next step with her husband.

Chapter Fifty-six

Pal, Ice, and Rambler responded well to Finn hanging around the kennels and yard since they already knew him. But Irish's trio was skittish, barking and acting wary of him. When he pulled out a package of jerky, it worked like stardust to relieve their angst and help them calm down. Finn's ability to get along with the various dogs seemed like a godsend. "This gig will be a paid position, right?" he asked while petting Aurora's neck and chest.

Why did Lake's brothers doubt his willingness to pay them? Especially now that he had the inheritance funds? "If I hire you, it'll be a paying job."

"Good."

"Do you like working with the dogs enough to come to my next race?" He needed to move this visit toward a serious commitment. If Finn didn't work out, he'd ask Sunday. He'd advertise for the position if neither of his youngest brothers worked well enough. "It'll be Pal and Ice. Not the whole pack."

"Isn't Irish racing?"

"Aurora hurt her paw during the last race, so Irish wants to give her a longer break. And with her work schedule, she hasn't been able to practice with her dogs like usual."

"Aren't you two married?" Finn asked with a scowl.

"What's that supposed to mean?"

"What's hers is yours, right? Or is it just what's yours, namely your money, belongs to her?"

"What's this about?" Was Finn going to say something rude to get him riled like Wilks and Spur had? He wasn't falling for that trick again! "Why the remarks about Irish?"

Finn moved on to Rambler, petting the dog and making his tail flip back and forth like a fly swatter. "I think the marry-the-girl-for-the-money thing stinks."

"I'm sorry it bothers you. Let it go, will you?"

"You, Hud, and Coe said you'd never go that route." Finn's expression resembled that of a grumpy teenager more than a twenty-two-year-old man.

"I know. All right?" Despite his self-lecture, Lake tensed.

"If she gets to do what she wants with your money, why can't you do what you want with her dogs? What's the big deal about you training her dogs if she doesn't have the time?" Finn thrust out his hand toward Lake. "I thought you had more—"

"More what?" Maybe taking on his punk brother as an employee was more trouble than it was worth. Hiring someone outside the family sounded more inviting by the second.

"Strength. Fortitude. Male prowess." Finn grabbed the wooden-handled shovel and scooped up a pile of dog droppings. He forcefully tossed it over the fence onto the heap.

"Because you 'might' work for me, I'll say this once," Lake spoke stiffly, not only from the chill air but from the anger strumming through his veins. "Irish's dogs are like her kids. The same goes for mine. If you agree to work at my kennels, you'll do what I say about my dogs and the property and do what she wants with her dogs. Irish and I are a team."

"Seriously? I'll be taking orders from her?"

"Yes, you will! She and I are partners—real married partners! Just like Dad and Mom raised us to be respectful and loving to our spouse, just like they were respectful and loving to each other, Irish and I are going to be that way with one another." Lake's voice rose stronger with each point. "Now, tell me if you don't like this arrangement of working for both of us, and I'll look for a more willing employee."

The silence was powerful. Finn continued shoveling for several minutes without speaking.

"So, what's it going to be? Can you abide by our terms for the job?"

"Yes. Fine." Finn abruptly returned the shovel to the corner of the shed. "What else do I need to learn about this job?"

Despite the tension between them, Lake finished guiding his brother through the feeding routines of his dogs, then of Irish's dogs. He showed him how to clip Pal to a hip belt for skijoring.

"You want me to run only Pal?"

"Pal and Ice. Rambler doesn't know what he's doing yet." Lake thought of the scrapes he'd received from the young dog trying to break free. He lifted a leash off a hook. "Walk him once daily to get him used to being clipped and doing what he's told."

"All right."

"Feed and water Irish's dogs per her specifications. Unless she tells you to run her dogs, don't."

"I get it. She's the queen and—"

"You'll show respect for my wife or else find other employment!"

"Sorry." Finn grimaced like the word was distasteful.

What was with him today? Did Spur instill this angst toward Irish in him? He thought of Laurie's younger sister, Bella. Weren't she and Finn friends?

Lake clapped him on the shoulder. "What's got your goat about Irish and me?"

"Other than you breaking the agreement with your brothers?" Finn jerked away from him.

"Yeah, other than that. Is it Bella? Have you two been comparing notes?"

"Sort of. We were dating undercover."

"Undercover?"

"You and Laurie. Me and Bella."

"I don't care if you and Bella like each other."

"Fat chance of that happening now." Finn cast him a cold, glinting gaze. "After you and Laurie broke up, her parents threatened to disown her if she went out with any of the North brothers. Some reputation we have."

"Laurie's the one who broke it off with me!"

"For good reason, right?"

"What's that supposed to mean?" Lake demanded in a low tone.

"Like you don't know!" Finn blew out a noisy breath. "Her folks said you flirted with Jazzy the whole time you dated Laurie."

"That's not true!" Lake's fists tightened, his fingernails digging into his palms. "We've been friends since we were toddlers."

"Laurie told them she caught you holding Jazzy's hand. Sitting close on the couch."

"No way!" A memory hit him, and he released his clenched fists. "She'd just found out she was pregnant. Going to raise her child alone. I was feeling—"

"Responsible?" Finn shot Lake a judgmental glare.

"No! Why would I? Wait. Are you implying I'm Jasmine's dad?"

"Laurie's parents thought so."

"That's not—" Lake groaned loudly. "Don't you think I would have stepped up to being a father by now if Jasmine was mine? Is this some prank you're pulling?"

"No! I'm not pulling a prank! You probably wanted to keep the North name unblemished." Finn's Adam's apple bobbed up and down. "Hide the affair because Dad's a pastor."

"Oh, good grief! Seriously? You thought Jazzy had my child, and I did nothing to help her? All to save face? Unbelievable!"

"What about holding her hand? Taking her to doctor's appointments? Providing groceries?" Finn ticked off the points as if they were grievances.

"Doing kindnesses for a friend doesn't mean I was unfaithful to my fiancée." Lake pointed at Finn's jalopy. "Maybe you should go. We should rethink the job idea."

"I'll say. It's hard for North brothers to keep their word."

"Finn, you are trying my patience!" Lake clenched his right fist, ready to sock him in the nose.

"Going to put me in my place, now that you're the big rich landowner?"

"No, I'm going to put you in your place because you listened to lies about me and accepted them as truth. Because you thought I might care about the North name more than I cared about my daughter!" He punched the air instead of Finn's nose. "When you first heard about this from Bella, you should have asked me. I thought we had honor among the brothers."

"Is that what you think you have? Honor?" Finn thrust out his arms demonstratively. "Marrying a woman for money? Marrying her outside of love? I'd say you're honorless! Integrity-less! I'm out of here!" He jumped into his car, started the engine, and sped out of the drive, his tires spinning and squealing.

Lake fought the urge to roar in frustration. Laurie, Bella, their parents, and Finn thought he had fathered a child and then went on with his life as if he were an irresponsible parent? That burned in his chest like a consuming fire.

Who else knew about this lie and believed it?

Chapter Fifty-seven

Ever since Irish arrived home to prepare for dinner at Liv and Smith's house, Lake had been acting sullen and non-talkative. He answered her questions in one-word responses and avoided meeting her gaze. She couldn't think of anything she said or did to bring on this level of moodiness.

It had been only four days since their date and passionate kissing. Things had been going well between them. What happened to bring about this change in Lake's feelings toward her?

Now they sat in his pickup outside his parents' house, the engine running, him staring forward with his hands clutching the steering wheel.

"I have something to tell you," he said glumly.

"All right. What is it?"

The door to Smith and Liv's house opened, a flood of light splashing across the porch. The door shut again.

"Rumors are going around town."

"About us having a fake relationship?" Irritation spiked through her. Was this what Benson was talking about yesterday?

"No. About me and … Jazzy." He said the woman's name as if it were painful to pronounce.

"What about you and her?"

"I'm only saying this in case the topic comes up tonight." He met her gaze then, and his brows wrinkled. "She and I never dated."

"She told me that. So did you." Most of Irish's tension drained away. "Didn't I already tell you I believed you?"

"Yeah, but we never—"

"I know. Jazzy assured me she was a pal to you. Nothing more." She patted Lake's arm. "So what's the rumor that has you all tied up in knots?"

He cleared his throat. "That I'm her daughter's father."

"What? That's crazy!"

His eyes filled with moisture like he was a breath away from bawling. Pain and anguish oozed from his expression.

She wanted to wrap her arms around the big oaf. But she also needed to hear his explanation, so she didn't move. "Tell me about it, please."

"Finn says there's a rumor going around Thunder Ridge that I'm … that I'm Jasmine's dad. A deadbeat dad." His lower lip wobbled. "I haven't seen Jazzy much for the last couple of months. But that's because she's been busy being a mom and I've been busy with the dogs and everything. Not because I'm avoiding her or her child! The rumor is all a lie!"

"Ah, sweetie," she whispered. "You can't let what other people say about you bother you like this. You and I know the truth."

"You do?"

"Yes, I do." She gave his shoulders a little shake. "I can testify to you being an honest man. If you were a child's father, you would own up to it immediately. I'm one hundred percent certain of that."

He exhaled a shaky breath. "Thank you. That means a lot to me. More than you'll ever know."

"I think I understand the gravity of this. And the reality of small-town gossip." She moved her palms to his warm cheeks and smoothed her fingers along his scruffy jaw. The pads of her fingers tingled with the caress.

"Thank you for understanding. I was so worried." Lake didn't look quite like the wounded puppy he did moments ago.

"Who do you think is behind the rumors?"

"Bella. Laurie's kid sister."

"Which means Laurie?"

"Maybe."

"It's going to be all right." Irish kissed him softly on the lips, moving her hands to his chest. "We won't let the rumor ruin our time with your family, okay?"

"They've probably heard of the speculation and kept it from me."

"We don't know that." She scooted closer to him, smoothing her hands over his shoulders. "I think what you need is a little distraction. Something to get your mind off the gossip."

"Yeah?" His breath seemed to catch. "Are you offering to be my distraction?"

"Maybe I am." She kissed him again, taking her time, teasing his lips, and stroking her fingers through his hair.

He made a muffled groan and pulled her into his arms. His lips met hers tenderly again and again. He tasted of mint and coffee. She enjoyed being in his arms, being close to his heart, kissing him as warmly and passionately as he kissed her.

Someone pounded on the window. "What's going on in there?"

They drew slightly apart.

"Wilks," Lake growled.

Irish didn't even glance out the window. "So, was that a good distraction?"

"I'll say." He brushed his lips across her cheek. "Thank you, Irish."

"Any time."

They stared into each other's eyes as if they'd never done so before. Lake's eyes glistened, a tender smile playing on his lips. All she wanted to do was stay right here with him. They were so close to the precipice of falling in love—she could sense it in every touch and kiss between them.

Finally, Wilks got the hint that they weren't in a hurry to leave the truck. He trudged back toward the house.

Even though Irish wanted to forget about tonight's dinner and continue kissing Lake, Liv must have the meal ready by now. It wasn't polite of them to keep everyone waiting.

Still, she wanted to do something first. "Before heading into your parents' house, do you mind if we pray together?"

"Not at all. That's sweet of you to suggest it." Lake smoothed his fingers down her cheek. "You're really something, Irish."

"You're pretty special too." She took a breath. "I like us talking to God together. Praying and believing for good to happen in our lives and our marriage has encouraged me."

"I feel that way too. Like praying together is binding our hearts closer." He clasped her hands, then took the lead in their prayer. "Lord, I'm sorry for how overwhelmed I became today. Thank You for sending Irish to be my wife and share my struggles. I thank You for her." He smiled at her again. "Thank you for being here with me, sweetheart."

"I wouldn't want to be anywhere else." She peered through the windshield at the dark sky. "Lord, please help all the gossip Lake heard about today to quiet down and dissolve into nothingness as if it never happened. We give it all to You." She squeezed Lake's hands and gazed into his eyes.

Accept Lake as the man God planned for you. Accept this marriage as a perfect answer for both of you." Trish's words floated through her thoughts.

"Also"—she closed her eyes for a moment—"thank You for giving me Lake to be my husband. For giving us each other to journey through this life together."

"Amen," he whispered, then kissed her again.

When they left the pickup, he kept his arm around her all the way into the house. He helped her remove her coat and pulled out her chair at the long dinner table laden with baked salmon, fried rice, bacon-and-onion french beans, and homemade applesauce. Once they were seated side by side, he clasped her hand beneath the table.

She sighed, thankful for the chance for their hearts to meet on a deeper level this evening. Seeing Lake as distraught as he was in the truck, she saw another side of the man she married. His tortured expression made her want to kick Laurie in the backside. Or else thank her profusely. After all, the gossip brought Irish and Lake closer together.

She'd heard of God taking bad things and turning them into good. Something about beauty for ashes. It seemed He did that tonight. And she thanked Him for it.

Chapter Fifty-eight

After his discussion with Irish and their kissing in the truck, Lake couldn't keep his gaze off his wife during the meal. In a matter of seconds, she'd neutralized his feelings of worry over how she might react to the rumors. Her taking them in stride, saying she believed him, and then kissing him as she did? How had he been so blessed to marry a woman as beautiful and understanding as her? And one as passionate!

If any of his brothers said a bad thing about her in the future, he'd make them eat dirt!

Finn sat kitty-corner from Lake and Irish. Hopefully he wouldn't bring up anything about their discussion from earlier. Right now, Lake was incredibly thankful for Mom's rule about no troublesome topics being discussed at the table.

His gaze met Irish's a few times as they ate. Once, she winked at him, and he nearly choked on his fried rice.

"So, what's the news?" Spur asked as soon as everyone's plates were empty.

Dad clasped Mom's hand, and their gazes met. Only then did Lake notice the strained looks on their faces. Something must be troubling them. Was one of them ill? Had they heard the gossip about him and Jazzy?

Lake clasped Irish's hand beneath the table, preparing himself for bad news. She gave his hand a slight squeeze like she understood his worry.

"After much prayer, I've decided to take a sabbatical from pastoring," Dad said.

A sabbatical? That wasn't such bad news.

"Aren't you old enough to retire?" Finn asked in his dramatic fashion. "You're what, nearly eighty?"

"Finney!" Mom said.

"You aren't coming to Hawaii with me, are you?" Spur asked in a mortified tone.

"Definitely not." Dad shook his head.

"What a relief!" Spur wiped imaginary sweat off his forehead.

Lake chuckled at his overreaction.

"The break will be for two months," Dad explained. "Plenty of time for me to think about retiring."

"So you are considering it?" Sunday asked.

"I am. Lake and Irish gave Mom and me a lovely gift." Dad nodded toward them. "We'll be taking a cruise. Spending time together on a Caribbean beach. Won't we, Livvy?"

"Yes! And maybe we'll sit at the lake here and stare at the sky for a few days straight." Mom chuckled. "We've been on the go for thirty-five years!"

Mom and Dad smiled tenderly at each other, sharing one of those private moments Lake envied.

"Whenever you retire, will you stay in this house?" It was hard to picture his folks living anywhere but here.

"The house is ours." Dad shrugged. "We can keep the place or sell it."

"We may put the old girl on the market and get a smaller house for Granny Trish and us." Mom patted Gran's hand in a loving gesture. "A place that's easier for seniors to take care of."

"Who are you calling a senior?" Gran asked in a faux offended tone.

"Just Smith and myself." Mom winked.

"For now, this will be a time for us to talk and pray." Dad scuffed his chair closer to the table. "When we return from our trip, hopefully, we'll have decided what's next. I hope you'll all be praying for us in our absence."

"Of course we will," Gran said.

Everyone else agreed.

What would it be like if Dad wasn't pastoring? Or if he and Mom moved away from Thunder Ridge? Had something happened in the church to cause him to consider retiring now?

"Hey!" Wilks snapped his fingers. "If you aren't a pastor, maybe people will stop calling us the preacher's sons."

"Wilks North, you boys will have that honorable nickname for your whole lives." Gran smiled proudly at Dad.

"Your grandmother's right. I'll always be a preacher at heart. When I was young, I wanted to be a pastor and have a big family." Dad gazed around the table. "I've been blessed with both."

"That you have." Gran dabbed her napkin beneath her eyes.

"Never got your championship baseball team," Sunday said teasingly.

"No. But we had fun trying."

"If it weren't for Stone, you would have!" Wilks chortled. "Too bad he got banished from the league."

"Now, now. He isn't here to defend himself." Although she sounded serious, Mom smiled. "I remember the day he stormed off the field with an umpire on his heels."

"Me too!" Dad rolled his eyes.

The group laughed at the shared memory.

"If there's one reason the Lord hasn't called me home yet, it's because that boy needs my prayers." Gran sighed.

"I have a burden for Stone, too." Dad nodded at her. "And I hope you are still with us for a long time, Mom."

"Me too," Lake agreed, feeling the emotional tenderness between Dad and Granny Trish.

"You've been a good dad to your boys, Smith." Tears flooded Gran's eyes. "You know Stone's wandering isn't your fault, right?"

A quietness settled across the room. It seemed everyone awaited Dad's answer.

"It's hard not to wonder what I could have done differently."

"Every parent wonders that."

"We heard from Coe," Mom said, steering the conversation to a lighter topic.

"What's that scallywag up to?" Spur asked.

"Feeding the hungry, helping build an orphanage, and repairing houses after flooding destroyed some homes. Pretty good for a 'scallywag.'"

"He plans to come back soon." Dad clasped his hands together, shaking them like a victory sign during their old baseball games. "Maybe he'll apply for a certain pastorate that might be available."

Coe pastoring at Thunder Ridge Fellowship? That didn't seem like him. But Lake didn't voice the objection.

"Except he isn't married!" Wilks said.

"Why is that a problem?" Irish tugged on Lake's arm.

"Unless the church board changes their expectations about the pastor being married, Coe is out of luck."

"Some staunch members still hold to the old bylaws." Dad rubbed the back of his neck. "I hope they'll ease up on the next pastor."

"Coe may find the perfect girl before then." Mom's smile looked wistful.

"Maybe he'll pick one out of a hat like Lake did," Wilks muttered.

"Wilkerson!" Mom exclaimed.

"Sorry." Wilks leaned toward Irish. "We like to pick on Lake."

"Why is that?" She linked her palm into the crook of Lake's arm. "From what I've seen, he's a great brother. Why do you like to pull pranks and make snarky comments toward him?"

"Yeah, why is that?" Lake sat up straighter.

"The guy at the top needs to be taken down a peg." Wilks wagged his thumb between himself and the other brothers. "We are the chosen ones for the job."

Lake groaned.

"They've always sparred." Mom picked up her plate, signaling it was time to clear the table. "I hope my sons remember to be kind toward each other, no matter how old they get."

"That's right, Olivia. They are the best friends they'll ever have." Gran's gaze encompassed them all.

Lake smiled at the phrase he'd heard many times growing up. Thinking of the closer friendship he'd like to develop with Irish, he put his arm over her shoulder. He'd thank her later for standing up for him the way she did. But right this minute, he enjoyed the envious looks being shot in his direction from his brothers.

Chapter Fifty-nine

Irish sat on the loveseat in the cabin, sipping her hot tea and wondering if Lake would come out of his room. Maybe he didn't trust himself after their kissing in the truck earlier. Perhaps she didn't trust herself either.

She had more intense feelings toward him than for any other man she had ever dated. No doubt about it. She was falling for her husband. Once she lost her heart to him, there was no going back.

When he'd acted so worried before entering his parents' house that someone might be rude about Jazzy and him at dinner, she fell more in love with him.

Fell more in love? That's what was happening, right? She was falling head over heels for Lake. But was it a lasting love like Smith and Liv had found? A love that could survive all the ups and downs of married life?

Suddenly, Irish longed for the happily ever after she had wished for before she got jaded about marriage. Back when she believed in love's power to heal and breach the gap between two wounded souls. Did she even think that now? Was she willing to risk her pride and all the emotional armor she'd surrounded herself with to keep from ever needing a man like her mother did so many times?

Was she willing to risk everything to be vulnerable with Lake? To love him as her husband?

She blew out a long, slow breath.

A married couple probably had to become vulnerable and tenderhearted to love one another. And with that openness would come all the possibilities of getting hurt emotionally. All the chances of their marriage not working, too. Yet, the only other option was for her and Lake to live in protective mode, indefinitely wary of love and true intimacy.

Which way did she want to live her life? She told Lake she believed in him. She defended him to his brothers. She felt lucky that he'd married her. That he shared his wealth with the animal shelter and with her too. She truly felt blessed to be a part of his life, including his commitment to his dogs and family.

But where did that leave him and her?

Lord, please help us. Help me to love You more. And to fall more in love with my husband.

She'd been talking to God more since her discussions with Liv and Trish, and since she and Lake had been praying together. The faith and grace they spoke of made sense as she saw it expressed in their lives. She found herself yearning for something more. A deeper relationship with God. And a deeper connection with Lake.

His bedroom door clicked open.

The scuffing sound of his bare feet crossing the room sent tingles up her spine. He proceeded to the kitchen counter without speaking.

She should try to tell him what she was feeling. Was she brave enough to be that honest with him? What if he wasn't falling in love with her like she was with him?

Gripping his steaming mug, Lake dropped down beside her and let out a long sigh. She watched him in profile. His jaw muscles tightened and released, then tightened again. What was he thinking about with such a serious expression? She thought he'd gotten over his angst about the rumors. Was this about his dad possibly resigning? Or was it about him and her?

"I hoped you'd come back in here."

He met her gaze. "Is that right?"

"When we kissed back in the truck?"

"Yeah?" He blinked slowly.

Was he sensing the emotional drawing together she was experiencing? At what stage of love was he? Step one—butterflies in the tummy? Step two—wanting to kiss all the time? Step three—wanting more than stealing kisses in his pickup?

Their gazes held, and Irish felt like she balanced on a precipice. Tell him? Or not?

"When we were kissing, I realized something." She set down her cup on the end table, wanting her hands free to clutch together in her lap. Or to wrap around Lake's shoulders *if* they kissed again. "I'm, uh, well—" She huffed. "I'm falling in love with you."

"What?" His cup almost to his lips, his mouth dropped open. "You're falling—"

"You can't be that shocked about it!"

"But I am." Lowering his cup, he stared wide-eyed at her. "You are falling in love with me already?"

Already. So he wasn't falling in love with her yet? Not even after what happened between them in the truck? A pang of disappointment rushed through her, but she squelched it. It would be nice if they fell in love with each other simultaneously. But she couldn't expect his feelings to coincide with hers.

"Yes, I'm falling in love with you," she whispered. Heat rushed up her neck and arms.

A wide grin crossed Lake's lips, replacing his serious look. He set his mug on the end table, bumping it against hers. "You're telling me this now because—"

"I want you to know how I feel. I want us to be honest with each other about it." She clasped his hand. "I'm falling in love with you, Lake! There. I said it boldly and honestly!" She grinned widely too.

"Oh, sweetheart." He pulled her into his arms and kissed her softly.

What started as a gentle kiss quickly turned more passionate, and Irish kissed Lake back as heatedly as he kissed her. The warmth emanating from his chest through his sweatshirt reached her, warming her even more. She ran her hands over his hair, his scruffy face that she loved to touch, and then settled her palms on his shoulders.

"What about you?" She took a shallow breath. "You don't have to say the same words just because I told you. But what are you feeling? If I'm way ahead of you—"

"You're not."

Good. He felt something. But what?

He stroked his fingers down her cheek. Then he smoothed some strands of her hair between his fingers, staring at it like he was lost in thought.

"Every day I lose focus thinking about you and our future together." He pulled her gently against his chest again, her cheek leaning against the dip in his shoulder. "I imagine what it will be like when we fully share ourselves with each other." He settled her back slightly and tipped up her chin, their gazes meshing. "I mean in more ways than our bodies. Although, heaven knows I want that too."

She grinned, feeling joy coming straight from her heart.

Then they kissed again, slowly, tentatively. Their lips traveled across each other's cheeks and back to their lips again.

She was immensely taken with him, wanting more emotion and passion yet feeling cautious. Was she ready to ask him to share her room? Or should she put on the brakes until he gave her more verbal assurances of his feelings? His cuddling and kissing were sweet and provocative. What about love? Should she hold out for him to feel the emotional powerhouse she was experiencing?

"Lake?" She scooted away from him slightly, gazing into his shadowed eyes.

"Hmmm?" His lazy-sounding tone tickled her ears.

"You said I wasn't alone in how I feel. What about you?" She didn't need specific words. But she desperately needed to hear his heart.

Clasping her hands in his, he asked in an almost melodic tone, "How do I feel about my wife? That she's beautiful. Has a fiery temper I find challenging and alluring. I admire her passion and determination to go after whatever she wants." He took a deep breath. "Irish, I admire how you care for your dogs, putting their safety and needs before your wishes or dreams of victory. I appreciate how hard you've worked at the shelter. Being kind and loving with all the animals. I appreciate how you stood up for me tonight."

She leaned in to kiss him, grateful for what he said, but his index finger landing gently on her lips stopped her. What was wrong? What wasn't he saying?

Chapter Sixty

Lake held his finger lightly over Irish's warm lips. Everything within him wanted to kiss and kiss her. Maybe to carry her into their bedroom and spend their first night together. But he knew what she was hoping to hear first. His saying he loved her mattered to her. He knew it like he knew his next breath.

"Irish, I care for you too much not to be completely honest with you."

"Okay." Her shoulders heaved with her sigh. "Is this about Laurie?"

"What?" The woman's name startled him. "No, it has nothing to do with her! The day at the coffee shop when you kissed me in front of her ended any emotional ties or tender feelings that I carried for her. Your kisses, understanding, and how you've prayed with me lately have shown me that you are the person I want to be with more than anyone else."

"That's sweet, Lake. So what is it? What's troubling you?"

When she smoothed her hand down his cheek, he wanted to press his lips into the center of her palm and kiss it. Kiss her until morning.

"I know you want to hear—"

"What you feel toward me. Not any specific words."

"Are you sure?"

"Mmhmm." She brushed her lips over his jawline. "I'm your wife. You are my husband. Are you still planning to stay married to me?"

"Oh, sweetheart, yes." He kissed her three times in a row. "A hundred times, yes!"

"Then what are you feeling?" She set her palm gently over his pounding heart.

Leaning back against the couch, he raked his fingers through his hair. He dug within himself for honesty, even if it hurt. "After Laurie ended things with me, I gave up on ever finding love again. I was fine with never marrying! Then, when you and I agreed to get married for a cause we both believed in, I figured that was enough. I hoped we'd fall for each other eventually. Maybe even like my folks did." He clasped her hand loosely, toying with her wedding ring. "I'm falling for you faster than I thought possible, Irish. And that's the truth." He met her moist gaze and gulped at the tenderness he felt for her.

"Oh, Lake."

Instead of kissing him passionately, she wrapped her arms around him. He held her close, her heart beating against his chest. Their embrace was comforting. They cared for each other and were falling in love with one another. Love was a journey. One they were traveling on together, but they hadn't arrived yet.

"Thank you for believing in me." He needed to say this. "About Jazzy. About Laurie, too."

"You're welcome." She broke the embrace and settled back into the couch cushion close to his side. "In the past, I dated some rude and abrasive guys. I gave up on ever having a real relationship. That's why I pushed for that first kiss between us. If all I had to look forward to in marriage was chemistry, it had better be good!" She smiled, then sighed. "But I still want the other stuff. The deeper parts of marriage.

The sharing of good times and bad. The blending of bodies, souls, life experiences, and laughter."

"Me too. And that takes time." He clasped her hand again. "We married quickly, but I've learned so much about you in the last few weeks. I care deeply for you. I'm committed to you and our marriage. I promise to pursue you, and along the way, I will fall completely in love with you. And you with me." He kissed her lightly, hoping to engrave the promise on both their hearts.

She responded with a deeper kiss, which he eagerly returned. Their kisses heated up again, a sweet tenderness becoming more passionate and intense. Irish was the first to break away and stand. Lake took a deep breath.

When she smiled warmly at him, invitingly, and held out her hand toward him, he leaped to his feet and linked their fingers together. Their lips found each other's again like magnets that couldn't stay apart. Then his wife led him across the room and into her bedroom.

Chapter Sixty-one

"Go, Pal! Run hard, Ice!" Lake dug his ski poles into the packed ice, working his thighs harder than he had since his last race two weeks ago. His team was in the lead after passing another team on the trail—not Irish's since she decided not to compete today.

"Let's go, Pal! Good job, Ice!" he shouted as the finish line came into sight beyond the snow-covered field.

The competition for this two-day event wasn't as challenging or energetic without Irish yipping her victory calls. Nevertheless, Lake still enjoyed the camaraderie among the racers and the thrill of his dogs running in tandem, skiing hard, and the wind brushing against his face. He almost tasted victory, so long as he didn't hit slick ice or Pal didn't stop to relieve himself.

The cheers of the small crowd gathered to watch the skijoring and mushing event in Priest Lake, Idaho, rose as his team approached the finish line. Irish and Finn were both here to cheer him on. After some coaxing and honest discussion between them, Finn had agreed to stay on as his assistant and dog handler, for which Lake was thankful.

"Go fast, Pal! Bring us home, Ice!" He couldn't wait to cross the finish line and receive his wife's victory kiss. That would be a first!

The cheers grew louder, and both dogs ran faster as if the applause energized them. Lake dug his poles in, skiing for all he was worth, hoping to make a strong finish. Accompanied by shouts and cheers from bystanders, his team crossed the finish line in first place, as he'd hoped to do!

Finn was there to unclip Pal and Ice and lead them away from the line where the other racers would soon be crossing. "Good job, guys!"

Lake released his skis as Irish reached him, threw her arms around his neck, and kissed him.

"Great job, honey! I knew you could do it."

"Thanks." He was pleased she came to cheer for him and support him even though she wasn't racing herself. Next time, when she was participating again, he'd face more formidable competition.

Irish petted Pal and Ice. "Sweet babies, you were amazing! Good job, Pal. Excellent work, Ice."

"What about me?" Finn asked jokingly.

"Good job cleaning up after them, Finn." Irish thrust her arms around her youngest brother-in-law and hugged him. "What would we do without you?"

"Clean up your own dog—"

A forceful masculine throat clearing stopped Finn from finishing his statement. His eyes widened.

Lake whirled around to see who it was. "Hud?"

"Surprise!" Hud thrust out his arms.

"What are you doing here?"

"Watching your race." Hud held out his hand, and Lake shook it heartily.

"You remember my wife, Irish." Lake set his arm over her shoulder, thankful he felt comfortable doing so now.

"Hud. It's nice to see you again." Irish smiled.

"Likewise." Hud met Lake's gaze with a sheepish grimace. "She and I have talked recently."

"You have?" Lake glanced at Irish. She shrugged.

The howling of dogs and the cheers of the crowd rose again. Another racer was coming in.

"We'd better get out of the way and continue this conversation at my parking area."

Finn was hanging onto Pal's and Ice's harnesses ahead of them and both dogs nearly dragged him back to their tie-out lines. Eventually, he'd master the trick of directing them, but not today.

"When did you and Irish talk?" Lake asked as soon as he reached his truck. Irish didn't meet his gaze. Did she feel awkward about the question?

"We spoke on the phone," Hud said evasively.

"You mean when you weren't taking my calls?" Lake grabbed his sweatshirt and parka out of the cab of the pickup.

"Maybe." Hud clenched his hands tightly, either fighting the cold or his angst.

"I called him to explain," Irish said.

"About what?" Lake quickly donned his warmer apparel.

"You and me. How you did a good thing by accepting the inheritance and sharing it with the animal shelter." She made a gulping sound. "How you are sending your folks on a cruise."

"Sweetheart, Hud and I already discussed those things."

"Minus the cruise part," Hud corrected.

"Why'd you come back now?" Lake adjusted his knit hat and peered at his brother. "I thought you were too busy with your work in Alaska. And the five-foot-three woman."

"I can't deny that. But there were extenuating circumstances." Hud shivered and grimaced. "Can we discuss this later? Let's celebrate your win. You did great out there!"

"Yes, you did!" Irish kissed Lake's cheek. "Don't be mad at me, okay? I wanted to help you and Hud work things out."

Her moist, deep green eyes met his gaze with such a loving expression that he was putty in her hands. He settled his arm over her shoulder again and tugged her against his side. Even though he didn't understand her reasoning for contacting Hud or why his brother showed up at today's race, he wasn't letting anything ruin the closeness he felt with his wife.

"How long are you staying?"

"Long enough to conduct some business." Hud glanced away as if he felt uneasy with the admission. What kind of business did he need to do here when his work was in Alaska? "It was fun watching you race again. It's been a while since I saw one of these events."

"Thanks for coming out. That means a lot to me."

It was time for Lake to give his dogs some treats and after-race attention. They'd worked hard, too.

Irish strode over to Pal, petting and hugging him.

"You're lucky." Hud lifted his chin toward her. "I'm surprised at myself for saying it, but you two seem happier than I thought."

"Yeah. Me too." Lake met Irish's gaze, and a feeling of tenderness rushed through him. "So, we'll talk sometime this week?"

"Absolutely." Hud moved his shoulders up and down in a tense movement. "I'll be staying with Mom and Dad for a couple of nights. Then I'm hightailing it north."

"I guess you heard Dad's news."

"About the sabbatical and possible retirement?" Hud checked his cell phone, then groaned. "Yeah. A lot is happening in our family."

"Are you okay?"

"'Okay' is debatable." Hud laughed humorlessly. "It's like you with the dogs out there on the racecourse. You make instant decisions. Do you ski around an obstacle or quit and turn around? Some things work out. Others don't."

"That's true. What are you facing, Hud?" His brother wouldn't appreciate him pushing for details, but he seemed troubled. "I'm here for you, man."

"You have your hands full." Hud nodded toward the dogs or Irish. Maybe both. "We'll talk soon." With a slump to his shoulders, he crossed the path and trudged around the snow berms toward the parking lot.

Lake silently prayed for him. Then he glanced at his wife. Did she know why Hud was here in North Idaho? Had she known he'd be at the race today? A tightness formed in his chest, combatting his affectionate feelings toward her moments ago.

They needed to talk, but not with Finn around. Which meant his questions would have to wait until later.

Chapter Sixty-two

It was late when Irish sat down on the loveseat with Pleiades resting by her feet. Hopefully, Lake would join her. As soon as they got home, they had tended to their dogs. Then they hauled Lake's racing gear and stored it in the outbuilding. Finally, they ate some heated leftovers for dinner. But it was a silent meal.

Lake had been acting more reservedly toward her ever since he and Hud talked earlier. Was he miffed with her for calling his brother? She didn't mean to go behind his back. The other day, she heard him praying for Hud and knew his heart ached for the closeness of their relationship before he accepted his grandfather's money and she became his wife.

If there were any way she could help mend the breach in the family, she would, other than backing down from her marriage to Lake. She was too much in love with him to allow that to happen. Even though they hadn't exchanged those tender words yet, she felt them burning a brand in her heart. *I love you, Lake. You are mine for keeps*. At some point, she'd tell him. But not when he was angry with her.

Silently, he dropped onto the couch beside her. They both sipped their hot tea, as they'd been doing lately before going to bed. She prayed whatever irritation he felt toward her wouldn't hinder their steps toward getting closer.

"So, do you want to talk about it?" Irish took note of her husband's tight-looking features and petted Pleiades to keep herself calm.

"What's 'it?'"

"You've been giving me squinty eyes since Hud spilled the beans about me calling him."

"I was surprised, is all." His shoulders lifted, then fell. "Not giving you 'squinty eyes,' whatever those are."

"I think you're more than surprised." She held Lake's gaze without wavering, expecting honesty between them. "You should own up to your anger."

"Okay." He moved to the edge of the cushion. "Your calling my brother irritated me a little. I wish you would have spoken to me about it first."

"You would have said no or told me to leave it alone." She stopped petting the dog as tension rose in her neck muscles.

"Of course, I would have."

"So, he's not my brother-in-law? Are you saying I'm excluded from the family relationship?"

"No. What I'm saying is there are rules." Lake growled out an exhausted-sounding moan. "Not rules. You should have talked to me first, that's all."

"So, do I have to run everything by you?" An emotional firestorm ignited within her. She shoved away from the loveseat and brought her partially empty cup to the sink. "Do I have to ask your permission to buy groceries? What about putting gas in my car? Or taking my dogs for a run? Do I need to ask you about that, too?"

"Irish. Don't be ridiculous."

"Ridiculous?" She glowered at him.

Lake's footsteps landed heavily as he walked across the small space. "Look. We're both tired. Let's just go to bed."

Going to bed with him was the last thing on her mind!

"You have to control everything, don't you?" She clutched the back of a chair at the table.

"What's that supposed to mean?" He set his nearly full cup in the sink with a thud.

"You don't want me to make decisions at the animal shelter. Nor about our house plans." She drummed her fingernails against the chair, which brought Pleiades to her side. "Now I'm not supposed to call members of your family? What am I allowed to do in this marriage?"

"I never said you couldn't make decisions at the shelter." He leaned his backside against the counter and raked his fingers through his hair. "You still work there, worked there even when I didn't want you to, so you're making your own choices."

"As well I should," she said through clenched teeth. "I'm not going to be some wimpy wife who can't take three steps without her husband's permission."

"That's an understatement."

"If you don't like how I am, too bad!" She'd had enough of this conversation. Irish patted her leg so Pleiades would follow her. Then she strode toward her room, planning to slam and lock the door. Lake could sleep in the guest room for the next month!

"Hold on. Irish, please." He ran around her, blocking her entrance into the bedroom. "I didn't say I don't like how you are."

"Then what? Are you still comparing me to Laurie? Still wishing for a compliant wife who will say, 'Yes, sir. Of course, sir,' to all your wishes?"

He snickered, and she glared at him.

"Just go to bed!" She pulsed her finger toward the guest room. "We can resume this argument in the morning."

He held out his hands in a surrendering gesture. "Sweetheart, we are married. Even if we fight, I would still like to sleep in our room with you."

"Then I will stay in the guest room!" She let the soles of her shoes hit the floor hard as she marched into the tiny room, waited for her dog to follow her, then slammed the door behind them. Her breaths came in giant heaves.

A quiet knocking at the door twisted more angst in her.

"In the morning, Lake."

"Are you sure? I thought you loved me."

"I never said that." How dare he bring up love!

He knocked again. "Irish?" His soft tone stirred a primal response in her gut. "My beautiful wife, whom I care deeply about, I'm sorry for getting grumpy and rude. Please, can we go into our room together?"

"You just want me to share your bed!"

"Of course I do. You're my wife. I want to be close to you. Come out here so we can talk some more, okay? Let's not go to bed angry."

"It wouldn't be the first time." Nor the last.

"Please?" His tone sounded little-boy sincere. "My parents don't go to bed angry with each other."

"So what?" She was tired of him mentioning what his parents did and didn't do. This was their marriage. Their lives. Not a replica of his parents' marriage.

She was about to tell him that when it sounded like he scooted down the door and landed on the floor with a soft "oomph." What was he doing?

"The Bible mentions something along those lines too." He yawned. "I'm sorry for making you feel like you weren't important or not a part of my family. I want to make things right with you. Can we talk?"

"In the morning." Irish dropped onto the twin bed, and Pleiades leaped up beside her. The dog circled, then flopped down next to her.

"I don't know why your calling Hud bugged me," Lake said in a sleepy tone. "I want to work out by myself whatever is off between him and me."

"Sorry for messing up your perfectly laid plans."

"There's no perfection in family stuff. It's complicated, messy, and challenging sometimes. Forgive me for being insensitive toward you?"

Did he want to make up so she'd wilt into a puddle of emotions and go into the bedroom with him? She said they'd talk in the morning. That's what she meant!

A few minutes later, she heard snoring. He was asleep on the floor? Unbelievable!

Chapter Sixty-three

Lake fed the dogs the following day, then fixed cheesy scrambled eggs, biscuits, and bacon. He was on his second cup of coffee when Irish opened the guest room door. Without speaking to him, she shuffled into the bathroom. Would the delicious breakfast and his humble apology make up for last night's tiff?

She had been so furious with him. And he reacted badly to the whole situation. He and Hud needed to work out the issues between them. He didn't want Irish interfering. But she was right about her being his wife and, therefore, part of the North family. She could call Hud anytime she wanted.

"Morning." She padded across the floor in her socks with Pleiades following her.

"Good morning. I made you breakfast. My peace offering."

"Is that what this is? It looks amazing." Her hair was messy, and she had that just-waking-up look he loved. Her beautiful jade eyes blinked in his direction a few times as if she was trying to figure out if he was still grumpy this morning.

He opened his arms to her and smiled, hoping his contrite look spoke to her heart. She walked straight into his hug. Sighing, he wrapped his arms around her, and they held each other.

"I'm sorry about what I said last night," he whispered. "I overreacted. I blew it."

"I overreacted too. Sorry." Releasing a trembling breath, she stepped out of his embrace. "The food looks wonderful."

"Coffee's good too."

"I'll have three cups, please."

"You got it."

"I just have to take care of Pleiades." She led the dog over to the door, opened it, then waited while the dog ran outside for a minute.

Lake poured coffee into a large mug and added a generous serving of creamer. Once Pleiades was back inside, eating the food he left in a dish for her, he handed Irish the cup of coffee.

"Thanks." Yawning, she sat down at the table.

"Rough sleep?"

"I could ask you the same question."

"I'd say yes. Sleeping on the floor without a blanket is for the dogs!"

They both chuckled.

He spread out his hands toward the array of food. "Eat up. Enjoy."

"I plan to." She had her plate full in seconds but didn't start eating. She clutched her coffee cup and sighed.

"Is something wrong?" Sitting in the chair across from her, he dished up his food.

"This heat is soothing after being in the chilly guest room. Good thing I had Pleiades to keep me somewhat warm."

Lake regretted that he wasn't the one keeping her warm last night. He cleared his throat. "I forgot to make sure the door was ajar so the warmth from the woodstove would flow in there." He stuffed a bite of buttered biscuit in his mouth. "I fell asleep and—"

"I know the rest of the story." She winked at him.

Thankfully, the irritation between them had dissipated. Still, he could have handled last night's disagreement better. He was a husband who loved his wife and—

He paused with his biscuit halfway to his mouth.

Loved his wife?

Glory to God! He loved Irish!

Of course, he did! He wanted to spend all his time with her. Deep feelings for her strummed through him whenever he held her in his arms or kissed her! He loved her passion, her flirty ways with him, her zeal for life, and even her fiery temper when they argued. He loved the way she gazed deeply into his eyes, like now.

He loved every part of her.

Oh, Irish.

Barely able to keep the words from exploding from his mouth, as soon as she finished breakfast, he asked, "Can we talk?"

"Sure. We might as well get it over with." She sounded like she was about to hear the worst news ever.

They sat down on the loveseat, and he scooted closer to her.

"I'm sorry about calling Hud," she said before he could say anything. "I didn't think you'd react so strongly."

"I shouldn't have. Hud's been distant with me since he heard about us getting married."

"I know. I felt like my presence in your life was a thorn in his side. That's why I called him. I don't want to be the woman who comes between brothers. I won't sit by and—"

"Irish."

"I mean it, Lake. If we want this marriage to work, and I do, then I must get along with the most important people in your life."

The way she met his gaze and smiled sweetly at him sent heat and chills alternating through his core. He wanted to tell her he loved her and kiss her.

"You still want our marriage to work, don't you?" Her vulnerable tone made his heart ache.

"Yes, I do. I was perturbed last night because I'm the one who broke the pact Hud and I made as kids. I caused the rift. Not you. Now, can we not talk about Hud for a second?" He tugged Irish nearer to him, tipping up her chin, and gazing into her eyes. "Sweetheart, you are the most important person in my life."

"Is that why you slept outside my door?"

"Mmhmm. I wanted to be as close to you as I could get."

"You have an odd way of fighting with me." She stroked her fingers down his jawline, then nestled her hands against his chest. Each movement was like a dance that captivated his attention.

"I like the making-up part." He kissed her slowly, enjoying the taste of bacon and jam on her lips. He wanted to keep kissing her and stop talking. But he needed to tell her what he had just realized. "I have something else to say to you too."

"What's that?" She trailed kisses along his cheek, momentarily distracting him.

"I love you," he whispered.

She stilled and met his gaze. "You love me?"

"With all my heart. I love you with every part of my being."

"Oh, Lake. I love you too."

They kissed tenderly. Then he stroked his fingers down her long red hair. "I'm so thankful we took a chance on marrying each other. I thank God for bringing you into my life."

"I feel the same way. I thank Him every day for you." She touched his wedding ring. "I want to spend my whole life with you. You are mine for keeps."

"Ah, sweetheart." He kissed her again, stroking her cheek, her hair, and drawing her closer to him. He wanted their emotional tenderness to continue forever.

Irish leaned back a little. "What would you think about taking a walk with me?"

"A walk?" He had other ideas about what he'd like to do with her that didn't involve wearing winter attire.

"It looks idyllic outside." She kissed the corner of his mouth. "Let's hold hands and say we love each other again and again. I'll never tire of hearing you say it."

"A walk and talk? And more kissing?"

"Sounds perfect, doesn't it?"

"Pretty close." Since he wanted to pursue his wife's heart and not just his wishes, he grinned and nodded. "Let's get our gear on and take a walk together."

Minutes later, they strolled down the snow-packed lane in front of the cabin with their gloved hands clasped. Their dogs barking in the background and his and her boots crunching against the snow created a cacophony of sound that resembled musical harmony.

As they walked, Irish tugged on his hand. "There's something I'd like to discuss with you. But I hate to bring up a troublesome topic after we just told each other we love one another."

"Sweetheart, I'll still love you, no matter what you say."

"Thank you for that." She leaned into him and kissed him. "I love you."

"I love you. I'm the luckiest man alive to have you as my wife."

"I hope you always feel that way."

"I promise I will—that's a pledge straight from my heart to yours." He smiled at her and tucked her hand into the crook of his arm. "Now, what did you want to talk with me about?"

"I'd like to keep working at the shelter." She gnawed on her lower lip. That action alone tugged on his emotions. "I love caring for the animals and matching pets with great owners. Even the challenge of daily operations is fulfilling. Can we talk about me working as the manager for a while longer?"

"We can talk about it, but we don't have to." He led them farther down the road. "I think you should do whatever you feel in your heart to do. While I didn't imagine us being involved with the shelter to such a degree, I understand why you can't let it go."

"You do?"

"You care deeply about things—that's how God made you! You're enthusiastic and compassionate. You see those homeless animals, and you want to help them. I love you for having so much passion." He meant about the shelter, but his thoughts raced homeward, too.

"Thank you. I don't know if anyone ever got that about me before."

"Well, I do." He paused on the road, holding Irish's hand and gazing at her. "You should talk to the board about being the permanent manager at the shelter if that's what you want to do. I mean that."

"Thank you for understanding." She hugged him.

"You're welcome." He stepped back from the hug. "I want what's best for you. For us together, too."

"Me too. I *really* love you."

"And I *really* love you. Are you ready to head back to the cabin?" With just a tad of encouragement from her, he'd scoop her up and carry her. Maybe spend three days locked away in their honeymoon suite together.

"There's one other tiny request."

"Your wish is my command, as the saying goes."

Irish was minimalistic, so she probably didn't want anything extravagant. It wasn't like he didn't have the funds to buy her something nice if she wanted it.

"His name is Little Dipper."

"Who?"

"He's a darling husky pup I helped Doc Cooper deliver at the shelter. I know we don't have the space right now."

"No, we don't."

"But I want to adopt him. Would adding one more dog to our group be okay before the kennels are built? Please?"

How could he deny her anything? "Can we talk about it some more later?"

"Absolutely. But did I say I really want him?"

"You did." He chuckled. Then he gazed longingly toward the cabin with its spiral of chimney smoke rising toward the sky. "Shall we head home?"

"Sweet lips, I'll go anywhere with you."

"I like the sound of that."

At the cabin door, Lake paused before going inside and removed Irish's left glove. With his gaze on the woman he loved, he brought her fingers to his lips and kissed her wedding ring. "Irish North, will you be my wife? To have and to hold forever?"

"Lake North, I will gladly be your wife."

She kissed him tenderly. Then she kissed him passionately, like there was no tomorrow and she needed his kisses as much as she needed air to breathe. Lake kissed her back, matching her kisses with gentleness, love, and a hunger of his own. The steamy air swirled around them as their affection intensified.

"Lake? You holding me forever sounds like heaven."

"My thoughts exactly."

One more kiss. And another.

Then, to the music of dogs yipping and baying, Lake clasped his wife's hand, led her into their cabin, and closed the door.

Epilogue

"Dear Mom," Hud typed the email greeting he had already written and deleted three times over the last two days. He should have called her before now. But how could he tell anyone in the family what he was going through until he decided on the next step? Now that he had, what he agreed to do went against his pact with his brothers and against his own moral compass.

He closed the email without finishing it. Writing Mom with the news was the wrong way to go about this.

The disastrous financial situation he found himself in had not only created immense trouble for him but also adversely affected Trista, his business partner. Losing everything he owned was one thing. Causing her to lose what she needed for her and her daughter to survive was quite another.

One week ago, he had watched Lake's skijoring race in Priest Lake. Then he spoke to the lawyer and set his plan into motion.

Today, he was getting married.

By evening, he'd be a billionaire.

How was he going to explain *that* to his family?

Thank you for reading *Lake*, Book 1 of The Preacher's Sons!

Hud, Book 2, is available now!

The Preacher's Sons series is a spin-off from *Liv & the Preacher*. If you haven't read Liv and Smith's tale yet, you might enjoy reading their love story in *Liv & the Preacher*.

Special acknowledgments:

Thank you, Paula McGrew, for editing this story and adding depth to the characters. I appreciate your help with my writing so much! You have been a blessing beyond blessings to me.

Thank you, Suzanne Williams, for the fun cover and artistic effects! I appreciate you sharing your talent and time with me again.

Thank you, Mary Acuff, Kellie Griffin, Joanna Brown, Beth McDonald, and Jason Hanks, for being wonderful, supportive beta readers. I appreciate your generosity in sharing your time, comments, positivity, and critique with me. I appreciate you!

Thank you, Jordan Bailey, for proofreading this story and helping polish it. I appreciate your part of the process so much!

Thank you, Dan Hanks, for going over my racing scenes and offering pointers in this fictional tale. Your love for your dogs and your joy in skijoring have been an inspiration to watch!

Thank you, Jason, for always reading my work, going over special scenes again and again, and chatting with me about creative ideas for my stories. Your support means the world to me.

Thank you to all the readers who have read my stories and "got" them. A million times, "Thank you!"

This is a work of fiction. Any mistakes are my own. ~meh

Christian fiction by Mary Hanks:

Liv & the Preacher

The Preacher's Sons Series:

Lake, Hud

Restored Series:

Ocean of Regret, Sea of Rescue, Bay of Refuge, Tide of Resolve, Waves of Reason, Port of Return, Sound of Rejoicing, Shores of Resilience

Basalt Bay Series:

Callie's Time

Second Chance Series:

Winter's Past, April's Storm, Summer's Dream, Autumn's Break, Season's Flame

About Mary Hanks:

When Mary isn't exploring the world through her characters' eyes, she is singing toddler songs and playing with her grandchildren. Vanilla lattes, gardening, and taking walks with Jason, her husband of 40+ years, rank high on her list of favorites. Telling stories is a huge part of Mary's life, and she hopes to continue writing heart-warming tales of grace, mercy, and love for a long time.

www.maryehanks.com

Made in United States
Troutdale, OR
03/01/2025